THE ALLEYS OF EDEN

"SUPERIOR...NIGHTMARISH...
AN EXTRAORDINARY NOVEL...
REMINISCENT OF
GOOD HEMINGWAY."
Cleveland Plain Dealer

"HARROWING...
The book transcends topicality
in its troubling portrayal
of people confronting a world
of only negative options."
Women's Wear Daily

"ONE OF
THE MORE INTERESTING
VIETNAM NOVELS,
certainly, as well as one of the finer
first novels of recent years."
San Francisco Chronicle

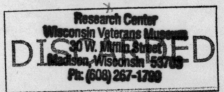

THE ALLEYS OF EDEN

ROBERT OLEN BUTLER

BALLANTINE BOOKS • NEW YORK

Library of Congress Catalog Card Number: 81-82842

ISBN 0-345-30774-7

This edition published by arrangement with Horizon Press

Manufactured in the United States of America

First Ballantine Books Edition: February 1983

for my parents

BOOK ONE

*T*HE DOGS HAD FLED. THE ALLEYS WERE QUIET because the rockets had fallen on Saigon until the dogs had stopped barking at them and felt the terror of the people and joined the refugees rushing out of the city into nowhere. Cliff imagined it this way. He had a vision of the alley outside his window as the center from which they all rushed, like all matter in the universe rushing from the center in the big bang. But he knew this didn't fit. The refugees were pressing into Saigon, pressing into all the corners and cracks and awaiting the end. Maybe a dog would yet bark tonight.

He felt Lanh's naked flank against him. He listened to the silence of the alley. He felt a moment utterly different from this but on the surface different only in a dog barking. A night in this back alley countless nights ago when he lay for the first time in his own and alien home and listened to a dog barking in the night, the only sound in Saigon, Lanh awake, he knew, listening with him, the faint drip of water in her tiny bathroom where she'd crouched after they'd made love and she'd sponged down her body. The paddle fan moved slowly in the dark above them pressing ghosts against his face.

But now he found his heart racing suddenly, his throat clamping shut. He could be the last American left. He had heard only panicked rumors of the helicopters rising day and night from the roof of the embassy. But he knew it was so. In the chaos, he could have gone to see, but he didn't know what there was for him to do and he couldn't face the scene without a decision. He could not panic now. Not after these years of careful choice. He could not yet bear to see the throngs of doomed Vietnamese besieging the embassy, doomed by their embrace with those who now rushed headlong away from them as the enemy of a generation advanced to take its revenge. But not on me, some corner of Cliff's mind asserted, to see if it sounded true. He could not tell. Cliff wanted to jump up from the bed but he pressed himself back again. Quiet, the night tarred against the sky, the cement walls of the room cool, the bombs of the B-52s crackling on the horizon like heat lightning, Lanh beside him. She was awake. She seemed always to be awake in the stillness beside him. Sensing his thoughts on that night long before this one, she turned on her side, her hands coaxed him erect, tugged him into her.

But now she slept. She'd been sleeping from early evening well into the day in recent weeks. And Cliff had too. Even as the nights cracked with the rockets and the end neared, they'd begun to feel tired, begun to sleep long and deep. But Cliff would not sleep on this night. He knew this night could be the last. Thieu was gone a week; the ARVN was in chaotic retreat; he had to decide tonight. He could be the last deserter from the U.S. Army left in Vietnam and time had run out. These alleys were once full of deserters but he'd held to this place—and the place had held to him—better than any before, and the very things that had let him be strong now turned against him. He'd done what he'd needed to do in his heart and mind to let him stay. His instincts now preserved his place here and he'd not been betrayed. Could he undo them? Suddenly he heard Fleming's voice. Telling him—was it on Cliff's first night in Vietnam?—that he had to adjust to survive. Cliff nearly laughed at the irony of thinking of Fleming on this point, but the sound of Fleming's voice was too clear. Cliff wasn't prepared to face him. But he listened again to the captain's little fable. Fleming told about a monkey that was the mascot of an airborne company. Once, the men decided the animal should make a jump with them. They

4

rigged up a parachute for it and they all went up to ten thousand feet and, just before their jump, they threw the monkey out of the plane and pulled the ripcord. Forced into a strange, intense world, the monkey did what its natural instincts told it to do—it climbed. The monkey climbed right up the risers, grabbed the parachute, and plummeted the last five thousand feet to its death. Cliff had applied the lesson in a way that neither he nor Fleming could have ever dreamed of at the time. And he would not panic, even now. He could still hear Fleming's voice. Quiet, frighteningly quiet all the time, no matter how terrible the substance of his words. Cliff could not face Fleming yet, though he knew he'd have to before the night was done.

Cliff thought of his own death. No one else's. His own alone. But not in an alleyway at the hands of a VC's triumphant rage. Not falling from the door of a helicopter over the South China Sea, unloaded from the evacuating party by a Marine guard. Not in the darkest pit of an Army prison. These hovered close to him, but he thought of the death he imagined in his first days in Vietnam. They were days in the countryside learning the intelligence distribution route, days passing in an open jeep through the little villages around Homestead, days following the hot, quiet country roads, his stomach tight from fear. He was afraid, but at the same time he felt a simple, undeniable freedom. The bright sun, the dark-earthed ditches with dirt clods at hand, a stand of trees. The smell of earth and heat, the feel of the road, were the same smell and feel of the days of summer vacation from grade school. The dirt clods to stockpile, the ditch to hide in, the trees to assault as a boy. Cliff had thought in those first days in-country—and it was the death that touched him now—that he might die on a day with the smell and feel of the days of play-war, years ago, when falling dead to the dusty ground was done with relish, grandly, to do again and again. Falling, Cliff smelled the fall, the dust filled his lungs falling, and even as a boy

5

he closely considered death; he wondered, even as he feigned it, whether death could hide him.

And that play-time death, too, was far from home. Too far: his father rushed upon him, slung him under his arm. Cliff watched the ground, the thrust, of his father's right leg, the dirt road-shoulder changing to blacktop gutter, to the beaten dead grass of their yard. His father hit him once, softly, on the butt but the words were worse. Words from much later—but Cliff was still barely more than a child. His father sat in a room thick with late afternoon shadow, no lights on, Cliff squinting against the dimness as if the problem was his eyes, as if he was going blind. He dared not move. His father sat, a dark shape against the window, and talked about his own father lying in bed for five years paralyzed, twitching the thick hands that once built a house. His body betrayed him, Cliff's father said. I know it's coming to me. I know it is. Cliff wanted to bolt from the room but that would let his father's tears come and Cliff would hear the first sob and so he stayed, blocking the purest release of his father's fear, making him talk it out instead. Please understand when I can't talk to you anymore, his father said, when I can't turn my eyes to you. Cliff felt his body go weightless as his father snatched him from the ground. This time he whipped Cliff hard, whipped him long and very hard and Cliff wrenched at his mind.

The man is dead. Dead and long ago disintegrated in a spot of earth ten thousand miles away. I don't have to face him tonight, Cliff told himself. Not at all. What is it that I do need to think through? Lanh stirred, her foot slid up Cliff's calf, and he laid his hand lightly on her thigh. He touched her to banish the ghosts, to bring himself to the beginning of this life with her. He had to understand that life tonight, for one thing. He gave himself over to the first meeting. He tried to hear the words. He'd thought of the first meeting many times but always in fragments. He re-constructed it carefully now; he knew her voice, her ways.

—I'm a friend, Cliff said in Vietnamese. A friend of Xa at the bar. May I come in?

He'd interrupted her prayers, though he didn't realize it until she'd turned her torso around from where she knelt. Her hands were pressed together before her, incense wisping up from her fingertips. The line of her black hair fell long across her shoulder and down her back and Cliff shivered imperceptibly from his first desire for Lanh.

—You not GI? she asked in English.

—I speak Vietnamese. You can talk Vietnamese.

—All right, she said with a crooked smile. You're *not* a GI then.

—Are you Lanh?

—Yes.

—Xa said I might come.

—You speak Vietnamese very well.

—I saw her today. She said it would be all right.

Lanh looked at him for a moment, then raised her hands to show him the incense. Go and sit down, she said.

—Yes. Of course. I'm sorry.

Cliff now remembered sitting in silence watching Lanh move the incense slowly up and down, her face—delicate as the faces of the roadside children that terrfied the GI truck drivers—was raised toward the plastic shrine on the top of her dresser. Candles flickered in her eyes. Then her face turned to Cliff and he said, I'm sorry to disturb you.

—That's all right, she said.

Cliff now heard Lanh's voice very clearly, as if she spoke aloud in her sleep beside him. She was always quick—like many of the bargirls—but she had an edge to her mind, to her feelings, that the others couldn't even begin to understand. Her mother, gone too soon, had helped give her that. Her mother had opened her, given her books, taught her the vision she had demanded from her own once-mandarin grandfather. Lanh had been much more than the other bargirls, but in this place she'd become as purposeless without parents or men as anyone else. Perhaps that, too, had been passed down from her mother's

7

grandfather. It seemed odd to Cliff, this sudden comparison of Lanh with the other girls from the bars. It was a function of his intense return to those first moments together, for though she worked in the bars for some time after they'd begun to live together, she stopped being anything but his mate almost at once. After they came together she earned what she could at the bars strictly from her cut of the Saigon Tea that GIs bought for her. Then finally she got an office job and took in some sewing and all of that life before had been utterly forgotten. I'd forgotten it, Cliff corrected himself. In those years Lanh learned things in ways that knew of no recollecting or forgetting. Cliff again gripped at his thoughts. He could let himself start with the moments that were good and that meant something to him. He let Lanh's words, her sensibility, return. He let her face stay turned to him and they spoke to each other on that first evening.

—Should I come back another time? Cliff asked.

—Where did you learn to speak Vietnamese so well?

—I went to school.

—Are we a simple language? she said.

Cliff heard a taunt in this, but he answered truthfully. Very simple, he said. Then he motioned to the incense. I can come back.

—No, she said. This is a good time. You are Xa's boyfriend?

—No. I'm just a friend. I've only talked with her a few times. I didn't go to your bar very much before.

—That's too bad.

—Anyway, she has a boyfriend. One who lives with her.

—I know.

—I'm not him.

—I know. I just asked because you might *think* you're Xa's boyfriend and American GIs are crazy jealous.

—A trait not unknown among Vietnamese women.

—That's true, I guess. But then, you're not a GI anyway. Right?

8

—Yes. Right.

—And I'm not a Vietnamese woman. Just a Saigon bargirl. So we have no jealousy, you and me.

—The bargirls I've known have been the most jealous of all . . . That is, a bargirl is a woman too.

—Don't try to go back on what you said. I wasn't fishing for sweet words from you. I *am* a bargirl. Ask the Vietnamese. They'll tell you we're different.

—But do you feel jealousy?

—Of course . . . But don't believe it.

—If you don't want me to.

—And GIs are human too, I guess. But I'll never admit that to anyone.

—It would interfere with your work.

—Yes. And lead me to feel jealousy.

They laughed lightly together.

—Why are you so skinny? Lanh asked.

—What?

—Skinny. Why are you so skinny?

—I don't know.

—Americans are fat.

—Are they?

—You're skinny like a Vietnamese.

—I eat a lot of Vietnamese food.

—Maybe that's it, Lanh said. You weighed more when you first came here.

—Yes.

—Three hundred pounds. Right?

—Yes . . . Uh, yes, three hundred pounds.

—Very fat. Typical American.

—Then I ate cha gio and bun bo and banh xeo.

Lanh laughed at his knowing the foods. Good, she said. Good. And you lost two hundred of your American pounds. The one hundred left is the Vietnamese who was inside you waiting to get out.

—Vietnamization. Cliff used the word that filled even the Saigon newspapers.

—A wonderful success, Lanh declared.

9

—Do you think I will begin to lose height too?

—I don't know. You are tall now. Very tall. I don't know.

—And my eyes?

—There is only so much bun bo can do, she said smiling, but then she turned surprisingly grim. I hope you don't change. Blue eyes are very good. The Vietnamese people are all the same, all dark. And you have golden hair. We are dark corners, deep wells. You are sky and fields. She was mocking him ever so slightly now, he decided, but as soon as he thought it, she changed again, waving her hand lightly in the air, the first recollection he now had of the hand moving after her prayers. And besides, she said, if I get pregnant by you, the government gives support to girls pregnant by Americans. I only sleep with blonds and redheads. Easier to prove that the father was American.

—And do you have blond children?

—Why of course. Every bargirl in Saigon has to have at least one baby. Don't you know that? We are a backward country. We have no contraptions, no medicines for that. My friends and I believe if you don't come at the same time as the man there will be no baby. But there are always babies. The whole thing is a mystery to us.

A moment of silence passed between them as he felt oddly shamed, an intruder. He thought about going, even as he asked, Where is your baby?

—I have none, she said and her voice was soft-edged though she looked at him hard and he felt her drawing him back, turning his mind back from the door.

—You said . . .

—I lied, she said. Why don't you sit down. You look very tired.

—All right.

—You're very nervous.

—I haven't slept for several days.

Lanh stirred now in her sleep. Cliff lifted his hand as she turned from her side to her stomach and then he placed his hand on the back of her thigh. He realized he was sweating. The night was close and he laid the sheet back off them. She'd chided him that first night about the heat. Americans are always fighting at the heat, she said. It's not something to beat away or run from. He'd told her, about then, that he'd lied. He was really a GI, like all the rest.

—Why do you have civilian clothes? she asked.

—A special job.

—You're CIA.

—CIA aren't GIs.

—Why do you carry a gun under your shirt?

—This is a country at war, you know. A stodgy, silly answer, Cliff felt; and he knew it was from embarrassment at her noticing the pistol.

—You carry it for your special job, she said.

—Yes.

—You shoot Saigon cowboys who try to steal your watch. Right?

She was helping him through an awkward moment again. Wrong, he said, picking up her tone. I steal watches from Saigon cowboys.

Lanh laughed. Good, she said. That's okay. I don't like the cowboys. They always make trouble . . . You hate Saigon, don't you. She'd turned suddenly serious.

—No. Why would you say that?

—All GIs hate Saigon.

—All GIs aren't the same.

—All right . . . All Americans hate Saigon.

—Wait a minute. I'm down to my hundred Vietnamese pounds. Remember?

—That was a joke. The heart doesn't change.

—But not all American hearts feel hate . . .

—I don't blame you. Not anymore.

—I really don't . . .

—One time I saw the city in a different way, she said. I would have said no, you're wrong. When I came as a child from Tay Ninh province, Saigon was important and busy.

11

It was connected to faraway worlds. But it was friendly as our village; people filling the sidewalks with their wares, and cars and motorcycles going by with smart people. And the girls were all so beautiful walking streets as wide as our yard in their ao dais, not just white ao dais like my school clothes but all colors and with flowers. Then I grew up and you Americans came who knew other ways, more advanced. And I learned from you. I began to see the city through your eyes. The city is choking on filth from machines that are treated like lovers by fools with sunglasses and pointy shoes. It's filled with these tiny brown animals always grubbing after anything they can get to hoard to themselves. Sleeping and pissing and grabbing at arms in the streets. Heat even. I didn't used to get hot but I get so hot now sometimes in this alley with these nosy old women high on betel nuts.

Even lying in the bed in the city that was his home with Lanh, long after she'd spoken those words, Cliff felt a surge of warmth in his eyes, his legs, that left him shaking. He'd not thought of those words since she'd spoken them on their first night—it had taken him a long time to exorcise them—but their effect now—now when the choices were even more terrible—renewed itself unexpectedly. Cliff wanted to thrash his way from the bed, but he lay still, clutching at his memories. She'd not known when she'd spoken on that first night that he'd only a few days before thrown away his past life—gladly, yes gladly, Cliff now shouted silently to himself—had only a few days before chosen as his new home the very place she derided so strongly. And she'd learned that derision from the ones I'd grown up with and only so recently left behind, he thought, trying to still the quaver in his chest with this irony. He liked Saigon very much, always had, still did; he loved Lanh even on that first night and he sought her face again on that night. He had to convince her anew.

—You're serious, aren't you? he asked.

—What?

—I thought for a while you were joking about the city and your people.

—I tell you I changed my mind. I'm convinced.

—But you weren't joking. You believe it.

—So do you want to stay tonight? she asked abruptly.

—You can't be convinced.

—Sure . . . You want to fuck, GI?

—But the things you're convinced about now. What fraction of truth is in them was caused by us. We changed things.

—I don't think Vietnamese ever had beautiful big breasts, skin pure white. •

—When you came to Saigon—when was that?

—1957.

—Remember . . . remember the trees then. Even now Saigon is the greenest city I know. Remember back then. I've seen pictures. When you could walk in tamarind shade all the way down Tu Do to the river. Do you remember that?

—Yes . . . But that means nothing. I was a child. A child will always remember the trees. I can see those trees from before. But most of them are still here now. A child will see only what she can know. And I didn't know the truth about things.

—You still don't know.

Cliff knew what he had to do, for himself, as much as for Lanh. Even now, even as he lay in the room beside the woman he'd shared a life with for nearly four years, he needed these words again.

It bothers me, Cliff said to Lanh on that first night, your being convinced by Americans to hate this place. Vietnam is . . . intense. That scares some people. Repels others. But it's alive here. The place pulls you into it. My god, the first day I came to Saigon—I was out at the American base near Bien Hoa, Homestead. I came into Saigon in a jeep at the bottom of a deep sky with the hot wind snapping the canvas top. And people on Hondas all day gliding up and back, up and past—at arm's length, suddenly,

13

these smooth small people, these Vietnamese. And I knew the language, so I smiled often and no smile was unreturned. I would shout a word of greeting in Vietnamese above the roar of wind and motor and they would reply long, laughing, talking, and waving their arms even as they glided away. I passed tiny villages deep under groves of banana and rubber trees, water buffalo lolling in yards like housecats. And ancient tombs, miniature towers and walls of pitted dark stone in the fields. Farmers buried where they toiled—no, I distort in my American way—not toiled. Buried where they lived and worked the earth, now to become part of their field. And finally into Saigon. The stores and ground floors of houses near and open full on the street like large-mouthed shallow caves. And the people's lives open too and there on the street, crouching with friends, laughing and eating at sidewalk food stands, and carving wood or tinkering with motorcycle engines or selling cloth, all outside, out under the hot sky and always returning my smile or word. We passed the narrow, twisted alleys with naked children running and old women playing Chinese cards and then down the streets dark in shade of tamarind and banyan. The city buildings in faded pastels set far back behind walls. And the young women moving with absolute grace, slim, and long, long black hair, the panels of their ao dais fluttering behind them and the silk of their black pantaloons shining like the flanks of sea mammals. I walked the streets for hours constantly touching and smelling and hearing intense human life. So intense you knew it would never stop. So intense and settled you knew it would always be here, always be the same. And it was life lived simply and with joy. Amazingly with joy. In spite of all that's happened. Amazing only to an American, maybe. But thank god I did see the joy.

The rush of Cliff's words stopped. His sudden terror had stopped. But his finding the things that made his decision bearable gave him the words to a catechism that he'd have to repeat many times to survive. He knew that.

—You're a crazy man, Lanh said after she'd seen he was finished.

—Why?

—You talk crazy.

—What did I say?

—You like it here?

—Everything I said, I felt.

—You're crazy. You have to be.

—All right, Cliff said.

—All I want in the world is to get away from here.

—And to be somebody else.

—American women are beautiful.

—Not as beautiful as Vietnamese women.

—I've seen them.

—Why am I crazy?

—I've seen pictures of them.

—Lanh, you liked Saigon once.

—I've seen the pictures of women that were so beautiful they would not be denied. They would not lose a man to anyone like me. They had beauty to make nothing of a present happiness. They make nothing out of a life together with no past or future but some joy now.

—And you call me crazy for maybe wanting to stay?

—Yes.

—You don't really feel that.

—Yes I do. I understand beauty like that. I don't mind. It's the way things are.

—It's not the way things are.

—You want me to believe it's just me?

—No. It's not you at all.

—Don't tell me how deep down everything's good here, Lanh said. It's not. I know it's not. The ones who made me understand what they knew, I didn't love them for it. The fawn can't love the tiger for explaining to it its place in the world. But don't you tell me now it's a lie, because it won't work. Leave me alone.

—All right, Cliff said. I don't care about changing your mind.

15

—Good.

—Are you angry with me?

—No.

—I'm glad.

But Lanh flared at once. Where were you and these words before? You're a liar.

—It's all right. I'm sorry.

—A liar, she nearly screamed.

—Do you want me to go?

—No, she said, suddenly very quiet.

—Are you sure?

—Yes, I'm sure. You're too skinny. You have to eat.

She made a bun bo for them and they spoke very little for a long time. I'm a wonderful cook, Lanh said after a long silence while mixing the beef and noodles on a hotplate. Cliff laughed. After another long silence, she said, You speak Vietnamese better than I do. Cliff said, Nonsense, and he wondered at her mind's silent wandering.

Lanh brought the food to him in china bowls with chopsticks. Cliff sat on the floor. Lanh crouched in the ubiquitous Vietnamese squat—legs bent and spread, the knees beside the shoulders, with both feet flat on the ground. They ate and did not speak but watched each other closely. She giggled when he faltered once with his chopsticks and dropped a piece of beef. He brushed a piece of rice from her hair.

After they'd finished eating and been silent for a time more, Lanh asked, Why didn't you come to meet me at the bar?

—I don't like the bar.

—You went there to find out where I live.

—Yes. But I didn't want to meet you there.

—How did you know about me?

—I didn't. I knew Xa.

—And she had her boyfriend tonight.

—I wasn't interested in Xa, Cliff said.

—She told you I'm a good lay, to come and see me?

—No.

16

—She told you I'm not a good lay?

—We didn't talk about . . .

—She lied.

—Nothing was said like that. Believe me.

—What are you so sincere about? Lanh asked, seeming to concentrate hard on her harshness. You think it would bother me if things like that are said?

—No. I don't know.

—What do you take me for?

—A beautiful woman.

Lanh paused briefly at this and then said, Maybe I am a good lay. Maybe I'm proud of it.

—You don't have to play your role for me, Cliff said.

—What role? You want to fuck tonight, GI?

—It's not that simple.

—It's very simple. You want a little break with a shortime girl. A little fun for the night. That's what you want, GI.

—Listen, Cliff said, let's just forget the whole thing. I enjoyed the food.

—What's wrong with you? Lanh asked, but her harshness was gone. You *are* crazy.

—Really. Just forget it. I wasn't interested in a GI quickie.

—Cliff. What do you want from me? I don't want you to go. I just want you to tell me straight. Don't treat me like somebody I'm not. What do you want?

—I . . . I like you, Lanh. I felt from the moment I came here . . .

—Straight.

—What is this? You ridicule me for talking to you with respect?

—No.

—I'm not telling you you're the fairy princess of Elephant Mountain or a mandarin's daughter or a virgin. I'm telling you that I like you. You've made me feel quiet here. Good here. You can believe that much, surely.

—You want to live with me, Lanh said.

—Yes.

17

—All right.

Cliff was struck silent for a moment by Lanh's immediate acceptance. Then he began to stammer, I . . . have some money saved, but . . .

—Don't talk about it. You live with me till we get tired of each other. Do what you want, when you want.

—But . . .

—I'm not just a whore, Lanh said sharply. I make all the money I need in the bar. GIs like to talk to me. They buy me Saigon Teas and I do all right.

—Of course.

—But for you I can make an exception, if you want. You can live here all right, but you pay by the hour. Okay?

—I wish you'd make up your mind what you want from *me*, Cliff said. You're angry because I talked money. But talking money is talking straight, isn't it?

—I'll give you a special deal. The hours out of bed— half price. Pretty good, GI?

—I think we were too quick in having me stay. Maybe I better go. I won't be a GI to you.

—And I won't be a whore to you.

—Good.

—Yes. Good.

The two suddenly realized that they were shouting and they fell silent for a long moment.

—Well, Cliff said. I think we have that much understood. He smiled at Lanh and she reached out to touch his hand. They held each other for the first time, they kissed. But the kiss—as much as her body stirred him—merely made Cliff afraid. He had one terrible thing to confess to her before he could lose himself in her body.

—Lanh, he said, pulling gently away. I should tell you something before you agree to let me stay.

—What is it?

—I will understand completely if you want me to leave.

—Tell me, Cliff, she said and there was no harshness.

—I'm a deserter.

Lanh looked closely at Cliff but somehow he knew not to be afraid. She came to him and gently touched his face. She said, No wonder you try so hard to love it here.

Cliff turned now to Lanh lying beside him deep in sleep. He wanted to wake her, to enter her, but he knew that, clutched in her hairless loins, he would lose hold of himself for the rest of the night. They'd clung together so often in sweet oblivion that he could never recover in time to decide. He wondered at how quickly that first night they'd sensed what they would mean to each other. But she'd had men living with her before. Cliff and Lanh talked little with each other about their pasts, but he knew there'd been others, and from her clinging, from her frightened visions of their being separated, he knew there was a need in her to have someone in her bed, in her body, that transcended their own individual love. Even now he felt a surge of anguish—jealousy—at the realization, just as he'd felt it the first time he'd realized this about Lanh. But as then, too, he felt closer to her in an odd and surprising way. He understood her terror. He came near to asking himself if it really made any difference—even with Lanh's quick mind, with the way she set her jaw, whatever—if it made any real difference to him who he was with. He would not pursue that thought. He had finally shut his jealousy out of his heart, particularly as Lanh proclaimed feelings that she said she'd never felt before—she had sensed his struggle with her past. And the jealousy had died as the time passed. Cliff turned sharply away from the thought that he'd loved her for this long, steady time because he'd had no other options. No. He loved Lanh. Even as the self-doubts came, they made his feeling for her clearer, stronger. He loved her.

He was lying in a bed in a motel in Carmel. Night, and he could hear the ocean breaking in the dark. Francine slept beside him. They had not touched each other since he'd gotten into San Francisco. The city had seemed all concrete, hard and clean. Alien, after five months in Vietnam. The streets were deserted, to his eye. Even at midday, there was so much space unused by people. Then down the Pacific Coast Highway. The trees looked sculptured, the hills modeled, the highway was hard and sharp-edged and no one was in the fields, no one was buried there or moved there. It all seemed alien. This was the foreign country to his eye now. On the return to San Francisco, this impression had weakened and Cliff had turned his eyes from the fields. Even then, even before he knew what he would do, he knew to preserve his sense of the rightness of Vietnam.

He lay beside his wife in Carmel and he listened to her breathing. They'd talked—casually, almost indifferently—all around the idea of divorce and had never actually spoken it. But they knew it was the only thing for them. They would speak it on the coming day. He held still. He tried to press himself back to his hootch at Homestead but he remained in Carmel. He'd stood on the curve of beach near the motel in the heavy haze of sunset. The sun was not clearly visible. An edge of the haze was spotted red like the yolk of a fertilized egg. The sea was the color of bronze, slick; he was surprised that the sound of the surf was not metallic. Down the long beach, people were lighting fires. He and Francine walked along the shore and he turned, once, to her. He found that he'd been walking far into the breakers, the water splashing up his rolled pant legs. He'd somehow assumed Francine was near his side, but she was split far off, walking parallel to him but just beyond the edge of the dying foam. She walked watching her toes. He was stirred by his wife. He feared her distance from him—he'd always feared her sense of detachment—but he'd found that that same detachment crawled in his genitals. He wanted to grab her to him, fight his way through that invisible space, thrust himself into her now. When they talked of literature and music and scenery so terribly well, he felt like a starving man suddenly fed.

He listened to her breathing in the dark and he wanted her to stay. Little things, little goddam things plagued him. Those slow, whispered breaths, her eyes puffed from the

20

afternoon on the beach, a penlight she brought to read the roadmaps in the dark of the car—her thinking of that kind of detail—these things made him want to grab her close and deny that anything was wrong.

Someone was making love in the next room. Alchemy. Her moans of grief transmuted into giddy laughter. Francine slept on, Cliff drifted off, and the room was dark still but for a thin vertical slice of grey. He lay without moving as his mind cleared. It was morning, he knew. He thought to rise and as he did he sensed she was gone. He opened the drapes and the room was very still. The dresser top was empty. Her bag was gone. He felt he could not stand. Her leaving could not have been a surprise, but he trembled. He wanted to sit, sit on the floor, lean back against the wall, but he would not. He searched for a note. There was none. Then he sat on the bed. Later, back in Vietnam, there were letters working out the details. It was only fitting that way. Her letter in his second month in Vietnam had prompted their meeting in California on his leave, but begun the ending.

Cliff veered away from that letter now. It had nothing to do with the decision of this night. Francine was dead to him. Though he knew she'd helped in some way to bring him to this back alley in Saigon. She'd had something to do with deflecting him from the Student Alliance and Burr Gillis.

He saw Burr for the first time at an organizing meeting for Gillis' Chicago West Side tutoring group. Twenty minutes late Burr strode into the meeting room at Scott Hall wearing a corduroy suit with a work-shirt and a tie. He still had his political science department teaching assistantship then and he had to be more restrained in how he dressed, and so he ended up looking like a radical from the 1930s instead of the 1960s. He scanned all the earnest underclassmen for a long moment and then said in a very low voice, You're not going to understand a thing. Not one of you in fifty. I don't know why you're here. You're not going to understand what I say or what the kids on the

West Side say or even what you say to each other. It's like I'm a ventriloquist up here, throwing my voice. You'll talk a good game, some of you, but it's my own voice I'm going to hear.

He paused and surveyed the fidgets and hiking throats and little sideways glances he'd set in motion.

—Can you think for yourselves, any of you? he said, his voice rising just a little, the voice still low by objective standards, but in contrast to what went before, with his glinting green eyes, with his body oddly stiff as if from some powerful repressed force, the words clanged in the room. Can any of you hear what's going to be said to you? He paused again, briefly. You better, he said. The country better, because there's a whole lot of shit we've got to make up for and I don't know if we've got time.

Then one of Burr's assistants was on his feet with a clipboard and talking and taking names. Cliff approached Burr Gillis after the meeting broke up. The others would not go near him. They only peeped at him as they cluttered about in the hallway outside the room. Cliff caught Burr Gillis mid-stride.

—That was a cheap trick you used in there, wasn't it? Cliff said.

Burr turned on Cliff and grinned at him briefly. Then he said in dead earnest, It was a trick, man, give you that much. But it wasn't cheap. It hurt to say that. Much as I'd like to have us all march out of there arm in arm, it'd be a lie. I want to find one good one in the bunch. Just one connection.

Cliff turned out to be that connection. He saw a dingy winter night on the West Side. Dingy even with new-fallen snow. Cliff remembered the chill stepping down from the bus. The snow hadn't been on the ground even three hours and it was gritty. The row of tenements facing the Youth Center spewed their darkness into the snow. The sodium lamps made the drifts the color of a State Street whore's hennaed hair. Cliff saw Burr's long arms scoop in a clump of boys juking and shivering on the walk before the Youth Center and he took them inside.

The glint of linoleum, frosted glass, a cubicle. Cliff couldn't shake the feel of a church basement. He sat across a table staring at a black boy who twisted and shouted sudden obscenities at passing forms beyond the door that laughed and shouted back. Cliff looked down at the mathematics textbook fuzzing away to pulp at the edge of its pages. What were the mysteries of long division to either of them? Cliff didn't know what to say. He rose, stepped out of the cubicle, stood in the hall for a moment and heard all along the corridor the faint pokings of the tutors' voices and the whistling, stamping, shouting of the black children. But in the hall Cliff's sense of futility in all this passed. The voices of the other tutors fretting at remainders and Columbus' three ships and verb tenses were all linked, they linked him, the people were one, here, doing what they could.

Going out the door that night, heading for the bus, Cliff saw Burr stop at a boy standing on the sidewalk. Cliff wondered at Burr's perception, for this boy seemed like any other but Burr pressed at the boy's ears and then took off the black watch cap he was wearing and put it on the boy's head. He pulled it down over the boy's ears, then over the boy's eyes and rapped him on the shoulder, laughing. Cliff thought about Burr's action all the way back to campus on the bus and he thought of it in odd moments through the week. But before the winter was over he saw Burr do the same thing five more times. Cliff had a clear vision of Burr's closet stuffed full of watch caps, of him walking down Roosevelt Boulevard pressing caps on shivering bums and then pulling refills from his pocket. But Cliff rejected strongly any felt criticism in this vision. It was a simple, very practical act of generosity and some of the other tutors began wearing watch caps, though Cliff didn't see any given away. He wore one himself and it never occurred to him to give it away. Cliff sat a few rows back in the bus and watched Burr in the front row aisle seat. Cliff watched Burr sit there unmoving, watched him as much as he watched the lights of the city passing. Burr was distant at that moment, unapproachable. Cliff felt chilled, perhaps a first premonitory fear. It would all end abruptly and Cliff would make a drastic reversal, he would go into the Army and the sequence that brought him to this room would begin.

Burr would be gone and then there was David Fleming. He saw Captain Fleming, his face impassive against the glare of the sun as they drove the perimeter road of Homestead, the Army base camp near Long Binh. Fleming was briefing Cliff on his first day with the intelligence unit. Cliff was still feeling odd in civilian clothes, odd at being called "mister." Even then the transparency of their cover as "technical advisors" was laughable to him. But he felt odd and it struck him how quickly he'd gotten accustomed to the uniform, to being an Army enlisted man.

Fleming stopped the jeep and turned to Cliff. He spoke in the same level tone that he always used but Cliff could see something in Fleming's face—he didn't know what; a cast to the eyes, the angle of the head, maybe—that made him know Fleming was going to say something he felt deeply about. Then it turned out to be something that seemed incidental, an anecdote almost, and Cliff was surprised. They had stopped just before the turn at the main gate that led off the perimeter road and into the central street leading into Homestead. Outside the main gate lay Highway 1A, a busy four lanes that went to Saigon. Across the highway was a grove of coconut trees.

—You'll likely never be here when he asserts himself, Fleming said, but you should know about One-Shot Charlie. He's suspected of being an ARVN soldier who deserted. Every morning at 0200 he fires a single round from somewhere in that grove of trees across 1A, through the main gate, and straight down the street. You can set your watch by him. Any vehicles on the street at 0200 know to

24

just pull off to the side. He never does anything more. Just his one round and then silence.

Fleming was smiling faintly at this and he glanced away toward the coconut grove. The odd little story was the closest Cliff had seen Fleming come all day to showing some kind of personal feeling and Cliff wanted to pursue it.

—What do you think about that? Cliff asked. Fleming turned his eyes back to Cliff but showed no sign of answering the question. Is the man crazy or what? Cliff asked.

—Oh, that's how everybody treats him. They returned his fire the first few nights but now the guards just know him and wave the unsuspecting off the streets and let One-Shot have his moment.

—What do *you* think? Cliff pressed.

Fleming smiled at Cliff as if the smile was an instrument he'd turned on to evaluate him. Then he said, I like One-Shot, myself. He's no more crazy than any of us. Out there alone in the trees at night. He has what he wants.

It was not the answer Cliff expected. And hearing it, Cliff found himself, too, having a strong feeling about One-Shot Charlie, a feeling at odds with Fleming's. But Cliff said nothing. He just thought that One-Shot most certainly did not have what he wanted. That nightly rifle round was a hand groping through the fence. He didn't particularly want to kill anyone. Everybody knew that. But they couldn't think farther. They didn't see that the rifle shot was a way to try to connect.

Cliff's thoughts now stayed with Fleming. Even on that first day, Cliff felt a link to the Captain. Fleming was Cliff's contemporary—only a few years older than Cliff. And Fleming's seriousness about his job, about the Army, included a strong sense of protective comradeship that Cliff found in many of his superiors. It was the one thing that he'd least expected about the Army when he'd gone in; it was the one thing that touched him the most. He saw briefly the face of the first sergeant in his basic training

25

camp—a black man, rumored to be the third most decorated man in the world. The man spat and swaggered and bullied the trainees but Cliff helped bring one of the trainees who had badly broken a leg into the orderly room, and he saw the first sergeant examine the leg with gentle hands, with his brow and eyes pinched in deep concern, and the first sergeant raised his hand to let the trainee grab it as the pain twisted through him. The first sergeant's gestures, his looks, were subtle but they were terribly clear to Cliff and Cliff felt a brief but strong bonding there in the orderly room—the boy with the broken leg, the first sergeant, Cliff, and the other trainee who'd helped bring the boy in, were all fused together in that moment.

It had been the same in Vietnam at first, but erratically. Then, more and more often, other moments stopped him, held him, shaped him; not the connections to people—other things, crazy things. Cliff thought of one of the Vietnamese agent handlers they worked with. They called him Cap'n Andy, a little man who had a dozen informants of his own who gave him mostly tactical intelligence, like the movement of troops in the area or planned rocket attacks.

Andy sat in a chair in Captain Fleming's office, his voice pitched low, flat. He had none of the ebullience of most Vietnamese. He was somber and slightly pedantic, with occasional digressions on Vietnamese history. He had a vague occupation that involved carpentry but mostly he lived by gathering information for the Americans.

This was Cliff's first contact with Cap'n Andy. Fleming was out somewhere and Wilson Hand, the shop's other enlisted man, who'd been in Vietnam several months already, ran the briefing. Wilson's mouth was shaping wordlessly, mock-sympathetically, to Andy's flow of talk. Below the eyes, Wilson's face was tugged soberly down like an astronaut going through the heightened gravity of a take-off, but his eyes were wide and intense in their relish of this little man.

Cap'n Andy paused after a few low-priority bits of information and then he pitched his voice even lower to say that this next item was from his best source. He said that the nearby Bien Hoa airbase would be rocketed at dawn from a place near Honai village. He gave exact coordinates.

Cliff carefully noted down the coordinates and Wilson sat back in his chair, his face loosened, his hand flapped out to draw Cliff's attention to him. You know, Cap'n Andy is a lucky man, Wilson said.

—That so? Cliff said.

—He has a beautiful wife. Very beautiful.

Cliff looked toward Andy and the man was smiling and his head was bobbing and his shoulders were moving deferentially.

—I've seen her, Wilson said. She's stunning.

—A beautiful wife is sometimes a very great burden, Andy said.

—Andy's right, Wilson said. He's made that point to me several times. Others see she's beautiful, right Andy?

Andy's body ceased its movements, his smile disappeared. But he grew no graver than he'd been throughout the interview so far. He simply resumed his former manner. He said, That's so.

—The husband of a beautiful woman always lives in fear of a rival. Right, Andy?

—Of course.

Wilson paused and looked closely at Andy, then at Cliff, as if he was deciding something. Then he said, still smiling, still in Vietnamese, You know, Captain Fleming said we never take a chance, we can't afford to miss a single bet on these potential rocket sites. That's the policy. So sometime just before dawn the Air Force is going to blow the shit out of these coordinates. But I've always wondered what would happen if Andy here found out his wife had a lover. Andy would just come in and give us the coordinates of the lover's house or the place the lover cuts wood or whatever and say the VC are going to launch a rocket from there. And we'd blow away his rival.

Wilson turned his eyes to Andy and Cliff looked at the little man and Andy returned the look gravely for a moment and then he crossed his leg without moving his eyes and he began to smile.

For as long as Cliff stayed at the camp, whenever he heard distant bombing, friendly fire, he thought of the U.S. Air Force blowing away the lovers of Cap'n Andy's wife, maintaining the domestic balance in the household of the somber little man. Cliff was inclined to laugh over this, but the laughter was an isolating thing, it held him apart from the madness, alone.

And there was the making of the cassette tape that happened later on. The camp had its official whores who were cleared, like all the Vietnamese nationals who worked on post, through the MP checkpoint. The whores came on each night to ply their trade and leave by midnight. Cliff was caught one night in the hallway of his hootch by a supply clerk from Davenport named Mark. Mark's great moon of a grin pulled Cliff along to the clerk's room.

—A little favor, Mark said. You speak the language. I need you to interpret for me.

Mark opened the door to his room and went to the table by his wall locker. This is Kim, he said.

A Vietnamese girl in a bright red mini-skirt was sitting on the lower half of the bunk bed. Cliff had seen Kim around, had exchanged a few words in Vietnamese with her on occasion. She smiled up at him and said hello.

—I want to make a tape, Mark said, holding up the mike for the cassette recorder on the table.

—A tape? Cliff said.

—For my wife.

Cliff shifted his eyes to a framed photo on the table. The wife. A pretty girl with a lunging, gospel smile.

—Julie, Mark said. That's her.

—What kind of tape?

—These girls sing so beautifully. I want her to sing some of the songs onto the tape for Julie.

—You want this girl to sing for your wife?

—Yes.

Cliff looked at Kim. She was still smiling at him. He

28

tried to visualize her singing to the wife in Davenport and he failed and so he sputtered about a bit before saying, He wants you to sing some songs into the tape recorder.

—Sing? What songs?

—Any songs. The kind you sing to yourself, I guess. Vietnamese songs. He wants to send the tape back to his wife in the States so she can hear Vietnamese songs.

—I can't sing to a machine, she said, and Cliff smiled at her being reluctant over the machine, not the wife.

—You'll be able to hear yourself, he said.

—All right.

—She'll do it.

—Good, Mark said and he waved Kim over and gave her the microphone.

As she began to sing, one of the Homestead patrol helicopters flew over, rattling the lockers. She stopped singing and Mark shut off the machine. He rewound the tape and Kim fretted with the microphone cord. She started singing again before Mark turned on the machine, but he stopped her with a quick wave of the hand.

—Not yet, Cliff said to her.

When Mark was ready he nodded his head. Kim turned to Cliff and he nodded too. She began to sing.

She sang a current popular song about a girl whose boyfriend goes away to Cambodia to fight and she writes him a letter every day and he's killed and she vows never to marry. Kim finished the song, paused only briefly, then began a second song about a girl whose boyfriend goes away to fight in the highlands and she writes him a letter every day and he's blown to pieces but survives and he's discharged an invalid and they get married.

Kim fussed about, trying to decide on the next song, thoroughly caught up in the project now in the room. Cliff thought of slipping out of the room, but he liked Kim's voice and instead he climbed to the top bunk and lay down to listen. Kim began to sing an older and more cheerful song, about a country marriage betrothal. From where Cliff lay, he could see the top of the door below his feet. While Kim was singing, the door swung open and closed and Cliff sat up on one elbow.

A new girl had entered the room. Cliff had only seen her in the company area a couple of times before. She stood quietly by the lockers listening until the song was finished. Then Kim chattered an explanation to her about the recording session. Wouldn't she like to sing to Mark's wife too?

She was a beautiful girl, without a trace of makeup, and Cliff watched her closely. She looked at Mark and the picture beside him.

—All right, she said and took the microphone. Mark beamed and Cliff lay back down to listen.

At first he just listened to her voice. It was deeper than Kim's and she phrased the simple tune slowly, thoughtfully. Then the words began to sink in. She was making them up, Cliff realized. That's why she sang slowly. Their rhythms were sometimes crude and they seldom rhymed. But they were a song. A rough-edged song, but she sang.

—You've sent your man to make us whores. You've sent him to take our pride, she sang. You stay at home and are chaste and pure, while your man comes to us and makes us soil ourselves. You let him come, you make him take us to bed. You make him use our sorrow and hunger. You smile at us from your picture as he screws us, and we are harmless toys. You are both safe from harm. You both make us whores.

The new girl stopped singing. She handed the microphone to Kim. No one spoke. Kim stared at her hands. Mark felt something wrong.

—Won't you sing another one? he asked. That was a very sad song, I think. The girl didn't answer.

—We go now, Kim said in English. Very late. You have songs now.

Cliff wanted to leave quickly too. He deflected Mark's thanks for the help but by the time he got out of the room the two girls had disappeared. He went to his own room and for a time he felt closer to the girl with the deep voice than he did to all the Americans here whom he was supposed to be attached to. But he couldn't approach her. He felt excluded by her bitterness. It never occurred to him to try to sleep with her, though he wanted her very much, he found, and he only saw her a few more times, from a distance, with other GIs, and he would turn away. Then he himself was gone.

And it wasn't the girl and her song; at the very end, it was his own act that finally cut him off. Cliff sat up in the dark Saigon room now, sat up and shook his head, listening for rockets falling on the airport. His mind had been too easy, too slack so far tonight. The city that sheltered him from torture and death, from decades of rape and assault in a stockade, from the madness he'd been part of, and from the guilt for a mindlessly terrible act—that city was under siege. The final siege. Saigon was falling and he had to clearly look at his real options—the options now.

Go or stay. Was it that simple? Not really, he sensed. Among the abstract phrases he gathered into his mind, flashes came of a shaggy head, frightened eyes, a curl of cigarette smoke. I can stay and embrace the conquerors, he thought. The first option. The face heaved, shrouded in white, Cliff felt the limbs stiffen beneath him.

Cliff lay slowly back down in his bed. All right. To stay or to go and how—these things could be decided only by first going back to that final act, the one that brought him to this alley.

It had started with Wilson Hand. Wilson had broken his arm on one of the trips to the orphanage in Honai. The place was run by a Vietnamese priest and nun and the buildings were strewn with pallets of abandoned infants, most of them part American; Cliff saw the infants sleeping there on the concrete floor like crabs washed up dead on a beach. His unit made a collection every payday for the orphanage and the following day the head of the intelligence shop and one or both of his enlisted man agents took the money out to the orphanage. It was one of a number of operational traditions Fleming had inherited from his predecessors. During one of these trips, on an impulse, Wilson had climbed a coconut tree in the courtyard. He'd gradually lost his hold and finally, just before his last grip gave way, he reached up with his free hand and gave the ground a crisp, military salute. Then he dropped and cracked an outstretched arm.

—That was a damn fool thing to do, Fleming said as they crouched over Wilson. But the rebuke was quiet and Cliff saw the same concern in the captain's face that he'd seen in his first sergeant's at basic training. Cliff felt instantly his link to Fleming, to Wilson. Cliff wondered: did men fight wars not for causes and territory but, deep down, for the opportunity for moments like this? And in battle these moments were only greatly enhanced. If Wilson lay there dying from a rifle round or a shard of shrapnel, wouldn't his death be transformed into a moment of intense connectedness for the men around him? And even for Wilson himself. In the final moments he would feel the grip of another human being on his hand, his shoulder, his head would be cradled by another human being and he'd be the center of that momentary, perfect universe beyond petty concerns, beyond trivial needs, a universe held together in empty space by the force of human connection. Until death betrayed the moment and the center departed and the moment dissolved. The pain beneath the tree subsided, Wilson pushed away help, supported his own broken arm, and he began cursing. But for as long as he could, Cliff held on to that moment of closeness to the two men. Even now, lying in the dark, caught homeless between the wrath of his former countrymen and the wrath of his former enemies, he was stirred by that moment—and whatever other moments like it he could find. His own likely death this night or tomorrow curled him up in the bed, pressed his hands to his face as his eyes grew warm; he wanted to let himself go to the tears for one reason—he'd die alone, before curses and sneers and no one to give him a hand to grab in the pain. He had an odd moment of regret at leaving the Army. If he was to die in Vietnam it would be better that way—beneath a tree, the hands of his comrades upon him, connected there.

Cliff uncurled. He sat up. He rose from the bed and crossed to the small window in the wall beyond the foot of his bed. His eyes touched the smudged air, the shapeless stretch of a rooftop. But his gaze turned quickly inward. His tears were gone, traceless in him, and he knew he had to harden himself. He couldn't begin to feel sorry for himself or he was lost for sure. He still hadn't examined his act. His complicity in the death of a prisoner. He'd been groping instead for moments that had meant nothing to him in the end, that had held no force great enough to let him prevent the killing.

Wilson had been captured. Captain Fleming left Cliff to tend the shop after the very next payday and he took Wilson, arm slung and hurting, with him to the orphanage. They'd done it once too often. Cliff had frequently laughed at their silly games, even in Fleming's presence. The uniform of PX slacks, PX shirts, PX Hush Puppies that was supposed to convince the Vietnamese they were civilians, then being given an Army jeep to drive the countryside in. And the patterns they established. Every spot report went to the same string of outposts all the way out to Bien Hoa Airport. Mabye there wasn't much they could do about that pattern, but then they created their own—like the regular trip to the orphanage. Finally the VC acted.

Fleming came into the shop and motioned Cliff into his office. He'd been gone a long time but Cliff hadn't wondered at it. He and Wilson could have stopped at a number of places on the way back—to massage local officials, to check up on one of their agent handlers, whatever. But Cliff watched Fleming turn on the fan and suddenly—though it was hot in the room, though it was absolutely natural for Fleming to turn on the fan—he sensed that the gesture was odd. That something was wrong and the captain was doing things by rote. Fleming sat down at his desk. His face was impassive. He began to speak in the same, even tone that he always used.

—They've got Wilson Hand. The VC have him.

Cliff felt himself gape. He wanted to make some kind of sound but couldn't.

—They came into the orphanage and snatched him, Fleming said. He was outside in the courtyard. I was inside with the priest and nun and it was done quick. There were four of them with AK-47s. I got out the back.

Matter of fact, quiet, the words were. But they clawed around in Cliff's head and he was caught by Fleming's impassive face. He wanted to shout the captain into some kind of feeling—rage even, something—but he still could not speak.

—They didn't kill Wilson. I know that much, Fleming said. But they gunned down the priest and the nun.

Cliff's mind twisted away in pain at this. His eyes drifted and then he felt something worse: with his own body he felt Wilson's separation. Cliff's limbs went cold and he wanted to draw into himself in the chair. Wilson was alone now. He hung in a tree ready to fall and no one could touch him. Even the plunge would be less terrible than that moment far off, out of reach of even the sound of voices that knew him.

Cliff could not bear his empathy any longer. He seized on anger for escape. They'd been fools here—the dedicated captain on down. They'd made stupid mistakes, exposed themselves, and Wilson had to pay for it. Cliff wanted to shout this stupidity into David Fleming's face, but he looked at the captain and the man was staring at his desktop and suddenly his impassiveness expressed the loss that he, too, must have felt, and Cliff said nothing. He sat for a long time with David Fleming that afternoon and neither of them spoke but Cliff sensed their minds coursing together.

Time passed—a day, two perhaps, Cliff couldn't remember. He had no sense of the time, really. He only knew that after a while he told himself Wilson must be

dead by now, and that thought comforted him somehow—
it seemed a more tolerable state for Wilson than to remain
sentient and alone. Now, in the dark room where Cliff lay
remembering, he sensed that this was too simple. Perhaps
because, even as the moments passed on this night, death
was drawing closer to Cliff himself. He sensed that alternative stalking through the alleyways leading to this tiny
room and it wasn't as easy now to embrace it. But Cliff
would not face that yet. He was determined to watch
himself kill again. He forced himself back.

Fleming had been out of the office most of the time just
after Wilson's capture. Cliff sat alone in the office with the
drone of the fans and often he found his mind blanking
out. He knew Fleming was trying to do something, was
pressing all his sources for information, but Cliff could
feel no hope.

Then Fleming entered the shop late in the afternoon.
Cliff looked up—the door had banged open, suggesting
strong feelings, but Fleming was standing before him very
still and his voice was steady.

—I've found somebody who may know about Wilson,
he said.

Cliff said nothing. He followed Fleming out the door
and his first flow of feeling was one of dismay. The fragile
peace he'd constructed had been set on the notion that
Wilson Hand was dead. Now the possibility that Wilson
was alive simply revived Cliff's raw sense of the man's
separation. He climbed into the jeep with Fleming. In the
back seat was a burly MP named Eddie Blake who went
with them on tasks needing muscle.

They turned onto Highway 1A and Cliff concentrated on
the fields, let his eyes skim sightless over the bent figures,
the buffalo, the tombs. The sun was low but hot, knotting
Cliff's forehead, pressing at his eyes. Fleming was pushing, pushing at the jeep until it wobbled all over the road
and the faces of children by the roadside turned to draw
back. They'd known to fear us at that moment, Cliff
thought now. He even feared himself as he saw the jeep

rushing through the long shadows of a stand of trees, saw himself sitting in suspension beside the captain who drove the jeep as wildly as his mind must have raced beneath the calm, implacable face that he showed to the world. Even now, years later, Cliff felt close to Fleming through the memory. He wondered if and how the man went on to destroy himself in his unimpassioned way. Cliff knew Fleming would betray him in the memory soon—would let Cliff betray himself. No, he knew he couldn't blame Fleming for his own part in the killing. They did it together, comrades, and that was the terrible irony, that was what shook Cliff so deeply: what Cliff wanted so much, what he knew was good, had been perverted that afternoon.

They stopped before a low stone building near dense woods. A South Vietnamese propaganda banner hung on the wall exhorting allegiance to the homeland. Beyond the building was a curve of concertina wire binding a windowless wing.

—Listen carefully, Fleming said, turning in his seat to look at Cliff and Eddie. The national police are holding a man here who may be a VC military cadre from Honai. He was caught on curfew last night. This is probably our only chance to get Hand back. We have to scare this guy. He's gonna be afraid of Americans anyway, pumped full like he is with his side's propaganda about us. Blake, I want you to stand near us and just look mean. Keep your M-16 in front of you and ready and anytime the prisoner looks at you, you look like there's nothing you'd rather do than kill the fucker right then and there.

—Wilson's dead by now, isn't he? Cliff asked.

—No, Fleming said. No, I've thought it out and they've got to have more than two days use out of him. I think he's alive.

Cliff regretted asking. It all started over again for him. He spun off into the silence and darkness with Wilson.

—Cliff, Fleming said, I'm going to pretend not to speak the language. Cliff.

—Yes? Cliff said, dragging himself back. He found

36

Fleming's face suddenly open, receptive. Cliff gasped yes again, thankful for where he was, thankful for David's sense of command. You'll pretend you can't speak Vietnamese, Cliff repeated.

—You interpret for me, Fleming said. I'll play it tough. You'll be the good guy. We'll Mutt and Jeff him. You know the routine. Tell him I'm a mad dog . . . Okay. Let's get Wilson.

A corridor of cells. Cliff's lungs filled with the smell of piss and caustic lime. He staggered in the dim light, heard no sound, though the cells were filled with shapes. They stopped—Cliff, Captain Fleming, Eddie Blake, and a Vietnamese police lieutenant—before a cell. The face in the cell was obscured by the dark. The police lieutenant went in, the figure rose on its own, moved forward through the cell as if avoiding contact with the lieutenant. The figure emerged, passed by without ruffling the air. Cliff could not be sure that the man actually existed, that he wasn't a trick of the light.

Then they were in a tiny room and the figure was flesh. He went straight to a stool in the center of the room. This isn't new for him, Cliff realized. A weakness washed over Cliff—we're amateurs, children playing, he knew. We'll learn nothing from this man. Wilson will live on wherever he is and we will not find him. The smell of the cells lingered in Cliff's lungs, in his mouth, and he felt dizzy. Fleming nodded Cliff to a stool near the prisoner. Cliff sat.

The little man was before him and the room fell away. The man's face was turned slightly, his eyes were cast down, seeking the thin slips of space between the bodies that surrounded him. Lying in the dark now Cliff tried to look very closely at the face in his memory. Even long before the afternoon of the interrogations, Cliff's eye had learned the ways in which Vietnamese faces asserted their individuality. But the face began to blur. Cliff lurched ahead. The face was shrouded in white. The cheeks were hollowed. He saw them beneath the cloth—sunk deep. The man was maybe forty, but it was simply a guess. The face was unlined, the hair—splayed from his head like an urchin's—was black. But the man's body had drawn tighter on his bones, was hard. That's how middle-age came to a Vietnamese man. He sat on the stool and his eyes did rise to the words of the police lieutenant warning him that if he ever wanted to return to his family he had better cooperate with these men. The eyes remained raised, shifted to Fleming, as the captain demanded in English where the American was who was captured at the orphanage. As Cliff translated the question the man kept his eyes on Fleming. The eyes were steady, unflinching, in spite of Fleming's harsh tone, in spite of Fleming's face drawing near. The man was measuring Fleming and Cliff felt a pulse of fear for the captain. And for Wilson. Lost among men like this.

—I don't know what you're talking about, the little man said in Vietnamese and he lowered his eyes again, though this time he looked straight ahead, not down. He crossed his leg.

—You're a goddam liar, Fleming growled after the translation. Then he shouted it. You're a liar, you son-of-a-bitch.

Cliff translated the cursing forcefully, colloquially, and the little man did not stir.

—Listen, I've seen this guy go crazy with prisoners before, Cliff said to the man in a low tone, confidentially. But the man did not even acknowledge Cliff's presence.

—I want to know where the American is, Fleming said. The man with the broken arm who was taken two days ago at the orphanage in Honai.

The words sounded temperate at first and Cliff translated phrase by phrase. Then Fleming's face suddenly appeared looming above the Vietnamese man and Fleming was cursing wildly.

—Let me talk to him, Captain, Cliff said to Fleming, overriding the curses. Cliff turned to the Vietnamese man and said, Even his own men are afraid of him. He's a madman. Believe me. He'll kill you.

38

The man would not respond. Would not even look at Cliff. Cliff offered him a cigarette. The man turned to him at this and reached for the cigarette. He glanced briefly at Cliff with an odd flicker of a smile about his eyes and Cliff realized the haminess of first suggesting the man's life was in danger and then offering him a cigarette, as if it was his last. Cliff knew the man was laughing at how transparent these Americans were in their act.

Fleming made a show of trying to deny the Vietnamese man the cigarette and Cliff said no, let him have it. But Cliff was already feeling foolish. He saw the smile still playing about the man's eyes as he turned away.

Cliff was soaked with sweat, he suddenly realized. He sensed the room tight about him. The little man before him was unruffled, with not a bead of sweat on him; he was in complete command here and Wilson was lost forever and Fleming and Cliff were playing a silly game, fooling no one but themselves.

The interrogation went on for a time and then Fleming said to Cliff, Let's take him outside.

They were in the woods. The trees were loosely spaced, though the sky was closed out above their heads. Late afternoon shadows draped the trees like grey crepe and there was no sound but their faint footfalls on the duff. Fleming led the way and Cliff caught a glimpse of a stream up ahead. The captain dropped back to walk by Cliff.

—Tell him I'm planning something terrible out here, Fleming said in a low voice.

Cliff wanted to say it was no use. Wilson is lost and we've been exposed for what we are. But he did not. He went back to where the prisoner was walking beside the police lieutenant.

The man was calm still. His eyes showed nothing—no amusement any longer, no fear, no secrets even, nothing but control, quiet. Cliff spoke to him and did not listen to his own words but listened for the little man's breath, his step. There was no sound. Nothing. It was impossible to tell, of course, with them all walking together, but Cliff felt that the man walked under the dark trees without making a sound, his footsteps silent, not breaking a twig. It didn't occur to Cliff until much later, until he was in Saigon, buried deep in a back alley, that as he walked there on the path he felt the man dead. The figure beside him had again become a thickening of the light, a flicker there isolated in the twilight, untouchable.

They were beside the stream. Cliff, Eddie Blake, the police lieutenant, Fleming, the prisoner—they all stood at the bank of the stream, pocked with late-day sunlight, and no one stirred for a long moment. Cliff watched Fleming looking about, deciding what to do, exposing the fact that indeed he'd had no terrible plan for the prisoner.

—Sit him down by the stream, Fleming finally said.

They sat the man down parallel to the stream. His hands were tied behind his back.

—Hold his legs down, Fleming said to Cliff.

Cliff sat on the man's legs—like sitting on rocky gound— and said, Tell him what he wants to know. Please. The man said nothing, did not look at Cliff, would not look at him directly again before the end.

Eddie Blake stepped behind the sitting man, crouched, and held his arms.

—Where is the American with the arm in the sling? Cliff translated for Fleming. He was taken by your friends. We want to know where he is.

The man looked up at Fleming, a gesture that startled Cliff, made him want to recoil, get away from the little man.

—I don't know where he is, the man said and Cliff's feelings swung sharply back—he knew the man was afraid. It was the only way he'd show the fear, by relating to his adversary. Relating with outward calm, but the very relating exposed his fear. Cliff knew the little man was ravaged with his isolation among these large pale creatures.

Fleming was looking at the man closely and Cliff translated the sentence with a rush, having nearly forgotten to keep up the ruse. In translating the sentence it suddenly struck Cliff that the phrasing had implied the man at least knew something about the incident. Fleming caught it, too.

—So you do know about it, he said through Cliff.

—No, the man said.

—You say you don't know where he was, Fleming said. But you do know *about* him.

The man lowered his head, looked before him as if he knelt with a gun at the base of his skull. Cliff knew he would say no more.

—You're holding out on us! Fleming yelled.

Cliff spun slowly away, toward the trees. Cliff was talking to the Vietnamese man, he knew, was pleading with him to tell the truth, but Cliff felt as if he had broken off, had risen into the dark tops of the trees; he was alone, as Wilson was alone. The prisoner moaned and Eddie Blake had been wrenching the man's arms back. Cliff saw Fleming motion to Blake to stop. Cliff was glad. Cliff approached the scene again. Fleming laid the man down. Gently, it seemed. Fleming was hunched over: in great sadness, Cliff believed, in loss; feeling, too, Wilson's isolation as if it was his own. Cliff again felt close to Fleming. Fleming laid his handkerchief over the man's face and was speaking Vietnamese to him. Where's the American? Tell me where he is. Please, he said, and he was splashing water on the handkerchief while Eddie held the man's torso down. It seemed such a little thing, this handkerchief, but Cliff had heard about the agony of it. No breath. No way to draw a breath. The legs vibrated under Cliff as he listened to Fleming's voice pleading. Cliff looked at the face coming clear under the cloth as the water splashed, the shape emerging minutely as if it were rising to the surface from a deep pool. Cliff felt the legs stiffen, heard the man gasping. It's just a handkerchief, a homely little horror, it will pass, Cliff thought. But tell us where Wilson is, let us bring him back, Cliff's mind shouted with Fleming. The face, the white face, gasped

41

and the chest heaved, the head the face rose and shook and jerked back and the legs went limp the body went limp the man was dead.

Fragments now. The police lieutenant listening at the chest, his head there as if resting. The heart was weak, he said. The heart was very weak. A weak man. Fleming pushed the lieutenant aside and pressed at the dead man's chest, pumped at him. But he was gone. Moving through the woods, the three of them, Fleming ahead, Cliff, the MP behind. The three of them moved in silence, there was no sound in the woods, no birds, no wind, beneath their feet no sound in the leafmass. They moved alone, Cliff was alone, cold, the two bodies moving nearby were far away, planets spun off from a nova in their separate courses, bound no longer, alone.

Cliff sat up in the bed now, gasping. He pressed at his face. The Vietnamese man's breath heaved in Cliff, strong, struggling, then desperate. Fleming did not breathe, never breathed, nor Cliff's wife, nor Burr Gillis, father, no one, there was no breath drawn but this man's and this man drew his breath through Cliff now, through Cliff's lungs and then it stopped. The breath stopped and there was nothing. Nothing but the night. Nothing but the rockets now in the distance, the sound of metal ripping in the dark. Then silence. Nothing at all, not even the night. Just the throb behind Cliff's eyes. Just his own trembling.

He turned his head to listen for Lanh. He could hear nothing. He laid his hand lightly on her hip. It was bare, the sheet was back, she lay on her side and her flesh was warm beneath his hand but he still did not hear her breath. He leaned down, drew nearer, his face passed her side, his face felt her warmth but there was no breath. His face passed her breasts and he drew near to her face and then he heard a faint sound, faint as the hiss of the stars but he heard her breathe. He stopped, leaning far over, his arms growing hot in the strain, his forehead tight, he listened on, and, as if in response to his attention, as if to touch him and soothe him as she did when she was awake, Lanh expelled her breath suddenly, sighed in her sleep, drew Cliff's mind to her, touched him, let him pull his body away now, clear-headed.

He'd not slept that night of the killing. He lay awake—even as he lay this night—to decide what to do. But there had been very little thought. He lay in the dark of his hootch and listened to the patrol helicopters hammering about the perimeter and he knew somewhere deep in his mind from the very first that he could not stay. He had seven months to go before the return to the States and he knew that his isolation in Fleming's presence would be unbearable. But even Fleming wasn't the worst of it. Cliff had sensed that even back then. Cliff had been part of the death of the prisoner and one death could not really be compared to another but the tortures of others in this country—the tortures with intent to kill—had been much worse. Fleming's stupid theatrics with the water on the cloth should not have killed—it was the man's heart—a heart that none of them had known was bad—and Cliff had begun to see it this way even on the night in his hootch. But his own heart had grown bad by then. That was the matter. He'd died, himself, to the life he'd been leading and that was what he'd known from the first on the night of the killing. He'd already gotten Francine's letter and he'd been to Carmel and it was a natural part of the flow of things, part of the wave that his father rode, his mother, Burr Gillis. He would turn his back and let the wave lift him, he would rise with it, rush on, away from the life he'd been trying to live, he'd run, fly, he'd join the deserters, he'd rush toward Saigon. Saigon. He knew the city. Yes. He loved the city, knew its language, yes.

The inevitability of the decision to desert seemed clear now, as Cliff lay in the bed beside Lanh in a calm moment. But at the time, these conditions pressed on Cliff without touching his reason. They swirled in the dark about his face, he drew them into his lungs with the sound of the dying man, and even the next day as he sat in the hootch with the monsoon squall blowing outside he could not rationally focus his mind. The stone in his shoe held him until the rain stopped. He sat for a brief time in the silence and then, without any awareness of a decisive moment, he knew there was nothing to go back to, there was nothing to do but go.

He'd returned to the CI shop just before leaving to get some things from his desk—Francine's letter, for one. The offices were empty, and as he drove off across the open space before the shop, he passed Fleming's jeep coming in. There was someone in the jeep beside Fleming and the glimpse of the face did not register at first because of Cliff's resolution not to stop. It was Wilson, he realized a moment later. He stopped briefly at the turn onto the perimeter road. He looked into his rearview mirror and Fleming's jeep was approaching the shop. Wilson. Cliff thought that he must have been mistaken. It had been just a glimpse. But no. He was sure Fleming had Wilson. He'd gotten him back somehow. It made no difference. If Cliff did not go back to the shop, Fleming would soon know something was wrong. But Cliff could not face Fleming. Could not face Wilson, either. And so it was done.

Lanh's breath again. She moved beside Cliff. He looked and she was lying now on her back, sheet down to her knees, her body as sleek in the darkness as an otter's flank. He drew near and her loins were a thickening of the dark as if from a deep churning in a night pool, swirling musk from the bottom of the pool to the surface. He trembled and bent to kiss her there, below the brief lick of hair. He touched his lips to Lanh, lightly, he could not wake her yet, his breath caught at the softness, she stirred and he drew back. He moved his recollection not to her touch but to her half-smile, mocking, that turned into a terrible flash of sadness quick as lightning showing in its colorless light the pain in her. He watched her body in the dark, felt her nearness plucking him erect. There was a sudden profuse popping far off. Distant gunfire. He leaned forward and covered Lanh with the sheet, pulled it up above her breasts.

He remembered telling her the story of the killing. He told her late in the afternoon of their fourth day together, after a long nap, entwined naked on this bed through the worst heat of the day.

—Can't you think of anything else to confess to me? She mocked.

—I just want you to know what you're getting into.

—And you? Shall I tell you all the things I've been paid to do?

Cliff could not tell if she was serious about this or still mocking him.

—You don't have anything to confess to me, he said.

—Or the things I did for free? How about those? She was clearly angry now.

—I'm sorry. It was me I was talking about. Not you. You know I love you for what you are.

—And can't I do the same? She was gentle now. You helped kill a man, she said. What did you expect when you came to Vietnam?

Cliff flinched at this and Lanh drew him close. Cut it out, she said. Listen to me. That man expected the same thing. He was more ready than you. Why was he so quiet when he knew he was going to die?

—He was afraid.

—No. Not just that. He was quiet because he is Vietnamese and he knew that dying like that was part of life. As natural as he can squat and take rice under a banyan tree and bury his daddy in the fields and bury a burned child, he can die from the way things are in this country. It was the way of your job here. It was part of his way too. He knew and accepted that. So he didn't speak when the water that had grown his rice squeezed at his heart. We're all alike in this place. We understand, you see.

Cliff pulled away from Lanh. He had to see her eyes at this. She was looking at him calmly. With love, even. He

45

could not even begin to fully understand what feelings lay behind her words. But he did know the look. She touched his face, pressed his eyes shut with her fingertips.

—You forgive me? he asked.

She kissed him on the eyes.

Another moment, much later. He pressed too hard to tell her his desire for her. You're beautiful, Lanh. So beautiful.

She turned on him sharply. You'd trade me in for the first pair of size 36 American breasts you could get your hands on, she said.

—No. Not true.

—I don't believe you. You'd be crazy to love a tiny little dark thing like me.

Cliff went deeper in, though he'd learned long ago he should just be quiet at times like this. You call me crazy, he said, because I appreciate you? Then are they sane men who come here to fight a war but find you small and yellowish and similar so they go with ease beyond just war and torture your people?

Even as he spoke of torture he realized how totally Lanh had let him forget what he'd done. The word burred in his mind but Lanh would not take advantage of it in the argument.

—Don't pity me, Cliff, she said. Don't do it. Don't pity the strange little people who need someone with sharp eyes to love them.

—I don't feel that way, Cliff cried.

—And don't talk to me about torture. You expect me to fall weeping now for my persecuted people? Must I weep for them all and never stop weeping?

—No.

—They understand. If I am in our fields and the sun wears me down, I go under a tree and sit quiet, feel warm, take my joy, but the hot sun is all around me. I see it, I know it's part of where I am. If there is no tree, I must sit in the field and accept it.

—We took your trees. We burned them away.

—Why is your coming to us any different from the

46

coming of the heat of the day? You live too. If you don't come, then that is the way of our life. But you did come, and if you kill me slowly, I will feel pain and die. But don't cut me off from the life around me, don't make me die bad, let me keep my acceptance of things.

—You know I've always fought you about your envy of American women. I love you, Lanh. I don't want you to look or think or act or feel like an American.

—Then speak to somebody else about the torture. I can't hear it again.

There was a long pause. Cliff sat on the bed staring at the floor. He hadn't really felt guilty anymore. She'd cleared that out of him long ago. That was the irony. But she was in pain and there was nothing he could do to remove it. Not as she had done for him. She was beside him on the bed. Her voice was gentle.

—We don't need to ever think about those things, she said. Not between us.

Cliff lay down beside her now in the dark room. He pulled the sheet over him and they lay together, side by side on their backs, hands at their sides, as if laid out together in death.

"We have to think these things now, my love," Cliff whispered in the dark. His mind dilated in fear—his body flushed hot. There was very little time left and he had no idea what to do. From what he could pick up in the newspapers he saw, from the complaints of two years of the Thieu government, the people in the U.S. had done all they could to forget Vietnam. That rang true. And to go back now would leave Cliff in the hands of a vengeful Army without the buffer of public opinion. He knew how quickly people could forget. They wouldn't care about the fate of a deserter from a war they no longer thought about, a war that they had decided never really existed for them.

But the obvious alternative was just as bad. The VC would have just as little use for him, would have a vengeance of their own. A few days before, he'd heard two old women down in the alley talking intensely for a long

47

time without any laughter, without any expansive cursing. He went to the window and listened. Even their betel nuts could not keep out their fear—they exchanged rumors about the terror of the VC. The VC were torturing everyone. Killing anyone who had had any contact with the Americans and torturing the rest just to make sure. One of the women wailed, My radio. It's American. Throw it away, the other said. Yes, yes, but I want my radio, the first woman said. Your life, the second countered and the first groaned in assent. The second grew grim. And me, she said. Every day I sold soup on the street before the hotel where the Americans put up their officers. The VC will know. Cliff had pulled away from the window, regretting he'd let himself listen to as much as he did. Foolish old women. Hysterical old women. Of course the wildest rumors would sweep the city as the end drew near. He could not listen to them. He had to keep his mind clear to make the best decision.

But he'd avoided making that decision, avoided even much thinking about it for the past few days. Until now. Cliff's mind began to want to flail about. The alternatives were difficult. But he had some hours yet. He forced his mind into stillness. He thought about America. He had, particularly in the past year, purged himself of any thoughts of where he'd come from. He'd made himself feel that nothing of what he now was remained in that country. He knew the time had come to examine the truth of this. Whatever he could think to do had to take into account what he'd been, what there might be left in him from the past.

He thought of Francine. He saw her sitting at the window looking out at the tiny rock garden of their apartment. He strode through her line of vision, approaching the door in his Army fatigues after the day's classes at intelligence school. His passage did not break her gaze. He stopped, waggled his fingers at her. They had no particular quarrel going at the time and so she raised her eyes, smiled her basic smile—it had grown to seem phony to him, constructed after the pattern of Rye, New York, families of substance and Tri-Delt sorority women. His own smile he knew to suppress. He constructed a put-upon look. Weary. She had demanded often to know why he was so cheerful coming home from a day being a soldier. He never had an answer for that.

They went walking after dinner. They talked about books. They were safe with books. Their rapport over books was intact. But they'd fallen silent after a time. Their time together of comfort—yes, of some joy, even still—had shrunk into the space of a twilight stroll in the streets of Baltimore. They turned in at a ragged little cemetery bound by row houses, a Chevrolet plant lot filled with semi-trailers, and a tank farm. They were on high ground and in the distance the city smoked by the bay as if it was the source of the gathering dark.

Cliff and Francine separated among the tombstones. Cliff stopped in an overgrown section where the graves were marked by hand-lettered wooden posts. One of the posts had a styrofoam cross wired to it. The ages at death of those buried here were very old. No relationships were noted. No beloved fathers of, no devoted daughters to or sons of.

—This is how I feel, Francine said.

Cliff looked up and Francine was standing some distance away, where the markers were marble. She did not elaborate on her statement, did not look up. Cliff moved toward her. He felt the ground suddenly bloat as he stepped on a grave hidden in the weeds and he recoiled from it, he shuffled his feet in the grass as the feel of the grave lingered there.

Francine was before two identical headstones. When Cliff was beside her she said, Look at these.

The stones had the names of a man and a woman, the dates of birth and death, and noted that they were husband and wife.

—He was fifty-two when he died, Francine interpreted. She was fifty at the time. But she lived on to be ninety.

Just before she died, it must have seemed to her that her life had broken in two. The married woman was a stranger to her.

They stood together in silence for a moment. Cliff waited for Francine to repeat that this was how she felt, but she did not. She must have decided it was unnecessary. He knew her meaning. They'd argued about it often enough. They'd had a life together when he first married her that had held them both tightly. They'd been on and off together through three of his undergraduate years at Northwestern. Then when it went bad with Burr—she'd always contended with that part of him—and he went to graduate school in Iowa, they married and she transferred to be with him to finish her own last undergraduate year. They were happy. Being linked to her by the institution of marriage was a revelation to Cliff for a time—they were closer than before and he felt content. But the Army came at last and Francine of all people could do nothing but encourage the acceptable path and then she was trapped. Cliff found attractions about the Army that he could never quite explain to Francine. And she grew more and more unhappy separated from friends, home, and graduate school. Her own life broke in two, she felt.

Then, his second month in Vietnam, the letter. She was in New York City, starting graduate school in art history. I'm unhappy, she wrote. It's not your fault. I'm not blaming you. But I need to exist. I need to be real. I have no creative talent. I have no religion. I have no profession—even what I'm majoring in now is made for college women who are just biding time. There are no museum jobs to speak of. I don't know what I'm doing here. So because I don't have any of these things I'm only left with other people to make me real. Do you understand me? You try to explain yourself, how you've changed, been able to be happy in the Army, and in Vietnam even. I didn't always understand. But I did try. So try now to understand what I'm saying and why, even though it maybe is difficult. I'm not a bitch. I'm not hard and cruel to write this to you. I just have to connect to people. Lots of people. So I know who I am. I've got nothing else because nothing else has been given to so many women. Including me. You spent your time marching around for a cause. You understand I'm not that way, marching around playing at games, but women need some breaks, too. And being married is death for a woman like me. *That* took some doing, to realize and accept that. My first impulse, being what I am, would be to say marriage is the real answer. But it's not. It's death. It stops me from really connecting to other people. And I have to connect as myself. Not part of a tandem. Not me in a role. Me. We're different, Cliff. Too different. Your cartwheeling around in your little Army is something I can't respond to. Like when you were cartwheeling around with your revolutionary playmates. I don't understand the wildness in you . . . Wow. I vowed not to say things like that. I'm sorry. I'm not critical of you, really. Even writing this I think of the good times we've had. We do share a lot. But I have to feel free to be myself. This year ahead seems horrible to me if I have to spend it alone. We have to resolve this. Please understand. Write to me. Please.

And so he went to San Francisco on his leave time and they drove down the coast and she disappeared from a motel room in Carmel.

He understood Francine's letter—understood her feelings, but the person she took him to be seemed a stranger. It wasn't him. Maybe we just create things—lie—about ourselves and about others to let us follow what seems to be a basic instinct to flee. Cliff sat up with this thought. It was an odd notion to him, one that had struck him only now, unexpectedly. He set it aside. It seemed clear to him that he himself had never wanted to flee. He'd wanted to connect. Even Francine's letter emphasized that she wanted to find others. Cliff had no anger at her now. He understood how she hurt, how she could feel the isolation so keenly that she would write to him while he was still adjusting to the terror at being in Vietnam.

He remembered seeing Francine for the first time. She

51

was sitting in a booth at an off-campus hangout with two of her sorority sisters. They were all three out of the Tri-Delt factory, it was clear. They were all willowy, all off-shades of blond. Their sameness aroused Cliff—their individual attractiveness was heightened for him by their clear, strong link to each other. Francine was in command, however. That, too, was clear. She sat on one side of the booth alone, and her hands moved strongly in the air before her, shaping her thoughts for her two sisters. Cliff could not hear Francine's voice from where he sat but he wanted from the very first to enter the circle of her resolute hands, wanted to become part of her, make her part of him.

For a year Francine would not let them go to bed together. It was 1964 and they were still part of the generations that had come before. She spoke with vigor of saving herself for her future husband. Later they laughed at that first not quite consummated year of passion. They knew then how narrow the generation gap had been—no more than a couple of years, and for a long time they had been on the far side. But Cliff saw himself walking back to his dorm after leaving Francine at the end of a date. They had agreed not to go to bed, but vertical, in the dark, with Lake Michigan washing away any sounds of distant passersby, they groped each other desperately. He smelled his fingers, smelled her most intimate link to him, felt again her sudden slackness, her suppressed moan, his hand soaked to the wrist, her softness clamping his fingers, binding him tightly to her. Of course he had loved her. Even now, lying in bed ten thousand miles and over a decade from that night, he knew how strong that joining had been. Just the smell of her on his fingers had made him feel close to her with an intensity that he never quite felt with her again. How sharply things impressed him then, he thought. He passed an alley on that walk and the dust and sour wood smell pierced him and he still caught very brief recollections of that smell in alleys—everywhere—San Francisco, Paris, Saigon—unexpectedly he would find himself pricked by that night, pricked by that sense of ecstasy. He thought now of when he held her on a sofa in the lobby of the sorority house. She was weeping softly over something he couldn't quite remember, a snub, something, a snub by the sorority itself, they'd passed her over for some office. She wept softly and he held her and when anyone walked by, Francine would look up briefly to see if it was one of the sisters that she should glare at, but then she'd remember her tears and retreat again. Fuck these children's games, Cliff said to her. You and I are going places. Her face jerked to him at this as if she'd heard a gunshot. Then she straightened, her tears were gone, and she whispered to him intensely, You bet your cock we are.

But where she felt they were going together definitely did not include the transformation of American society. She hated Burr Gillis and Cliff's involvement in the radical movement—though she did love his hair long and his great drooping mustache. Cliff was torn. He felt close to Francine but he felt close to those he marched with as well. In the summer after graduation from Northwestern he spent a month with Francine in a cabin on a Wisconsin lake and then Burr called and wanted him to go with him to the West Coast for a few weeks and he went in spite of Francine's threats. But he was not ready to relinquish his ties to the movement and he felt Francine would remain with him because he knew she thought she'd win in the end.

On the hitch to the west Cliff thought twice that Francine had been right all along. He found a pay phone each time and called her.

The first time was after a night in a crash house in Kansas City. The group there had the top floor of a Victorian home in a straight neighborhood. The main room was enormous with beveled glass and windowseats and no furniture at all. The floor was covered with naked mattresses stinking of spent semen. The women of the pad were all the same, all lanky with tangled brown hair and gnawed fingers and bruised arms. Cliff smiled at them, thinking of Francine's sorority replicated here but feeling drawn to them nevertheless and to one in particular. One with amber eyes and a crooked smile and Cliff watched her moving—rubbing her eyes, shaking her hair—through the evening's talk lounging on the mattresses. They stripped at last for sleep and Cliff watched where she was when the lights went out and the bodies began to move and the churning sounds began all around him. He crawled on his hands and knees, erection shooting down, to where she was and she came at him from an angle and they clung into each other. He wished the lights were on. He could not see her face in the darkness—they'd put blankets over the windows to keep the straights from going ape-shit— and he tried to remember her smile. Shit, he thought, as he came in her. Shit. I want to see her, want to join her with a view of her face. He woke in the morning still pressed against her and when someone took the blanket down he saw it was some other woman he'd made love to. This one was freckle-chested, pretty, but somebody else. Cliff didn't even let himself look to see where the one he'd wanted had ended up. He put his clothes on and walked around the block and he called Francine. He called Francine who insisted on keeping the lights on, who'd do it with him in a klieg light if she could, and he told her he loved her. He didn't tell her she was right all along. Already that notion— which had come in the first moments of light that morning— was beginning to fade. He just told her he loved her and he missed her.

But he still would not return. He didn't do that till Burr skipped the country on him. Cliff didn't linger now with Burr's abrupt departure. He remembered instead the second phone call.

—Where are you? she said when she heard his voice.

—San Francisco, he said.

—This just to say I love you?

—No. I'm coming back.

—When?

—I'm leaving tonight.

—How?

—Bus. It'll be a couple of days.

—Okay.

There was a long pause. Cliff waited for her to ask what happened. She must have sensed that she could say I told you so. But she didn't push it.

—Okay, he said.

—So you love me. Right?

—Yes. And you?

—I love you, she said and she was laughing. Phones are bad ways to communicate, Cliff knew. Cut off from gestures, inflections, postures, it was hard to tell how some things were meant. He couldn't quite place her laughter. Was she relieved? Gloating? Joyous in their love? Self-righteous? Any number of other things? He couldn't really say. He wanted to crack the receiver on the side of the phone box, pull the phone out by its roots and jump around on it.

—What are you laughing at? he asked.

—Why aren't you laughing? she answered.

—I don't know.

—Come home, goddamit, she said. Just hang up the fucking phone and catch a bus. I love you, goddamit.

So he went back to Francine and he married her and that was the end of Burr Gillis and social protest. But Cliff now did not let his mind return to Francine. He stayed with Burr, but not in that ill-fated last trip west. An odd moment, an intense moment.

They were watching television. Eight or ten of them in the office of the Youth Center. Johnson was addressing the nation on something—Cliff couldn't remember what. But Cliff and Burr and the others were hissing, they were cursing and shaking their fists at the screen, and Cliff remembered how he felt then, how he couldn't bear the Texas drawl, the sound of the dumb war-mongering gross Texan, and his pendulous ears like rooster wattles and his trace of a smirk—Cliff remembered hating the man, hating him and turning his eyes to the others who shouted in hatred too, hating the man wanting him to shit in his pants on the screen wanting him to fall down dead. And Burr looked at Cliff and the others too—they looked at each other in their hate for the image on the screen and they knew each other's minds and hearts and found their own reflected there, found the kinship of their cause and their ideas, found that it was this kinship they were shouting in the room. They felt close to each other in their shared hatred, they felt validated, even comforted. But Cliff's mind, even as he shouted on, began to pull back. Their cause was just and it was a human one, revering human life, upholding the brotherhood of all people, but how then could it inspire this hate? He could not answer this. He thought, suddenly, about the white bigots they fought against—did the bigots feel this intense comradeship with each other? Of course they did. They hated the blacks so they could love each other more fully. Cliff stopped shouting but his mind stopped too. He went no further. He stood in silence and stared at the face on the screen, which turned into a collection of features, no more, a face and voice flickering in a rectangle of light.

An ex-Green Beret who was a student at Northwestern— what was his name? he'd gained notoriety—Cliff couldn't recall the name—why did the man come to him at all? —Cliff was beginning to drift now, he realized. He was getting tired. But the Green Beret. Cliff saw him clearly in the little restaurant hangout near campus. He was a tall man, blond, boyish-looking, but with a very serious face. He'd been in the Berets and had gotten an honorable discharge and enrolled in Northwestern. Then he showed up unheralded, in uniform, at a big peace rally on campus. He burned his draft classification card or discharge papers or something and made a nervous but firm speech denouncing the Army. The wire services picked up his picture and it was splashed all over newspapers across the country. The Army was going to arrest him, they said. Two days after the rally Cliff was sitting in a booth when the Beret came in alone. He was in jeans and a workshirt with a notebook under his arm, but Cliff recognized him at once. The man went through the self-serve line and he carried a tray toward an empty booth. On the way he bumped into a surly, scuffle-footed old man who cleared tables. The Beret's pie ended up on the floor, his glass of milk shattered, splashing the old man's shoes. The old man began to curse the Beret, who retreated without a word of defense and bought another piece of pie. He passed through the glares and the mumbled threats of the old man and went to the utility table to get utensils. He couldn't hold on to them. He dropped a fork first, bent to retrieve it, straightened and pulled his tray away too fast and at an angle, dropping the fork again and a knife. Cliff watched the man bend to pick up the utensils. He thought the man stayed bent just a beat or two longer than he needed. He rose red in the face, his jaws clenched and pulsing. The man sat alone in the booth behind Cliff where only the sound of the man's eating came for a time. Then Cliff heard abrupt scraping noises and puffing. Cliff turned. Some of the papers from the Beret's notebook had fallen between the booth seat and the wall and he was trying desperately to get them back out.

Cliff stirred in his bed now. Why didn't I join him, tell him I respected him, ask him to come see Burr Gillis about doing more? Instead I let him remain isolated. His act had come out of nowhere, though. He'd been with no group, and after he'd said his piece to the press, he'd slipped away without letting anyone near him. Cliff realized that he had sensed something about the man that wanted to be alone. But remembering him now he pitied the man. Cliff shivered slightly in empathy with him, with his isolation, his struggle with the little things there in the restaurant that drained the significance out of what he'd done. Cliff's own life in Saigon for a long time had resolved itself into a daily obsession with keeping the room cool, trying to fight the shits with Vietnamese medicine, trying to keep his mind busy. Not till he started taking risks—going out for long walks in the street, using the old IDs that could still be on some MP's wanted list, meeting with the *Washington Post* reporter—did he free himself from the same kind of tyranny-by-the-trivial that tried to undo his mind, his resolve. He stood in the center of the sidewalk and watched a jeep of MPs approach and his heart raced and the jeep went by and Cliff clung to his home there, clung to the lichen-stained building walls, pulled into himself the rot and gasoline and sun smells and the swooping gabble of women near him and he knew where he was and why in the moment the MPs passed him on the street.

When the Americans pulled out at last, Cliff found himself discontented for a time. The life and values he had rejected were gone for good. At last he had to live his new life strictly in its own terms, not as an alternative to something else. The original meaning of all this had gradually worn off. He went for a walk early after the withdrawal had officially ended and he found himself staying in the alleys, crossing streets quickly, as he hadn't done since the very early days of his desertion. He went back to their rooms. He lay down beside Lanh. She looked frightened. She must have known his anguish then, though they didn't speak of it. He couldn't understand what was happening in his own head. They said nothing that afternoon but pressed their faces deep into each other's crotch their mouths swarming at each other for a long long time longer than ever before devouring each other till they could not breathe till they found that the rectangle of sun had moved from the floor and onto their flanks and then they joined each other and lay still, clamped tight face to face, chest to chest, gut to gut, and Lanh came again and again until at last she began to weep softly against his neck and he came, but held back his own tears.

—Why are you crying? he whispered.

—I love you, she said.

—I could live in you, he said, his penis still inside her.

—Stay. Yes, she said.

Cliff found his love for Saigon reviving. The people in the streets remained as open and warm to him as before and Lanh was herself his home within his new land. They had devised hopes for a time that as ties were severed and some strain even developed between the South Vietnamese government and the U.S., Cliff could ask for asylum and marry Lanh and he could be permitted to work. They held those hopes for a time and then things went bad in the South not only with the U.S. but with the North. The war turned and people began to grow seriously afraid in Saigon.

The war, governments, politics: Cliff thrashed now in anger at them all. He spit them from his mind like broken teeth. These things were meaningless in the end. He felt that very strongly. There were worse than these. Always. A man gasping by a stream, dying there. The big issues were just neutral media that carried men into these moments, just as their legs, their arms were not the cause, neither were the governments, the ideologies.

Cliff came in from a monsoon rain and found Lanh sitting naked before a mirror. Her breasts were cupped in her hands, were lifted up and she was crying. She did not look at him when he entered. Her hands fell to her sides.

—I can hardly see myself in the shadows, she said. My body is dark and I have to have the sunlight to see what I am.

These words drew Cliff to another memory, similar. Lanh's hands beat at her own face and neck. They'd been out briefly together—they'd walked in a park among the child-faced amputees in jungle fatigues—and Lanh had kept her purse raised to her face to block off the sun—like many young Vietnamese women avoiding any darkening by the sun—she was not alone in being affected by the Americans, Cliff thought. But back in their room, she sat on the bed for a moment and she was gasping, flushed, and she beat at her face and neck saying, The heat, this terrible heat, I can't take it anymore.

Again, her words lurched against him, prepelled him toward still another moment. She sat beside the radio and turned it from the smarmy-voiced American DJ on the Armed Forces station—she'd never taken up with American rock—and she found one of the adenoidal Vietnamese chanteuses singing about a parent-arranged marriage that threatened a true love and Lanh wept openly. She wept until she saw Cliff watching her and then she tried to smile and shrug at the song but she kept crying.

He remembered Lanh telling of how young people who lived in the old ways out in the countryside tried to see each other. She said, If the young people lived on the river, they went lantern fishing at night. We have a certain fish that can be caught at night by attracting it to lantern light from a sampan. So the young people all told their parents that they were going fishing and then met at the river. On clear nights the boys and girls sat in separate sampans and sang to the moon, debating in their songs whether all boys were butterflies who went from flower to flower never staying with one or whether all girls were the praying mantis insects who eat their husbands and children. And when the songs were done the boys could paddle their sampans close to the girls' sampans and they could kiss.

Lanh paused for a moment and her face, her hands, the sound of her voice lingering in the silence, had all been so mellow that Cliff did not speak for fear of breaking the mood with his own voice which seemed unchangeably, racially, flat and hard to him. After a moment Lanh laughed lightly and said, Of course, the boys had to bring a supply of fish with them to give to the girls to take home. So their parents wouldn't know what was really going on.

She was silent for a long while after this, and Cliff watched her face knowing with absolute certainty that behind its surface glow she was beginning to suffer at her loss. She'd never had a chance to go on the river and live out her innocence beneath a full moon—she'd come to Saigon instead at ten, half an orphan, then a full one at fifteen, and she'd become a whore for a foreign army, and then ended up living for an alien deserter who could not help her, whose very presence must surely perpetuate all the damage done her. Cliff knew this as he watched her sitting with her thoughts still on a river she never entered and he knew it now lying in his bed with the damage done her coming to some terrible kind of climax.

He turned to Lanh in the bed beside him and he was drenched in sweat and his eyes were burning. The scalds of sleeplessness on this night suddenly racked his body and he knew he'd harmed her.

Clanged the air clanged the room trembled and Cliff jerked double. A rocket. It was close. That was close, his mind babbled. Close. A close rocket. What now? He was sitting up. He was listening. More? In this room next? No. No. The seconds passed and nothing. The sound was gone. Then he heard distant screaming. Very faint. Very distant. And then nothing again. Not so close. No more sounds. Dogs barking. Distant, too, voices. He'd heard a dog tonight at last. It took a rocket to give him back the old sounds. Lanh was stirring.

"Cliff?" she said, her voice bloated from sleep.

"It's nothing," he said, but she had already turned over on her stomach. She was asleep again.

The rocket must have been far down Tran Hung Dao, as far as Gia Dinh, maybe. But it had cracked him open. He knew he had been insulating himself the past few hours. He'd been drifting. He was no closer now than at the start of the evening to an answer, a way out. Or was he? Pattern. He was looking for pattern, something to suggest a next step. But now his heart was pounding, he could hardly breathe, he gasped heavily, tried to draw a deep breath.

What pattern? All he'd done and been: could there be an answer there, a place to go? If there wasn't, then everything he'd ever done was random, meaningless, everything anyone had ever done. But that declaration flew out the crack in him and was gone. He was wounded now. Badly. The words were gone.

And his father came. Not who Cliff wanted now. His father was dead. Long dead. He had nothing to do with any of this. But his father strode through the breach and as if he'd found Cliff wandered too far from home, found him playing dead in a ditch far far from home, his father grabbed him—grabbed him now—slung him onto his hip—Cliff did not kick, fight, did not move, just watched the ground passing beneath him, his father's legs moving, heard the man's labored breath, and his father slammed open the door into a dim room, sat Cliff carefully on a chair, and then lay down on the bed, went stiff, gagged. Help, it's come, he gasped.

No. Cliff turned his face away. The times with his father were all fused together—all that the man had been to him collapsed with the stroke—collapsed into a timeless center of gravity like a black hole, drawing Cliff in from a great distance. He saw his father sitting in silhouette in the window, dark against gray light, and talking about his own father's stroke, weeping in fear for himself. And it had come to Cliff's father at last. Cliff sat at his bedside and it was night. The table lamp was on and his father had closed his eyes. Cliff wondered if he was dead. After months, dead. After his father had spoken again and again the request to his fourteen-year-old son to kill him, end this pain, finish what had come to half his body already. Cliff could not move. The thought that his father might have just died before his eyes ravaged him. He wanted him to die. Yes. That was his father's wish and Cliff himself was terrified of the man. His father hated him now.

Earlier that day his father said to him, Why looking? His mouth twisted to the side at each word, slurring them.

Cliff did not answer.

—Why not kill? And his father's eyes strained toward him.

Words thrashed in Cliff but he could hold none of them long enough to speak.

—Can't do for me? Father. Yours. Can't?

Then his father's eyes changed. Cliff saw the hate fill them like tears.

—You, he said;

then extended silence, but more coming;

—keep, he said, tiny, his will going;

62

—me, he said, gasping;

—like this, he said.

Cliff wanted to shout no, no. I wouldn't keep you like this. I'd do what you ask, but I don't want you to leave me, please, there is no one else, please stay, even if you hate me for making you stay, please stay. Cliff grasped at his father's hand and Cliff was weeping and his father did not pull the hand away—he was weak, but he did not even try—and Cliff looked at his father's face and he was weeping too, his eyes were softer now, his father was in control again. Sorry, he said, his voice faint as his breath, but Cliff knew his father was disappointed in him and then, as they wept, the door flew open and Cliff's mother was there and she said, Here here now what's so gloomy? The patient needs some cheer. And she threw open the shades to a sun-splashed smokestack on the roof of the next wing. The intrusion of his mother in the memory gave Cliff a moment's minimal control of his thoughts now and he pulled his mind back again to the night when his father closed his eyes before him and he thought it was over. The moment was Cliff's own. His and his father's. But he felt no relief for either his father or himself. This was the ultimate desertion. He felt that strongly and his own anger swelled in him. Cliff rose beside the body and wanted to strike it, he lurched beside it, his fist clenched. He pounded the bed once near his father's arm. There was a tremble in his father's fingers. Cliff's breath caught. He leaned forward, pressed his face near to his father's and he heard the faint but steady slip of breath. Cliff fell upon his father's chest and embraced him.

Dreams. Dreams since. His father died a month later but Cliff was not there. He'd never done his father's bidding and his father left at last without him, without warning. Cliff had wanted to be there. He imagined his father's hand groping across the bed for him as the end came, the hand on him would forgive him once and for all. No need now, my son. Forget what I asked. I can handle this myself after all, it seems. It's okay. But no, the man died by himself. Cliff was left alone and then the dreams. An unsodded grave. A wide plain extending to the horizon, a plain of manicured lawn, row upon infinitely receding row of tombstones, and the grass growing even and wide across all the graves but one. An unsodded grave in the center. Cliff moved to it trembling, his heart racing until his throat clamped shut. His father's grave, a rectangle of naked earth like an unhealed wound. And then Cliff was slung up again under an arm and he would wake with his chest nearly bursting.

Bursting now he sat in the dark and looked around him and it was unclear for a moment what he was doing. Had he drifted off briefly to sleep on this night at last? His heart still pounded in his throat. He held up his hands and they were trembling. The room about him was filled, the darkness was filled, with people. No. Just the thoughts of people—all those he'd been close to or had expected to be. All those who'd come already tonight. But come in thought only so that what the room was filled with now was their absence. They'd come only to remind him he was homeless, to breathe into his lungs the cold air of their oblivion.

Gunfire somewhere. Cliff rose. From the distance he felt the tidal lift of the night sky, moving toward him. His only home was here and it was about to be swept away. Fleming's voice. Quiet. Explaining life in this country. Explaining that the VC would show no mercy to us. They knew our faces, our names. My face is still with them, Cliff thought. My past is known by these shrewd little men far better than by anyone else. I'd never be able to keep it from them. The smell of cement—faint from the walls but unmistakable—the silence now, the dark. He was standing in the middle of a cell. Lanh's sleeping body in the bed behind him was a mere fragment of himself laid out there to keep him from going mad. But he was caught already. The alleys beyond would hide him no more. The door might as well be sealed; was sealed in reality. He stood in the room now, his eyes on the smear of dark window, and he felt his body flush hot then go cold then begin to sag. There was nothing now. Nothing. The country he left was empty, the country he was in was doomed, he was at the end of it all here, the rest shut off, a void for him, his life dwindled now to this room and to a few hours. And it was the same for Lanh. She was doomed with him. She'd lashed herself to his mast long ago. She was an American's whore. An American intelligence agent's whore. She slept now in her tomb. And how would it end? They'd stay here till they starved? Go into the street and be seized? Separated forever, taken to their isolated torture and death at the hands of others? No. Something moved his arms in the dark, his legs. No. His mind throbbed. He was weary. Very weary. He could hardly hold his body erect. He was dead now, he knew. That was his weariness. He moved in the dark to a trunk at the foot of the bed. He opened the trunk, his mind quiet now in its weariness. There was no answer, after all, in the patterns. Except to show there was nothing left. Life had run out on him. That's all. He cut off the words. He was tired. Tired. His hands plunged through cloth, paper, deep into the coolness, over to the grainy inner wall of the trunk, down to the bottom and metal. His hands came out and he had a pistol. He closed the trunk lid and turned. His body cut off the little light that came through the window and he could not see Lanh at all. She was invisible in the shadows. But he knew where she lay. Quickly. One bullet for her. One for himself. Better to resolve it himself while they were still together. He raised the pistol in the dark. He could not even see his hand before him. He had to draw nearer. He couldn't chance missing a fatal spot, couldn't let her have even a second's pain. He stepped to the side of the bed and the barest smatterings of light—from stars, from the invisible verging moon—gave him the long curve of Lanh's back, her sacral dimples—the faintest dipping of the flesh at the small of her back—his arm with the pistol dropped, he sat, the pistol fell, he wept now, wept at Lanh's beauty, touching her back lightly now, his fingertips resting in the slight depression there—she'd mock his weakness at this moment, he knew—she'd mock him—What are you crying for? I'm the woman. I'm supposed to cry, right? But I won't. You love me? Okay, love me then. Quit all your crazy talk. Quit your crazy thoughts. Just lie with me. Cliff's tears stopped, his chest loosened, at the thought of Lanh's mockery.

"All right," he said aloud. There has to be an answer somewhere in me. He thought of Lanh's face—looked at it to see if her mockery was gone. What would you have me do? Cliff asked her in his mind. Just tell me what you want, she said. To make sense of things, he said. What I've been. Then we'd know what to do.

Cliff was calm again. He sat on the edge of the bed and began with his father. He wanted to put him to rest now. But he did not know what to do. His mind led him down the carpeted hall of the mortuary and stopped him just before the entrance to the parlor. In a glass case in the wall were Little League trophies, photos of boys in rows with the funeral home's name on their chests. Inside, his mother was standing at the casket, her back to his father, but right up against the casket, as if protecting it from thieves. There was no one else in the parlor. He approached his mother and they did not touch, did not speak, for a long moment. Then she embraced him and, beginning to weep, she said, We're all alone now, honey. He put his arms around his mother but already he found it difficult to know what to say to her. Yes, he was alone. But he felt his aloneness for himself. She was not part of it.

He looked at his father's face. He'd been made up heavily, as if he was an actor ready for a role. Somebody later on, a cousin or someone, looking at the body—no, at the casket—Cliff remembered standing as the casket was slipped from the limousine in the grove of markers and hearing a cousin say to someone nearby, His health just deserted him. Cliff thought much later of the remark and said to himself, More, his life deserted him. That was what happened in the room where his father died alone—

66

his life up and bolted without warning, it abandoned him and Cliff could only stand in the chill of the void left behind and sniff for the fading scent of his father's life. For a time that gave him a way to bear what had happened: his father had not gone, something had gone from his father.

And what was left to his mother and him was very little. When he was in college she formalized the basic truth of their relationship. She loved him with a regular check sent folded in a piece of heavy, pale-blue letter paper with not a word on it but her embossed name. He went once, in an August, to meet the man she married. They were living the warm months at the Paradise Hotel on the south shore of Long Island. The hotel was on a spit all alone and was massive and pink like an obese society matron. Cliff passed through the lobby and out to the ocean side where he descended artificial levels of fake fieldstone, through throngs of reclining, misshapen bodies, snatches of talk—snubbed me at the Fontainebleau even though it was I introduced her to Ben, my god his inner ear was so bad he couldn't stand up straight, I sold at forty-five and the next week it was down three points, I cut her dead right there. He found his mother supine in a canvas chair before a cabaña. She saw him and smiled, struggling to rise from her awkward position.

—Stay, he said and she lay back and he kissed her lightly on the cheek that she turned to him while she kissed at the available air.

—Have you been getting my letters? she asked.

—Letters?

—The checks I've sent.

—Yes.

—I hope you're enjoying school. It's a wonderful time of your life.

Cliff looked off toward the massive triptych of the hotel. It had minarets that he'd not noticed when he first arrived.

—Have you been making some good friends? she asked.

Cliff looked at his mother and he felt a rush of something he did not understand. The question from her was the

67

first time he recognized so strongly the importance of his friends—of Burr and the rest, of Francine. He'd felt very close to them all, of course, but seeing them as "his friends" and feeling a sentimental pleasure at the phrase—a sentimental pleasure he was not ashamed of in the least—this had not happened until his mother asked the question. And he wanted very badly to clasp her hand and lean forward and say, Yes, momma, Yes I have, let me tell you—and she'd put her other hand on his. And she would, too. Cliff sat there and looked at his mother's face, her sunglasses raised onto her forehead to see him better, and he felt very strongly that she wanted to do the right thing but just didn't know how; he knew that if he'd talk giddily to her of his friends that she would know from her own instincts how to respond, how to connect to his thoughts, draw from her own present life. But he couldn't speak. He could not bear to look at his mother's face because of the sadness he was beginning to feel for her, but he could not say a word about his friends. He wanted to. He wanted to speak. He wrenched at his mind, tried to form the words. She was waiting to connect, but he only felt the comfort of those people he would see in a few weeks a thousand miles from this place. He could not tell her.

Some, he said. I've made some friends. He looked away again, down the beach. For all the bodies scattered along the sand, no one was in the water. And so where's your new husband? Cliff asked abruptly. And that was the end of it. Things went on from there as they'd always gone. He did not look back until he sat here in a dark room on the night that Saigon was falling. He was strong enough not to continue to look back now either. He absolved himself quickly. Too much had happened before that moment on the beach to have let him speak. And nothing would have been different five minutes later, even if he had been able to say something. What could be different? There would still be nothing there to suggest his return on this night. And that was what this was all about, he told himself. He rose in the dark room. He had to examine this whole thing rationally. The alternatives.

Saigon. He wanted to stay in Saigon. Maybe they'd let him stay. But his propaganda value would be nil. He knew that. The war was almost over. Nonetheless, for the moment he set that aside. How could he be sure? Maybe he could stay. Saigon was his home now. He felt that strongly. He loved the city. For its energy. For its life, moment to moment. All that he'd told Lanh long ago. He stood in an arcade in the center of the city. Sunday, the shops still sealed behind metal grids, the concrete cool around him, a few fruit sellers spreading their mangoes and papayas and jack fruits and shaking the stiffness from their limbs, young Vietnamese couples walking through, their eyes wide in the shade and in their love, and from inside a shop somewhere faint music—Vietnamese classical music whining and thumping like an Ozark hoedown. And peddler sounds. Scissors snapping from the woman with a pan of nougats, an old man clacking bamboo sticks before his spread of fruit, a woman carrying baskets of steaming rice at opposite ends of a long pole balanced on her shoulder and twirling a little drum chattering from a pair of balls dancing against it on strings. Entranced, he stumbled on a leper, the man's face wiped roughly clean of his nose, his lips. The man was not in the arcade. Cliff wanted to keep his mind in the arcade, but Saigon was amorphous, had always been, and he knew where he was. He stumbled on the man in the street and a tiny boy crabbed by, his stunted legs twisted beneath him, begging with an upturned Army bush cap. Cliff knew what country he was in. A column of diesel smoke from the traffic circle at Le Loi, sirens, from a block away he could smell flesh burning. He turned and people were running past him to see but he did not need to see. A bomb blast that he heard in his sleep though it had been at one of the American officers' barracks on the other side of the city. He could hear the flesh ripping, he thought. And the nightly rumblings of the horizon. He knew where he was. Saigon held all of that too. A throat cut in the mouth of his alley, the blood still smeared in a great crescent on the pavement the next day. Raking gunfire and a government minister assassinated and the old women in the alley read the papers to each other aloud and he could hear their voices pitch higher and he knew where he was. He thought of twilight in the countryside, the air mild as the sun flashed in the racing line of trees; they passed a procession of ox-carts carrying wood home, bells jangling, the people's faces turning to smile—their lives were simple in the village but they knew joy—these in the little villages were close to the land, to the pure joy of things—like a young animal running through high grass—running just to run—running to feel grass and wind. And that spirit was in Saigon, too, in its way; still in the hearts in this city. But animals tear at each other without remorse. They kill. They aren't animals, Cliff cried to himself. We were the predators. We who came from outside. But this place is half the world's conception of Hell. Even now that all the Americans are going but me. The terror persists outside these walls. Cliff felt his mind being pulled apart. Yes, Vietnam—Saigon—was filled with terror. Now as before. He'd chosen to embrace this place. Chosen it. Chosen to cut away everything he'd known, close all paths of return and stay in the place he feared the most. He feared it. Of course he feared it.

He remembered Martita Pells' shock. She was a Saigon correspondent for the *Washington Post* during the period when Cliff was at his most careless in roaming the streets of the city. One day she strode across the little park near City Hall—tall—over six feet—with a firm handshake that Cliff liked at once—and a heavy-lidded tightness to her face, as if she was standing into a stiff breeze. She saw him and asked who he was and introduced herself. I like to get as many angles on this war as I can, she said. From that introduction, however, she began a long dissertation to Cliff about the horrors of the war. She wanted to do for the *Post* what Gloria Emerson was doing for the *Times* she'd said. But she talked on a level of abstraction that had no real meaning for Cliff and he couldn't now remember a word, hadn't heard a word of her ideas even at the time. He was light-headed in talking at length with an American for the first time in several years and he was entranced by the mere tone of her voice. But he heard enough to trust her at last with the truth. I'm a deserter, he said.

—A deserter from the Army? she asked, showing her shock.

—Yes.

—My god. I've heard about you guys but I've never found one. My god. What would you desert *here* for?

Cliff could only shrug.

—I know, she said. A man's home is where he is innocent. You could never feel innocent again in the U.S.

He thought of the man dying by the stream—the first he'd thought of him in some time—and what she said rang true to him as nothing she'd said to that point had. But he could not endorse that reason—not for himself, not entirely at least. Nor was she waiting for his endorsement. She was already talking on, extemporizing her next story, and he had nothing to contribute to her.

—Well, she said suddenly. I've got to be off to write a Martita Pell special. Can I meet you here again?

—Sure, Cliff said, though he feared in some reflexive way becoming too accustomed to her voice, the pattern of her speech. It was foreign to him now, but he sensed a danger in letting it reassert its claim to the movement of his mind.

But he met Martita Pell often in the next few months. She told him about a friend of hers at a radical newspaper named *Free West*. It's national, she said, and getting attention. It's getting to minds that are only half open. She suggested he write some pieces for them about his views of the war. She'd be his go-between for correspondence and payment. He wrote, for a time, and he was delighted at being able to earn a little money to help Lanh with their finances. But he found himself dwelling increasingly on

71

the sense impressions of the city, wanting to write about Lanh's body, her mind, her feelings, and the editor of the newspaper apparently wanted him to rail, to rant, to analyze the war and international politics. Cliff could not comply. He saw things on a different scale. Martita tried to persuade him to write what she called simply "the truth"—as if what he saw in his own terms was somehow false. Maybe she was right, Cliff thought briefly, now that he was faced with a decision forced upon him by the war and international politics that Martita and her friend were so interested in. It would be easier if I saw things that way, he told himself. Easier to know what to do.

—I'm sorry, Martita, he said to her on their park bench. He could hear his own voice throbbing, I just can't.

—My god, she said, shaking her head. I don't see what you're here for if you can't see it that way.

They sat in silence for a time and then she turned to him with her normal exuberance renewed. Have you seen the displays at City Hall? she asked.

—No, Cliff said. Of what?

—Come on, she said grabbing him by the wrist.

They passed through a large scuffed foyer and up a fat-neweled stairway reminiscent of an old big-city public library. On the second floor was a vast open floor, with faded diaphanous paintings in the vault above, a remnant of French colonialism. Among potted plants and flags were glass display cases. The milling Vietnamese ignored Martita and Cliff.

—It's a bizarre parody, Martita said. Somebody in charge of all public events in this country can never resist having a cruel joke.

The two of them peered at lacquerware with scenes of combat, endless varieties and categories of medals, and— the goal of Martita's impatiently plucking hand—a long series of cases filled with glass eyes and artificial limbs— veterans' benefits.

—Oh, isn't this terrible, Martita said turning away from the cases as soon as she'd placed Cliff in front of them.

72

Cliff even thought he saw—out of the corner of his eye—the back of Martita's hand rise to her forehead. He did not look at her little demonstration but stared at a sequence of plaster casts showing the stages of making glass eyes, with one—just a single, finished eye imbedded in the white plaster—looking like a gynecologist's vision of womanhood.

—It's just too sad, Martita was saying. How can we do this to a country? And the Vietnamese come here and stand in awe of this stuff, she said without lowering her voice. Cliff looked about and still no one seemed to notice them. They think it's wonderful, she said.

The two of them edged along now, passing rows of artificial arms and legs of all shapes, sizes and colors ranging from dark cream to light brown. Aha, she finally said, and they were standing before two stationary versions of bicycles built for amputees. One had a motorized mannequin with artificial legs pedaling away, colored lights whirling in the spokes. The other bicycle was empty.

—It's a parody, she said again. It's theatre of the absurd. The idea was so strong in Martita's head that she had stridden forward to the bicycles. She watched the rise and fall, listened to the unremitting clack of the mannequin's legs, and her head shook in amazement as if it too was mechanized. Then suddenly she mounted the other bicycle and began to pedal.

—The sense of theatre is too strong in me, she said to Cliff, and then smiled over to her bicycling companion.

A clot of Vietnamese quickly formed and laughed with Martita Pell as she hunched over the handlebars, her feet jammed into the stirrup pedals, her long legs splayed practically akimbo on the bicycle, and she matched the mannequin stroke for stroke. Cliff heard neither ridicule nor anger directed at Martita from the Vietnamese but only remarks on what a funny sight this was. Cliff loved his new people very much at that moment. They were better than he—for he was edging away even then—they showed in their rancorless, unshakeable, child-like delight how it was that they'd survived. But Cliff was about to bolt when

Martita descended from the bicycle, nodding and waving like an actress at a curtain call, to the laughter and smattering of applause from the spectators.

—Children, she said descending the staircase. You see?

They parted on the street and she said nothing about this being their last meeting. But it was. He waited several times in the usual place for her and she never showed up. It took a while for Cliff to realize that he'd profoundly disappointed her the last time by rejecting the truthful path for his thinking on Vietnam. The display at City Hall had been intended as some kind of a final demonstration, a lesson, for him.

But she'd only made Cliff feel more certain about what he had in Saigon. And what was that? He looked about him now in the dark room. The glow of satisfaction from his recollections of Martita Pell dissolved into the dark. Another old Vietnamese woman—just two days before— Cliff had stood inside the door, out of sight, while the woman talked to Lanh. In DaNang, she said, twelve policemen were paraded in the street naked and then the VC made them all kneel down and they chopped off their heads one after the other. And they stripped the girls from the bars . . . Lanh stopped her. You're a foolish old woman, she said. You believe rumors at a time like this? Are you so bored you have to think about torture to feel alive? You'll be brought down yourself, the old woman said. Your high-handedness and that fancy American you slave for. Lanh slammed into their apartment, but she was shaken. They held each other and said nothing about the rumors, but Lanh was trembling and Cliff felt his own body picking up the tremor, either from empathy or his own fear—he did not try to decide which.

The recollection of the rumors drove Cliff around and around the floor now. Fleming's voice, low and controlled but in touch with horrors across the quiet fields, deep in the dark line of trees. The vengeance coming to the city, nearing even as he had idled in this room. He stepped toward the window. He let himself move beyond his alley, beyond his own memories; for a moment he listened with his full attention to the city outside and he heard a faint hammer of engines. They faded away but in a few moments grew again. He rushed past this sound and listened for rockets falling, gunfire. For the moment there was nothing beyond that trenchant pulse of engines. He found his eyes fixed straight ahead into the dark, focused on nothing. He was a long stride back from the window and he turned the city off in his mind. He began to feel the difficulty of staying. But the alternatives seemed just as difficult and so his mind would not let go of the option.

He thought of the opposite course—he and Lanh suddenly transported to the U.S. He remembered a conversation with her once about the U.S. She shivered. I'm glad you're not a good and true GI, she said. I'd love you and you'd have to take me back there. It scares me. I can't picture a country actually filled with such enormous people. Your women are bigger than our men. I'd be terrified to walk in the streets.

—And me? he said. Am I too big?

—No, she said. You're tall but you're too skinny to scare me. She leaned forward against him placing her forehead in the middle of his chest. You're a tree, she said. You shelter me. Then after a pause, without moving her head from his chest, she said, Let's not talk about America for a while.

And the time of the big sweep, she let her fear of the U.S. show again. He'd heard rumors on the street of the sweep. One of the old women who sold soup on the sidewalk pulled him to her with a flapping of the hand held low behind her pots. Squat, she said quietly. Beside me here.

—What is it? he said squatting. She was one of the women who lived in their alley. She knew what he was and he'd never heard her argue with Lanh about anything.

—I have a customer, a white mouse, she said, using the American epithet for a Vietnamese policeman. But she did not pause, as she usually did, to enjoy a laugh with Cliff over her knowledge of American slang.

—He has a loose tongue, she said. He talked to another white mouse with him. Loud enough for me to hear about the plan they had with the American MPs to find American deserters. They're going to go in the night through all the streets they think have the deserters and go into the apartments and look for them. The Vietnamese police are going to let the MPs search Vietnamese homes.

Cliff teetered beside the woman and said nothing.

—Have some pho, she said, ladling a bowl full of the soup.

His legs were suddenly too weak to keep him in his Vietnamese squat. He sat cross-legged back onto the pavement and cupped the bowl in his hands bending his head over the steam and finding a moment of empty respite in the heat in his palms.

—Our alley is sure to be on their list, the old woman said.

—Of course.

—I'll try to find out when they'll do this thing.

In the midst, that day, of standing in the center of the room with Lanh, their eyes gasping about looking for places there to hide him if they came, Cliff was suddenly struck by the fact that an old Vietnamese woman soup-seller was privy to the U.S. Army Military Police's secret project. He found himself grinning. They're as stupid as we were in intelligence, he thought, and he laughed aloud.

—Stop it, Lanh said.

—What?

—I don't care what you've found funny at a time like this, I don't want to hear it, she said and she glared at him.

—Hey. You're scared, he said as much to himself as to her.

—Aren't you? she demanded.

—Yes.

—I see them grabbing you. I can see them. With fat necks, fat arms, having to duck to fit in our door, pawing

76

at me, grabbing you and taking you back to that country of theirs. They'll break you like a twig.

She was standing taut and straight, her hands were clenched at her side and she closed her eyes for a moment. Cliff found his own body beginning to quake.

—I . . . he began but couldn't find any words. At the sound of his voice Lanh opened her eyes and looked at him.

—I'm sorry, she said loosening at once, coming to him. I'm selfish to talk about my fears when they just make yours worse. We'll hide you. We'll find a place.

Cliff held her for a moment, he sensed her drawing a resolve from the embrace and he noted even then that her worst fear for him was not them killing him but taking him back to the U.S.

Later, though, the thought of them trying to kill him on the spot must have occurred to her. It was twilight in the room. He was sitting on the bed and she sat beside him— Cliff thought now in the dark how he often remembered the places they were standing or sitting when something occurred; he knew from this how constricted his world was; he was very sensitive to this now—but they sat on the bed in the dusk of the room and she said, Where is your gun?

—In the trunk.

—You should have it when they come.

—I should kill them? he asked, though he already knew that she was suggesting that. He asked the question simply to pose the possibility for his own examination—that he might be put in position of having to defend himself or her and he would have to kill.

—If it came to that, she said softly, our life would have ended anyway. Let them kill us both.

They sat in silence for a moment and then she said intensely, No, I could have something done with the bodies. We can defend our life. I'll get rid of them somehow and we can go on living here.

Cliff turned to her and did not let himself smile at the

sudden image of Lanh dragging the bodies herself out the door and away. Knowing part of her would certainly try to do that and another part of her would not let her kill, he loved the wholeness of her that could contain both these impulses.

—You don't mean for us to kill them, do you? he said.

She turned to him and her voice was steady. If they try to hurt us I will kill them myself.

Cliff did not reply. His thoughts of the past moments, his repressed smile, the twinge of the slightly sentimental part of his love for Lanh, all seemed suddenly foolish. She could kill. Yes. He himself had killed. He could kill again, given the proper fear or confusion or distraction. He knew where he was, what country this was, who he himself was, who this woman was, this woman whom he loved in ways much stronger than a patronizing, idealized response to her surface charms. Hearing her say she could kill, knowing she could, pumped his chest suddenly full and he grabbed her to him. They stripped each other fiercely.

The MP sweep for deserters came a week later. The old woman came to them and knocked in the night. Cliff was in the bathroom in two strides but Lanh found the old woman outside. At the sound of the woman's voice, Cliff turned the light on in the bathroom and stood in the doorway. He calmed his breath, quieted his mind, but the woman said, Tonight. Now. They're coming. Lanh closed the door and turned to face Cliff. They looked at each other without a word and Lanh climbed back into the bed while the race of Cliff's body resumed and he went to the trunk. He pulled his pistol from the trunk and a roll of Vietnamese money, their savings, money he'd brought with him when he'd deserted. He went into the bathroom, pushed the door halfway to, and reached to turn off the light. But he paused. Their plan, crude as it was, with the barest consideration of only the most obvious contingencies, was that the pistol was to be used if an MP found him, the money, if a white mouse found him. Push the money into the Vietnamese policeman's hand before he had a chance to betray Cliff's presence to the MP in the other room. If the MP checked the bathroom himself, Cliff had the pistol. His hand stretched toward the light chain, Cliff thought that either way it would be better if the light was on. If the MP came into a dark bathroom he would be sure to be ready to kill, would force something for sure. If the white mouse turned on the light to find Cliff he would be more likely to gasp at his sudden sight and tip off the MP without having a chance to accept the bribe.

So Cliff pressed against the wall and filled his lungs with the ammoniac smell of their bad plumbing, filled his ears with the trickle of water, shut out any thought of the movement of forms to their door. He closed his eyes to the light.

When the knock came at the door, Cliff started as if it was completely unexpected. Lanh switched on a light by the bed and put on some clothes with the second knock. I'm coming, she shouted at the door. I just have to dress.

At that moment Cliff's mind seized on a fantasy that held him through all that followed. The MP had heard her say she'd been undressed. Cliff could hear the man's mind begin to work. The door opened and Cliff could see Lanh as if through the MP's eyes. He saw her beauty and the idea of her having just moments before been naked aroused him.

A male Vietnamese voice was explaining he was the police, this American was looking for deserters. Was she alone?

Yes, come in, Lanh said at once. Come in both, she repeated in English. Please.

And Cliff imagined Lanh thinking of sacrificing easily what she'd sold often before so that Cliff could be safe.

Heavy footsteps entering the room. Shouts out the front door, far down the alley.

—You alone? the MP said.

At the MP's voice Cliff began to feel his arms grow strong, begin to rise as he thought of what was inevitable. Let me fuck you and I won't look in the bathroom, the MP would say. And Lanh would see it as the way to save herself and Cliff, save their life together, and she'd strip off her clothes as she'd done how many times before? Cliff had never asked how many men had touched her but he felt them now crowding in, feeling her, licking her.

Yes, Lanh replied to the MP in English. Look around. Please.

—I don't know why you're alone, honey, the MP said and Cliff nearly moved. The shouting grew in the alley. Cliff looked at the pistol in his hand. And even as he looked at the pistol, as he saw himself emptying it into the MP, a shot rang out down the alley.

—See you some other time, honey, the MP said hastily and the feet clattered out the door.

Cliff and Lanh lived for months fearing the MP's return, but he never came back. The shot down the alley had been a Vietnamese deserter who tried to run and was gunned down. When Lanh told Cliff about the incident, which she'd heard from one of the old women, Cliff said, He's better off than I'd've been, right? Better dead than sent to America. Cliff was surprised at the time—and surprised now as he thought out his options—that he'd been struck sufficiently by Lanh's fear of the U.S. to chide her for it in a joke weeks later. Did he have a trace of defensiveness about his former country? Perhaps. But also he shared, for somewhat different reasons, her fear of the U.S. and sometimes he could not bear to have her reinforce his own fears.

He had those fears now, of course, as he sat alone in wakefulness trying to decide what to do about this coming day. Lanh slept on and Cliff knew the terror she would feel to wake to the U.S. He kept returning to an untenable conclusion—stay in Saigon, make the world in fact stop around them as it had often virtually seemed to stop for the past four years. But that wasn't possible. He was in Saigon and Saigon was falling.

He thought of Burr Gillis. Wondered if Burr was still as comfortable as Cliff had imagined him after he'd disappeared. All right, Cliff thought, feeling suddenly strong in reclaiming control of the direction of his own thoughts. I'll finish with Burr Gillis now.

That last trip west. Burr was going to meet with a number of his counterparts from a dozen campuses. Cliff alone hitched with him this trip.

Stoned, in a commune up near the Mendocino Forest, Cliff felt a viscous flow of heat clot at the back of his head as he bent forward and the flesh of his hands was strobing before his face. He was in the center of a large screened porch, the lamps filling the space with the color of watery piss, and he was with two dozen silent people, Burr somewhere out of sight. The whole day all these people had made broken attempts at talk—some phrases recited—and they smiled and clapped at each other's shoulders—and it all worked, they felt like a family, talked like one and it was here on this screened porch that they attained the highest expression of their lives together, here they gathered momentum for the next day of broken phrases and sudden embraces, here in the bare bulblight. Here in the silence Cliff felt the links to them but it was like holding hands with a woman he'd slept with for years, that was the feeling that he tried to understand, the feeling of commonness, but his thoughts had long intervals in them, he was not forgetting what he was thinking, there were just gaps and a blur in his eyes like the seconds before fainting but the sensation persisted.

The next day, his body feeling heavy, flaccid, rubbery, he sat on the back step with one of the men of the family—a thin young man in bib overalls. You goin' on into San Francisco? he asked.

—Yes. Soon.

—Oh man, you missed it. You missed heaven, you know. It's dead there now. Christ it was beautiful just a few years ago. A whole city in a city. And in our city you could stop anyone on the street and they'd grab you up, you know, and they'd love you and you loved them. The acid was beautiful. The people were beautiful. Then it all went bad. The Summer of Love and the acid went bad and the place filled with plastic hippies and somebody hacked Shob's arm off and man I freaked out.

There was a long pause and for the first time since they'd come here Cliff felt somebody had spoken to him straight. He felt the man's sense of loss. He felt his own loss. The image of the city of love gripped him—he turned his face away in regret. He didn't want to talk to the man anymore. He envied him his time in Haight.

As Cliff stood to go, the man said, We got ourselves a nice place here, though. We've got a little bit of Haight right here.

Cliff turned to him at this and wondered if the young man was deceiving himself about the nature of this commune or had deceived himself about the nature of Haight.

With Burr, Cliff found—as he'd expected, but with a strong sense of thankful relief nonetheless—that his own impressions of the commune were not mistaken. They walked together alone along a line of trees down the hill from the house.

—They're going bad, Burr said without being asked.

—I know.

—They're spending their undrugged time playing cards and sending out for pizzas. They're nowhere. They're an old folks' home. They're waiting to die.

Later, on the road again, heading south to San Francisco, Burr said to Cliff, We're doomed in this thing, you know.

They were walking through the outskirts of some little town. It was noon and they were going to resume hitching at the downstate edge of a McDonald's parking lot. What do you mean? Cliff asked.

—Don't forget it, man. It'll keep everything you do in perspective. We're making a mark now but not one of us is gonna be able to keep up our revolutionary act for a lifetime. We've been had. The priests tell you, give me the child till he's seven and you can have him forever after. The child will come back eventually as a man. That's what

82

the priest knows. Well, we've been had, Cliff. We've put our seven years in to the society. Day to day creature comforts is gonna get us all in the end.

Cliff understood the point with his mind but it seemed irrelevant to his gut and he would have forgotten it completely in time if a few days later it hadn't struck him that Burr's words were somehow self-prophetic. Burr went off to make a phone call in a booth at a gas station. He'd called somewhere several times during the trip but he never explained it to Cliff. These calls didn't seem important either, until the final one he made in Frisco. They'd had a long session during the day with the other campus leaders in a Victorian house on Stanyan Street. That night they went back early to the apartment of the San Francisco State University student leader where they were sleeping. It was a modest place, just the man and his woman lived in the two rooms and they slept in a bed in the other room with the door closed. Burr went out near midnight and Cliff realized later it was to make his last call. When Cliff woke in the morning in his sleeping bag against the wall, the woman was making coffee. She saw him and said, Good morning.

At the sound of her voice, the man looked into the room. How'd you sleep? he said.

—Fine, Cliff said.

The man came and crouched on the floor next to Cliff. Burr said the meeting will start at five today, the man said.

—Oh?

The man's mouth drew itself into a tight line. We're gonna miss him, he said.

—Miss him? What's happened.

—Didn't he tell you?

—No.

—I just assumed you knew. Burr's time came. They drafted him. So he's gone into exile.

—Exile? Cliff rose up.

—Canada. He's gonna be missed.

—Canada? Cliff couldn't get his mind to settle so he

83

could think all this through. He felt suddenly hollowed
out.

—Guess he wanted me to tell you the meeting time
because you're supposed to take his place.

Cliff lay back down. He couldn't understand. The Army
would be after him soon, too. Why didn't Burr tell him
what he'd planned? Cliff would have gone too. Gladly.

The man was talking on about something but Cliff did
not hear him. He closed his eyes and he gyred in the dark
and he couldn't breathe, he felt his will failing and he
knew he would stop breathing soon. It would have been
simple to tell me.

—He's left you a big responsibility, the man said.

Cliff sat up and the fantasy about his breathing had
passed—a foolish thing, like a grown man shocked by a
light socket and wetting his pants. Already Cliff saw Francine's face. But he staggered when he was standing, he
staggered and could find no words to speak to the man and
woman in the room with him who were rattling on, using
the stock phrases he'd lived with for a long time and which
never meant anything to him. Burr Gillis, his friend, had
gone without a word, without a glance back. That was all.
He put his gear together and he could hardly murmur a
thank you to these people he did not know and he went to
find a phone to call Francine.

And Cliff felt empty for a moment now in his dark room
and he called Burr a fool in his mind. And he was thankful, yes thankful, he found, that Burr had run out on him.
Otherwise, he told himself, my desertion would have been
phony. I would have gone to Canada with Burr and I
would have lived in another America, talking—in a sun-lit
apartment, my stocking feet on a coffeetable—about the
monstrosity of it all. Now it's done right. I've stayed here
where no American wants to stay. I've stayed so that no
inherited part of me can go back on what the best of me
knows is true. But that's in Burr's terms. Cliff balked.
There was truth in that rendition of his decision. But there
was more. Those first moments after his desertion—driving

fast down Highway 1A, the hot wind beating at him, as right as he knew what he was doing to be, he was caught by the throat, he could barely breathe from his aloneness. Place and idea, act and personality, they were all media for something more basic. He was driving furiously, he could barely hold the wheel steady, he was driving into the chasm, into a city feared by the world, and yet he knew there would be something there that could touch him. And there was. Lanh. But is she too a medium for something else? his mind demanded. In fact is Lanh really irrelevant to this ache in him? Were he and Lanh, too, doomed from the start, were they just waiting to die, at least die to each other? He could wake her and ask her—how long did she really expect him to stay? She can't go to America and he can't stay here. Things have changed. He has to go. He has to leave her. And what would she say as he stood in the doorway, the rockets falling, billows of fire rolling through the streets, the last helicopter waiting for him?

Go, she would say. What is this place and its people to you? The best of you, the most compassionate of heart, the most tolerant and appreciative of mind, have come here and used Vietnam as a stage to play the high drama of your own conscience. A place to suffer grandly, to define the limits of your own goodness, to confront the traces of your own evil, and then to leave. To leave utterly. And whether you treated us good or treated us bad, it makes no difference. You used us. You came and gave us scraps of your awareness, one year each of your heart. You came and made us feel, feel deeply, stirred us, set us seeking new things, and then you go. Vietnam is a foreign place to you. You feel here, suffer, for a time, but you return to a home far away. But there is no home away from here for me. You come and you make me suffer, I suffer with you, you give me joy, we share joy, and all those things alter this place for me. The sun shows differently on the clouds now, the trees are different. You go back to other places, old feelings. It was a terrible thing you suffered here. But it was only a dream, after all. It was another time, another place, the far side of the world, and it is all over. Go back. It is all you can do. But I hated you and loved you and I cannot be the same and there is nowhere for me to go.

Yes, Lanh, Cliff answered in his mind. You're right about us in many ways. And you're right to treat me like an extension of all the others. I only gave you a few more years of my heart. But what happened to you happened to me as well. And not just here. Not just here. I've spent a lifetime collecting scraps of awareness, changing my heart, seeing the world change around me, and I held people to me, held them close and then they were gone and I had nowhere to go. But I still have nowhere. What I've sought has always been on the far side of the world.

He saw his father in the dim room, felt his father's hand drawing away minutely, though Cliff could not see the hand in the dark, he felt its withdrawal in his own pores, felt his father receding and he wanted to seize the hand but he sat still, sat still on the beach and would not speak—it was foolish, this was such a trivial question for his mother, she could never connect, never, not even for the few moments he felt could be his while sitting on the beach before the Paradise Hotel but he wanted to speak, he was right, he knew somehow he was right. Cliff rolled his head now and the heat of sleeplessness dispersed briefly but he was weak, his arms were weak, his legs, and Francine touched him, he lifted the index and middle fingers of his right hand to his nose. She was with him, in his flesh, that night walking under the vault of Evanston's elms. Francine fell against his chest in the dark and moaned. She sat in the light in a booth across the way and she glanced at him while laughing at something he did not hear, she glanced at him and they were bonded for that moment, across that gasp of space, across their ignorance of everything they were eventually to find out about each other, they were bonded briefly. People shouted—the voices of children— down the hall and Cliff stood in the center of the floor and heard the voices of the tutors prodding at the squeaking chairs, the sudden curses and Burr appeared beside him, his hand on Cliff's shoulder and he said nothing, not a word of platitude, he seemed to know that those were not the important things.

And all of these people were gone. They all betrayed him, cut him loose, deserted him. Goddam them, Cliff said to himself and he felt the weakness in his limbs suddenly squeeze out, he felt himself rise. "Goddam you all," he said aloud and his fists were clenched. He wanted to pummel these faces that drifted in him, beckoning him, opening their arms now, all of them holding a promise of peace and then before he could either embrace or batter them they were gone.

Cliff pressed at his temples, pressed hard and he was aware that the consideration of options was over. There was nothing but emptiness. And so it didn't matter. He knew he'd be a dead man in Saigon. Let it be. And Lanh was dead too. Lanh? She was still here. He turned in the dark to see her. He could see her body in the dim light, the sheet was down and he saw the dark disks of her nipples. Lanh was here. He began to open again. She was still with him. He opened further and he heard the sound outside and he suddenly knew what it meant. He heard the hammer of engines—very faint—faint as the tick of the furniture in the room—but he heard it. Not so faint, now that his awareness had turned to it. He moved to the window. The sound was an old one, from Homestead. Choppers. Off to the north. The American Embassy. The helicopters were there as the rumor had said. They'd been running this whole night long, carrying the Americans and the special Vietnamese they were saving out of the country. They'd started yesterday and they'd been running all night. All night. His hands jumped to the window sill, his face pressed against the screen. God. How many Americans could there be? The helicopter he heard at this moment—it was clear in the night air—the only sound—this one he heard hammering up—he could perceive the direction now, it's changes in pitch—hammering up and receding—sweeping across the province and out to sea—this one he just heard could have been the last. He kept his head against the screen and he closed his eyes and he listened, listened for another. The silence persisted. Nothing. It was gone. It was decided for him. No. No. I don't want to roll over and die. This home of mine is doomed but I have to get out. The night was silent. He opened his eyes. Far out, north of the city—at the airport, he knew at once—he saw a great fan of red against the night sky. Burning. His legs wobbled. He clutched at the window sill. Then he heard the faint beat of a helicopter engine. Not done yet.

He turned from the window and he knew he had to go. And Lanh? He felt very clearly an impulse to slip quietly away. He knew her terror of the U.S. If he was gone, perhaps the VC would never know who she'd been with for these past four years. He would run through the dark streets and leap into a helicopter and they'd take him away and he could bury himself in a prison and wait for the ten years to pass or maybe for a liberal president ready to pardon. And then? Released to nothing. He couldn't look that far. Go. Just go. Don't put her through any more pain than need be. Just slip quietly out the door and away. Then she could start over again with some kind-hearted apparatchik.

Cliff went to his clothes draped on a chair. He put them on hastily but suppressing the sounds and he watched Lanh as he dressed, watched her turn on her side, her arm curl up to her breast as if she was drawing him to her. He stopped. I'm ready to leave her, he thought. I'm ready to desert Lanh. For her own good, I tell myself, but I'm ready to break it off this time myself. My feelings for her are undiminished and I'm ready to flee. And is it really for her? He sat down on the chair, quieted himself, shut out the sound of the helicopters for the moment, waited to understand what he was doing, who he was. It was he who could not speak on that beach, he knew, he who could do nothing for his father, and maybe he'd failed Francine too, never realizing what it was she needed. And maybe Burr's judgment on him was correct—he knew Cliff could never go with him to Canada—Burr knew something about me, Cliff thought. But I stayed in Saigon. I deserted here, not into a surrogate America. I deserted, yes. And I'm ready to desert again. Desert the love I've forged with a Vietnamese woman. Not a Vietnamese woman. Lanh. What does she herself want? He rose, went to the bed, sat on the edge and she stirred. In the areola of her scent, near the quiet of the mind that so often had pierced ruthlessly through to his unacknowledged feelings. Cliff felt suddenly calm. He touched her cheek and her eyes opened at once.

"What is it?" she asked.

"We have to decide now."

She sat up and fell against him, her arms pressed him to her, and he held her while trying to repress his response to her nakedness. There was very little time left. He heard the sound of the helicopters again.

"You hear that?" he said.

"What?"

"The noise outside. In the distance."

"Airplanes."

"They're evacuating all the Americans by helicopter from the embassy. The end is near."

He expected her to cling tighter but she drew back. She took his hand firmly in hers and she sat perfectly straight in the bed. There was only a barely discernible quaver in her voice as she said, "All right. What is there to do?"

"What do you want?"

She looked at him and her eyes glistened in the faint light. "I want you to get out of here."

"What?"

She let go of his hand. "Get out quick. I've got to be able to get myself ready for the new regime."

Cliff sat without even trying to find an answer for this. He fixed on the tone of her voice, a brittleness there that was familiar to him but which he didn't have the energy at the moment to place.

"Go on, now," she said and she rose and pecked a kiss at his cheek and drew back pulling the cover against her.

Cliff rose and moved heavily to the center of the room. He turned. She was sitting absolutely still, the sheet clutched to her, and she did not turn her eyes from him.

"You're afraid of the States," he said, though his feelings were still moving slowly, were not listening to his own words.

"That's not it. Get out of here now or you'll fuck up my chances." The words came hard and clear from the figure in the bed but she had seemed a ventriloquist—nothing had stirred there, she was curled in on herself and he hadn't seen the movement of her mouth in the dark.

"The old women. Some of them will inform on you," he said and even as he did he recognized the tone in her voice—you want to fuck, GI? That was the tone.

"I'll take care of them," her voice was saying, the words were coming from the motionless form.

"Oh shit," he said and he felt a grin cutting through the fear that suddenly surged in him as he understood what she was doing. A helicopter hammered in his head. One more gone.

"What is it?" she asked, her sheet dropping slightly.

"Oh shit," he repeated.

"Oh shit what?" she demanded, rising onto her knees. "What oh shit?"

"You better talk straight with me, goddamit," he said.

Lanh's body was suddenly fluid, flowing on the bed, she moved back from him but the sheet was down, her hands rose and she pressed at her cheeks.

"Don't put anything on for what you think is my benefit. We're way beyond that. Tell me straight. What do you want?"

She began to move her hand forward and he took a step toward her and he felt his tiredness fall away, her hand stretched to him and they embraced.

"You," she said. "I want you."

"We can't stay here."

"I know."

"Are you afraid of America?"

"Yes."

"You'll be alone, for years probably, if we go back."

"They'll put you in jail."

"Yes."

"You'll come to me when they let you go?"

"We won't be young then. It'll be very hard on you alone."

"But you'll come?"

"You know I will."

"So you me go," she said in English.

He drew back from her. They kissed in haste and broke from the bed. Lanh ran to the bathroom, Cliff knelt by the bed. His hands groped along the floor in the dark, then the light from the bathroom splashed before him and he saw what he wanted. The pistol lay near his right hand. He felt its weight, its coldness, a second before he touched it. He rose, went to the trunk, opened it. He heard water splashing in the basin in the bathroom.

"No time," he said. "Get dressed." The water stopped. He threw clothes, papers, from the trunk, found the small leather holster and he stripped off his belt, fitted the holster on, and fastened the belt to him. He found his hands steady but he heard the engines in the distance. Then a burst of automatic rifle fire. Far off. Back down Tran Hung Dao. He knew there was no use listening to anything but what would be in the alley ahead. He thought about the embassy. It was better than a mile and a half.

If they hurried, if they weren't delayed, they could be there in half an hour. How many more choppers were left for this night? He couldn't think about it. How to go?

"How well do you know the streets from here to the embassy?" he asked.

"It's on Thong Nhut?"

"Yes."

"Pretty good," she said.

"The back ways. The alleys. We should stay there."

"Okay," she said and her voice was distant, absorbed.

Cliff looked around him. He went to the tin can holding incense on the top of the dresser. He pulled the stalks of incense out and loosed a smell that stopped him. He saw her from the back, before she'd turned her face to him for the first time. The wisp of this smell curled into him and he stared at the soft panel of her hair. His hand dipped now into the can, pulled out a roll of money—some greenbacks, mostly piastre—and he put the roll in his pocket. He looked around the room and thought to turn on a light to see it for a last time, but he did not. There was nothing to this room. He felt that very strongly. There were just two people. For a time the place had held their scent, their words, had let them enter each other in peace. The place itself was nothing and he waited with his awareness turning again to the distant stroke of the chopper engines. There was silence from the bathroom. He heard nothing there and a fear lifted him. He could not define the fear but he was striding in terror to the bathroom and his face plunged into the light.

She was standing at the basin. She was biting at her fingers, scraping the nails. The fear changed instantly to anger. "What is it? What are you doing?"

She started and turned. "I don't have any polish remover," she said.

"Now . . . Why now?"

She looked down at her hands as if they belonged to someone else, as if she didn't know what they were. "If we don't make it," she said. "They said the VC will kill any girl with polish on her nails."

Cliff stepped toward her. She turned to him and grabbed him to her and she was trembling.

"We'll make it," he said.

"They'll do terrible things to you," she said, her voice breaking.

"Come on."

"They'll torture you."

92

"Lanh," he said shaking her, but he found himself trembling too, found his own voice cracking.

"We can't both go to pieces," she said, though her unsteadiness had not changed in the slightest.

"Neither of us can," he said and he squeezed her and let go. "We can run it off."

"Okay."

They stepped from the bathroom and looked around them. Lanh started toward the dresser but Cliff stopped her.

"Leave it all," he said. "Let's make the break."

She turned to him and nodded. "One thing," she said.

"Yes?"

"If anything happens to me on the way, you go on."

"Nothing's . . ."

"Promise me. Go on. There'll be no place for you to hide here anymore."

"Lanh . . ."

"Promise me."

"All right."

They were through the door and into the landing. Down a winding metal staircase, past the closed doors of other apartments, no sounds, the stench of piss, into the ground floor landing. There was always someone sleeping here at night. Missing limb often. Old often. Often different from the night before, but someone. Not tonight. The landing was empty and they were through it and into the alley with Cliff's mind lingering in the empty landing. Were the weak ones dead already?

The air was close, closer than their apartment. They splashed through the murky dark, running up the alley away from Tran Hung Dao. The dark beat at Cliff's eyes as they ran as the hot wind had beat at his face in his flight by jeep to Saigon. He could not see the objects passing nearby. His hand touched and withdrew, touched and withdrew from Lanh's elbow as they ran together. The buildings, tight, unbroken down the alley, passed by like a mountain range in the dark.

93

The first corner and they pulled up short. They knew to be cautious. The next alley was straight across and they pressed against a building in the deep dark of an overhanging balcony and Cliff looked briefly out—down the street both ways. Empty. Utterly empty. There was no sound anywhere. He heard his own breathing, Lanh's breathing—and that was all. They could have been alone in the city, in the world, for all he knew. And there was no sound from the embassy. None. Was it already too late? He wanted to wait, to listen, to will the engines to return. But they had no time. The street was empty and they crossed quickly into the darkness of the next alley.

A body ahead. Lurching. Lahn gasped, they drew back and a hand grasped at them. But Cliff smelled rice wine and his own hand stopped its move to his pistol. A face thrust close to Cliff's. There was still a fringe of light from the street and he could see a clean-shaven face, a middle-aged man.

"American?" the man asked in Vietnamese. "American?" he repeated, his hands clawing into life.

"No," Cliff said thrusting him away.

"British," Lanh said and Cliff unhooked the man's fingers from his arm and he ran, Lanh beside him.

"Save me," the man shouted after them. "Take me with you."

They ran in silence. The sky, lights, disappeared again in the unbroken row of buildings with stacked floors but dark, without shape. Cliff was sweating and his sweat smelled of Saigon, his sweat absorbed the sweet rot of food, the tar and stucco smells, the smell of the river.

"We've got to avoid the presidential palace," Lanh said as they ran.

"It'll be secure there."

"They'll be killing Americans now," she said.

"The VC aren't at the palace yet."

"The ARVNs will be killing Americans now," she said.

94

"Of course," he said low, more to himself than to Lanh. It chilled him briefly that Lanh would know this so instinctively. It was almost as if the possibility was in her, her knowing this. He grabbed at her hand. She took his fervently, squeezed it, held it until he broke the hold so they could run better in their own individual rhythms.

Another empty street and they ran along the sidewalk for a short distance, their feet ground broken glass, a streetlight splashed upon them and Cliff felt exposed, in rifle sights, then they were in the dark, approaching a corner. He let himself listen and he heard the hammer of engines—perceptibly louder now—the choppers were still flying. There was still a little time. But another engine, a second one, a different stroke, behind them, and Cliff's heart raced as he turned. His hand was on Lanh's arm as he saw a jeep turn the corner down the street. The jeep looped wide, the figures canted there, he heard loud voices. He pulled Lanh into a doorway, out of the line of sight. They were prowling ARVN soldiers. They'd kill from their drunken doom, Cliff knew. The voices were resolving from noise into words. Find a bar. A bar. Get the girls. Nothing of value there, another said. A stereo store.

Cliff and Lanh were pressed against a corrugated metal door out of the ARVN's sight but the jeep would pass straight in front of them. There was nothing to do but run.

"We'll go in the first open doorway in the next street and up as high as we can go," he whispered to her.

Lanh nodded. Cliff tilted his head in the direction of the corner and they were on the sidewalk, close to the buildings, finding the shadows, but running hard, exposed to the jeep and just before the corner Cliff heard one of the soldiers shout in surprise. Cliff and Lanh turned the corner, were in the next street, and a burst clattered behind them. Cliff's eyes groped for doorways. The jeep motor raced. There. Beside a stretch of stone fence, a doorway into a building. They leaped into the darkness, found a metal staircase with their hands, their eyes useless, their ears bringing them the grinding of the jeep's gears as it careened into this street. They climbed clattering for a ways. Then as if on cue they both slowed drastically, climbed softly as they knew the jeep was slowly drawing near, looking for them, they heard slurred voices in the street and Cliff and Lanh left the staircase on a floor, they stretched out on a frayed and dusty rug and lay quaking in their own heartbeats.

We're too small, too much trouble to them, Cliff told himself and thought to tell Lanh to help soothe her but he could not speak. His throat was clamped shut. He felt for her hand and held it and let it be. She knew better than he about these things anyway, he thought. They lay waiting as the voices passed and the street grew quiet again. They sat up. They couldn't see each other's faces in the darkness of the hall. Then there was a faint slip of light from behind him; Cliff could see it on his hand that rested on the floor. But he did not turn to the light, he looked back to Lanh and suddenly her face jumped from the dark, her torso was splashed with yellow light. Her eyes lifted beyond and behind Cliff and she gasped in fright. Cliff clawed around, his hand moving to his pistol.

A Vietnamese soldier stood in the door. Cliff almost drew to fire but the man's head drooped, the sleeves of his fatigues were rolled up, he was barefooted. Cliff felt Lanh moving toward the stairwell, pulling at his elbow. He moved.

"Who is it?" the soldier said thrusting his face forward.

Lanh was on the stair going down. Cliff was on the stair but he was held briefly. He knew what was coming.

"An American. You're American," the man said and his hands came forward, supplicating. "Please. Not me. My boy. Take my boy," he said in Vietnamese.

Cliff was backing down the stairs, slowly. The man teetered forward.

"Not for me. Don't let them take him from me."

Cliff could not speak. He staggered further down the stairs.

"You take him America." The man was speaking English now. "My boy. VC bad. You know."

Cliff turned and he wanted for a moment to let his grip go, to plunge on down into the darkness, but his legs moved, Lanh was waiting, and they hung at the door. Cliff looked into an empty street and they ran, ran into the next alley and on toward the embassy.

They worked their way north and east and the streets were largely deserted. They passed along a row of sidestreet restaurants and where other nights the street was full of sleeping indigents and the smell of cooking food there was now only debris—shattered plates, glass, garbage. And no people. No sense of people. No feel at all of people behind the doors and windows. No sense of the intense life that Cliff had always loved in Saigon. The life was gone, the city was comatose, the body was broken. Paper banners on a restaurant hung limp and colorless in the shadows as they ran. They'd been out of the alleys for several minutes and Cliff was getting nervous. A form in a doorway they passed. It was human but did not move. They stopped at a dark corner where food garbage was piled waist-high in the gutter.

"We've got to get back into the alleys," he said.

"They're tricky," she said.

"ARVNs are still around."

"I know."

Their chests heaved and they leaned together for a moment to rest though they both knew this was not the place.

Lanh gasped and jerked back. Cliff grabbed her and cried, "What?"

Lanh spat out in disgust and pulled him back further away from the spot where they'd been standing. "Rats," she said.

Cliff looked and saw two rats the size of squirrels passing from the garbage heap and into the darkness of the restaurant and then another from the darkness toward the heap.

97

"We can't stop again," he said and they moved on half a block more and then struck off to the east in an alley.

Down the alley, from somewhere in the indistinguishable twists of stair and balcony, came the smell of bun bo cooking. They ran on and the smell faded quickly but Cliff was heartened by someone cooking. There was still life inside the walls they passed. Then he was struck by the odd hour for the cooking of food—particularly bun bo. Then he knew that someone was expecting to die. Someone was living out of time because the approach of the end rendered time irrelevant. Just as Lanh and he had not waited till dawn to go to the embassy. Someone was preparing a last favorite meal, Cliff decided. The city was preparing to die. He ran pushing heavily through the clammy air and he knew that these had been his kinsmen, these people caught now in their rooms. That he and Lanh had gone into the streets did not change their own identity. He turned his awareness toward Lanh, listened to her heavy breath, her footfalls in the dark next to him, to keep himself from despair. He would not listen for the helicopters. He filled himself with the splash and clatter of their feet in the alley to block off any consideration of their chances for escape.

He had tried for a time to keep track of the streets they crossed but he was quickly into sections of the city he knew little about. He ran on faith now, keeping a sense of the northeast, following Lanh's better informed estimates of where they were, waiting to hit Nguyen Du or Hong Thap Tu or another major street he knew led in the direction of the embassy. But at each cross-street Lanh was getting progressively more nervous in her assessment of their next move. And his own notion of the direction of the embassy was blurred with the vectoring they'd been forced into by the alleys.

The shops were falling away now, the looming ranges of apartments as well. They were running along walls, unbroken walls, trees jagged blots against the dark sky. Walls, and Cliff felt no life at all about him, walls sweating, he sensed, a corridor, doorless, he grew uneasy, he fixed his eyes on each gap ahead, the street, sometimes faintly lit by a street light, often just a subtle remission of the dark. They ran and the smell of garbage had faded. Cliff grew unsettled but this was the kind of neighborhood the embassy was in, he told himself.

Then they stood at the mouth of an alley. Lanh looked both ways and across at the alley mouth before them. They started across but Lanh stopped in the center of the street. She looked both ways again and then at Cliff and he knew she was lost. She clutched his hand and her mouth opened to speak.

"I know," he said.

They looked about them. The walls were high along the street. Their view snagged in the trees but Cliff could force his view through to a large house set deep on the grounds of the estate next to the alley. He pulled back to the street. On the wall near an iron gate was a rectangle of metal. An official building of some sort. Then Cliff stiffened. His eyes went back to the house. It was visible. Dimly, but visible. He looked up to the sky. Overhead the sky was deep black, starless, but his eyes descended and the dark diminished till at the far end of the street he could see a thin band of grey. Dawn terrified him. He knew it was almost over.

Lanh was weeping beside him. She'd taken her hand from his and her hands were pressing at her face and she was beginning to cry.

"Come on," he said and she was beside him running at once and he looked to see the tears still coming but the sounds were gone. They ran up the middle of the street to the end and went to the blue tile rectangle in the corner wall and the intersection was Phan Ke Binh and Tu Duc. They looked at each other. The names meant nothing to them. Lanh leaned wearily against the wall. Cliff's hands flew up before him, clenched there, and he looked around sharply then swung his head back as if there was an answer hiding somewhere around them and needed to be caught unawares. His mind wobbled again. How many times will my hopes be picked up and cast down this night? he asked. Better to just stretch out on the street here and wait for the North's tanks to roll over than to feel these surges of weakness and terror over and over again. He turned wearily, expecting the worst, to the sky once more. There was silence for a moment. No, not quite silence, the engines in a mode he'd not heard before. Idling. Faintly. Then the engines surged and he could hear them clearly. Clearly.

"What is it?" Lanh asked.

He looked at her. She was standing erect staring at him. "This way," he said. "We're close."

They were running again, following the sound which was close enough now to mark their path. The engine he'd heard rose up ahead and swung away to the left. The air was moist. He knew there were still several blocks to go, but it was close. He had a fix on the place. The engine was gone, out of range, and silence held once more and Cliff found the emptiness swell through his chest. The sound of the engines was close and that spurred him on, gave him hope, but their nearness made these silences more devastating too. He put his head down and grabbed Lanh's hand, pressed it. Her hand was cold, clammy. He turned his face to her and saw her eyes fixed ahead and her mouth sagged open and she ran unsteadily. Her eyes. Her eyes were coming clear to his sight. The sky was lightening. He looked straight up. Dark still. Unstinted. He lowered his head, shut his eyes. They were at a thoroughfare. He went to the marker. Phan Dinh Phuong. Yes. Yes. He knew the street. Which way, though? It was subtle. Then he heard the distant beat of chopper engines. He looked before him. There was open ground across Phan Dinh Phuong and he looked at the sky, heard the engines. Then off to his left, far away, he saw two red lights, they were wiped away, then reappeared—the clouds were low—or smoke—but he knew it was the chopper. It moved before him and off to the right, paused, descended, and he lost it. But he knew where he was going now.

"There," he said, pointing.

"I saw," Lanh said, but her voice was faint.

"Are you all right?"

"Yes."

They ran on and Cliff listened to the faintly idling engine, listened and wanted suddenly to make this one, make this very chopper, this one that was so close, this one that could be the last. Past one more street, still running, bearing parallel to Thong Nhut, where the embassy fronted. They'd somehow worked their way too far north and too far east of the embassy. But now he knew. He was sure now. They hit Mac Dinh Chi and that was the one. The words of the street nameplate—clearer still, as the dark was fading rapidly—filled him up. They turned south and he heard the chopper's engines sharpen, the pounding began, the sound rose and he saw the red lights hover then swing away. A pistol shot. Up ahead. He thought for the first time of what must be at the embassy. The chaos. He slowed slightly as the chopper's engines receded.

"Stay close to me," he said.

Lanh said nothing and he turned to her. She was struggling. She was a glimpse at part of himself that he'd been too keyed up to be aware of. His own legs were tight, his side throbbed. They'd only jogged and they'd slowed often to a quick walk to catch their breath, but they'd come a long way.

"Are you okay?" he asked.

She nodded.

"We can't collapse at this," he said. "We'd be doomed in this city."

She nodded again. They'd both known that instinctively all along. But Cliff was worried about her as her chest heaved and she staggered on a dip in the sidewalk. He caught her by the arm.

"I'm all right," she said.

Cliff approached Thong Nhut with a growing, gagging fear. A helicopter hammered in directly overhead, the engines vibrating in Cliff's teeth. He could see no one in this stretch of Mac Dinh Chi who might have shot at the chopper before. There were the sounds of many voices now, though, but he kept his mind on the helicopter. There's one more at least, he thought, and that moved him into the broad width of Thong Nhut and he and Lanh staggered back from the sight.

Down the block, before the main gate of the embassy, the street was filled with people. The mob pressed tight at the wall and fanned back from there till the street was blocked and the mob dissipated in the walk across from the embassy. The air was filled with voices. The helicopter sat in the dark at the top of the embassy, its lights blinking, but its engines were matched by the sharp-edged babble of the people. The mob rose up where it impacted the wall and individuals were moving regularly from the rest, up the wall and then meeting darker forms at the top and dropping back, dropping with cries sharper than the rest, dropping with limbs flailing, clawing at the wall, at the air.

The chopper engines were revving and they woke Cliff from his stupor. He moved forward and knew Lanh was hanging back. He turned, extended his hand to her, she took it but her eyes did not move from the sight before her. They went slowly down the high white wall and approached the first fringe of the mob. Cliff shifted his hand from Lanh's hand to her wrist. He had her firmly and he looked at her face once more to see if she was all right. She looked at him and he saw her sense that he was looking for some sign. She smiled at him, though he could tell that the smile came from a great act of will.

"We're here," she said hoarsely.

They passed the first people, half a dozen men shifting back and forth, up and back, moving toward the mass of people then withdrawing in despair.

Cliff kept his face averted, his head ducked, and he

moved toward the seam between mob and wall. Against the wall, just before the people clotted together, a middle-aged woman sat. Three large, bloated leather suitcases surrounded her. She stood with one hand raised to her face, a heavy bracelet hanging down, and she stood absolutely still. A man pushed back from the crowd, glanced off her, and she moved a bit but retained her position and her hand did not fall from her face. Cliff blotted her image from his mind, resolved to look at no one. He tightened his hold on Lanh and shoved his way into the space between the crowd and the wall.

"Through. Through," he said to the people before him. "They'll open the gate for me. Through."

Faces turned at last to Cliff and started. An American, someone said, then another. More faces were turning. The crowd shifted, threw him against the wall, his breath gasped from him, he held Lanh tight.

"They'll open for me. They'll open the gate. Let me through," he cried.

Yes, yes, voices said. They'll open. People gave way. Cliff edged along the wall but the crowd crushed at him again, his chest sheered into a bevel of the wall.

Take me. Please. Take me with you. Please. Please. The voices pressed like the weight of the crowd against him, pressed his mind against the wall.

"Follow me. Let me through and they'll open," he yelled. "I have to get to the gate before I could help you."

More people gave way. Let him through, he'll get the gate open. The shouts were taken up all along the wall and the crowd wedged open slightly and he was moving again, his hand clutching Lanh tight. He looked back at her and her face was blank.

Engines battered his head. He heard the helicopter rise. His eyes darted up briefly and the night was lanced, the black was draining away even overhead. He could see the form of the chopper bound by the lights. It hung above the street for a moment and Cliff wanted to leap up to grab for it. Then it was gone, the crowd convulsed, he looked and

103

the gate was ahead, the last few people gave way and he and Lanh were before the iron bars of the gate.

A Marine was near Cliff just inside the gate. His M-16 lay across his chest, bayonet fixed. He was watching the Vietnamese pressing against the gate just to Cliff's left. But they were trying to breach the wall, not the gate. Here they were sticking their hands through with rolls of worthless piastres, jewelry. They cried the names of Americans. General Scott my friend. I am his driver. Mr. Craig. I was Mr. William Craig's aide. He knows me. Let me in. Please. He said I should come here. The Marine still had not seen Cliff.

"Sergeant," Cliff shouted. He waited a moment and then realized he'd shouted in Vietnamese. "Sergeant," he cried in English.

The Marine turned sharply to Cliff's voice. "Jesus, man," he said coming over. "What are you doing out there?"

Cliff laughed. He laughed and he watched himself laugh as if watching a stranger from a great distance.

"You *are* an American, aren't you?" the Marine asked.

"Yes," Cliff said without hesitating. "I'm an American." Cliff was holding the iron bars with both hands.

"I'll open up."

Cliff turned to Lanh, put his arm around her.

"Not the girl," the Marine said, his hands pausing at the fence. The crowd was pressing forward already.

"She's my wife," Cliff said, clutching at the fence again.

"I'm not supposed to let Vietnamese in," the Marine said but Cliff heard the regret in the voice, heard a crack. "You can come in," he said. "But alone. I've got my orders about Vietnamese."

"My wife, man," Cliff said wrenching at the bars, holding back his panic. "My wife. What is this, anyway? They'll kill her."

Cliff thought he saw the face soften, but then the Ma-

104

rine's eyes shifted and Cliff looked to his right and Lanh was gone. "Come on in," the Marine said.

Cliff turned to the Marine and gaped, his mind shut down, he was struck numb. He was lost. He was lost now forever. The crowd crushed at him, the bars ground into his chest, his face, he felt himself slipping, felt his grip going, he was alone, alone for the last time, he'd be trampled under the feet of these people. He felt the gate move, the Marine was opening it.

"No," Cliff shouted. Then he was moving, he was turning away, he was pushing off to his right.

"We're almost done here," he heard the Marine shout. "Come back."

Cliff clawed at the bodies in his way, they yielded, he moved along the wall, moved quickly, these behind were content to take his place forward.

He broke free of the mob and looked up the street, across the street, and he saw no one running away. He moved out from the crowd, he started off one way, then drew back and started off the other way, a mirror image of the Vietnamese men at the back of the crowd. The despair was returning, the urge to lie down before his isolation and let it all rush over him and past and wait there to die. But he knew why Lanh was gone. She heard the Marine say only him and she didn't want to stop him from going, she wanted him to escape, to be safe, even if it meant her own death. She was afraid of America; he knew that too. That made it a little easier for her to follow her deeper impulse, but he knew that Lanh loved him enough to return alone to the streets of this doomed city and face what her strongest instinctive fears were telling her was certain torture and death. Wherever Lanh was he had to go there even if it was to sit down with her and wait.

He saw an old man squatting against the wall. The man was alert. He was watching the crowd that roared in Cliff's ears. Cliff went to him, squatted before him.

"Sir," Cliff said. "Did you see a young woman running away from the crowd?"

105

The man's eyes moved slowly to Cliff's face. Cliff said, "I'm an American. Maybe I can help you. But I have to find that woman."

The man shook his head slowly.

"It was a strange sight, someone running away from here. Surely you saw it."

"You can't help me, young man," he said still shaking his head. Then he stopped and looked at Cliff. His eyes were almond-shaped, clear, black in the dawn. Cliff looked into the unflinching eyes and he nodded at what the man had said straight, true.

"Did you see her?" Cliff asked again and he felt the old man's pity, felt the old man's mind touch him through the faintest softening of his eyes.

"That way," he said pointing off toward the south extension of Mac Dinh Chi.

Cliff lingered a moment longer squatting before the man. They looked at each other in great sorrow and Cliff felt kin to this old man. Cliff put his hand briefly on the man's shoulder and rose and turned.

He ran down Thong Nhut and turned into Mac Dinh Chi. There were people here along the sidewalk sitting and crying, sitting and staring. He passed them, checking each face. Lanh was not there. An ARVN officer was stripping off his uniform, throwing the clothes into the street and moaning, his eyes wide, watching his own hands as they tore at his clothes. Cliff hurried on and he reached the end of the block and spun around. He looked back and the tamarind trees, tall and linked above the street, had emerged from the night. The sky was grey. Morning had come. He stood beneath the tall trees and there was no sun and Lanh was gone. Where would she run? It had only been minutes. She was exhausted and had nowhere to go.

He stepped into the intersection and looked down the street. A figure far off. Walking, aimless. A woman, slim. He took two steps forward. The figure was running now. Running toward him. He ran. It was Lanh, he could see her face in the light, and they ran hard and she was against him and they spun and she was crying.

"You're a crazy man," she said. "Crazy. Go. Save yourself."

A helicopter pounded aloft, swung away, and they stopped their spin, looked up.

"Not without you," he said watching the chopper. He turned to her and she too was watching the helicopter.

"You're afraid to go," he said.

She looked at him. "Yes . . . But only because you'll hate me back there."

He knew he wouldn't. Of all the things he'd tried to determine this past night about himself, he felt sure that his feelings for Lanh would remain.

"If you hate me," she said, "I'd rather stay here and die now."

"I love you."

"And what if I change there?" she said. "You love Lanh but if I go to a place like that, what if it changes me?"

Cliff could not answer. Lanh always went straight to the things that he was afraid to confront. But she was so unerring in this impulse, surely she would have the best possible chance to remain herself wherever she went.

"No one who loves another is safe from that," Cliff said and he knew the night had showed him that as well.

Lanh laid her head on his chest for a brief moment and then without a word they turned and began to run. They ran back up Mac Dinh Chi. The ARVN officer was naked and was wandering in the middle of the street. Cliff and Lanh ran hard, Cliff listened for another helicopter but the silence persisted and he felt a sinking this time, a letting go, there was no rush of fear, only a draining, but he did not slow his pace, they ran to Thong Nhut.

He looked up the street and the mob was still there, still besieging the wall, and on the top of the wall Cliff saw Marines still kicking and beating rifle butts at the Vietnamese who reached the top. They still have to get the Marines out, Cliff realized. There has to be another chopper.

And as Cliff and Lanh ran toward the throng before the gate he heard the engines far off. He sensed the end was very near. They circled the crowd to the other side so that he could work his ploy of getting the gates open to maximum effect. He took Lanh's wrist and went to the wall and began to push in.

"American," he shouted. "They'll open the gates for me."

The faces turned as before and they quickly took up the idea and the crowd opened but the faces were twisted. The faces were sharper as they confronted Cliff. They too knew how close the end was.

One face, a young Vietnamese man, lurched before Cliff. "You bastards," the man cried. "Bastards. Leave us to die. Bastards." The man grabbed at Cliff's throat. Cliff clutched at the hands, fell back, dark swarmed at the edges of his eyes, then he saw Lanh before him, his pistol jutted up under the Vietnamese man's throat.

"Let go now," she screamed.

Cliff knew the man was too desperate to care if Lanh killed him but the grip loosened for a moment of indecision and Cliff wrenched at the hands and he found a bit of space behind to move his leg and he thrust his knee forward into the man's groin. The man let go, fell back, Cliff grabbed Lanh again, and they pressed on. The helicopter swooped in overhead and the final cluster of people drew back and began shouting to the Marine inside. An American. Open up.

Cliff pressed at the bars again and he saw the chopper settling on the roof of the embassy. The same Marine he'd encountered before came forward. Cliff grabbed at his wallet as the Marine approached, he pulled out the old identification slick with wallet grease, ragged, and Cliff said, "Look at this, Sergeant. I'm CIA. You've seen IDs like this before. I'm CIA. My wife's an agent . . ."

The Marine didn't look at the ID, didn't listen to Cliff's rush of words, but went straight to the gate bolt.

"I'm sorry about before, man," he said. "It was my orders. I was afraid you weren't coming back. Come on. Bring her in. No one's gonna give a shit now."

Cliff's hands, his voice, trembled as he said, "Thanks."

Other Marines approached the gate as it inched open and the first Marine completed his thought in a low voice, "We've let plenty of these in already."

Cliff and Lanh were through the gate and immediately heard bursts of M-16 fire. Cliff turned. Two Marines fired bursts into the air before the gate, the half dozen Vietnamese who came in behind Cliff and Lanh scattered round the embassy grounds and the rest of the crowd drew back. Four Marines heaved the gate shut. Cliff turned away and he heard the thud of rifle butts on flesh, again and again, but he did not turn back. He faced the embassy, the great white facade partitioned into countless tiny baffles, maniacally regular, like the memory circuit board of a computer. He reached for Lanh, turned to her and saw her throwing the pistol away into the embassy grounds. He looked beyond her to a spiky, leafless, thick-limbed tree that rose in the grounds near the wall. It was a tree, a rampike, but it looked like a sculpture, cast iron.

Now a Marine spoke to him. "This way," the man said. "Follow me. Keep up."

Cliff took Lanh's hand and they were running again. Into the shadow of the portico, the engines idling high above, into the slick dark tile of the foyer, the place smelled of floor wax and burning papers. Down a wide hall, shredded streamers ankle-deep, into a stairwell, massive metal door held ajar by a desk.

They followed the Marine up the steps, behind them another Marine, his footsteps one beat slower. They climbed and one flight down heard a pop. They climbed and Cliff's chest heaved, with the helicopter engines coming closer, rattling the bannister, throbbing under his feet, his breath was giving out, his throat knotted shut. He turned to Lanh.

She was bent nearly double to the steps, climbing in great pain. There was a prickling in his eyes. Tear gas from below. His eyes began to feel swarming sharp edges, he saw Lanh's hand rise to her face.

"Don't rub them. It'll make it worse," he said. And they turned a corner and the Marine was at the top of the flight, looking down, a slash of grey behind him, the engines very loud. Cliff could hear the pistons beating, he smelled the fuel. His eyes cleared. They went up the stairs, his legs heavy, moving from a bog, up to the door, into the thick air, the light was grey but sharp, he flinched and they moved on the tarmac beneath the rotating blades.

A Marine in the helicopter gave his hand, pulled Lanh up, then Cliff. They moved to the far side, strapped themselves into seats, Cliff by the open side of the chopper, Lanh next to him. Cliff looked out across the tarmac, beyond the back side of the embassy. There was no movement but the slow columns of dark black smoke at the horizon. Before him lay Saigon, quiet, still, green. The trees. There were so many trees. He turned to Lanh. She too was looking out the side of the helicopter. She shifted her eyes to his face and her eyes were unchanged toward him, the love there was frank, direct. Beyond Lanh's head bulky forms were rising. Cliff did not look away from Lanh but his attention shifted beyond her. The Marines were boarding. Hulking men. Large men. Their rifles clacked against the seats. They sat, strapped in, and the helicopter shook, the engines pitched higher, beat away all sounds in the world. The helicopter lifted and turned.

Cliff looked out the side. He saw the front of the embassy swing round below him. The facade bled black and pink smoke, billowing, blotting the surge of people over the wall, through the gates, swarming toward the building.

The chopper hovered for a moment but an automatic rifle chattered below and the chopper swung suddenly away, rose, the embassy dwindled, disappeared, the trees spread and receded in Cliff's sight, turned into lichen on stone. They entered a low cloud and the outer world was gone. Surrounded by grey Cliff turned his face and Lanh was sitting upright, very still, looking straight ahead, and beyond her the Marines sat, thick arms moved, their bulk made Lanh seem suddenly very tiny. And Cliff felt tiny himself. His arms were thin. Too much bun bo, she would say. He waited and she turned her face to him and her head moved toward his shoulder at the very moment his arm rose to hold her.

BOOK TWO

BOOK TWO

*T*HE HELICOPTER SWUNG AROUND AND CLIFF couldn't understand why. The clouds broke and he saw the embassy once more beneath him, saw the crowd pulsing from the doorway onto the roof, the Vietnamese people bleeding onto the empty tarmac, arms raised, and Cliff felt the press of the restraining straps—he would have fallen in that moment through the open side of the helicopter. His hand went instinctively toward Lanh to hold her back as well. But his eyes remained on that chasm. Uprooted, flung into the air—he felt this strongly now and his limbs lolled helpless, weak before the gasp of space.

He remembered Lanh scraping frantically at her finger-nails, remembered his last look around their room. The room that had often seemed insufferably small had suddenly seemed protective, rooted, as comfortable as a crouch, as they were about to flee into the alleys, opening into streets, rising to the top of the embassy and now this leap into air that exposed them.

He should have stopped them, he thought. He should have said to Lanh before they went out the door, How can I rip you from this place. I don't know how to protect you away from this room. Be quiet, she would have answered. You're a fool. This room is lost to us no matter what we do.

The helicopter veered away, rose, the clouds closed, wiped the space away and Cliff sat back. He found his hands clenched tight, lying on his thighs. He loosened them. He touched Lanh's hand, looked toward her, but his sight turned inward. He saw her crouching naked beside him in the dark, bending to him in the tiny alley room.

—Are you awake? she said.

—Yes.

—I was at the window.

—I saw you.

—I was listening to the bombs falling.

—They're far away.

—I know that, she said.

Cliff waited. He didn't need to ask if she was afraid. He knew she wasn't.

—Is there anyone under them, do you think? she asked.

—The bombs? Probably not. They're killing trees and monkeys probably.

—I don't care. She almost whispered it.

—About what?

—If anybody's being killed out there tonight.

—No one is.

—That's not true. But I don't care, she said sadly.

—We're safe.

—Do you think I'm heartless?

—You can't be that, he said rising to one elbow, touching her shoulder. He began to be impatient with her words.

—We've been together two years now, she said. But I can't remember anything from before.

—Good, he said, thinking of the men she'd been with.

—I have no feelings for anything outside of this room.

—You don't need . . . he began automatically.

—Be quiet, she said sharply. Just be quiet.

—You'll hear the bombs then.

—I don't care.

Cliff turned away from that room. In the cloud now, in the roar of the helicopter's engines, he denied to himself the insulation that Lanh had felt. But the denial was glib, and he knew it—the clouds had closed them in again and he had to convince himself that Lanh would be safe. He felt thankful that she was not back in Saigon as the tanks rolled into the city bringing the vengeance of the North.

116

Cliff felt weary now. For a time he lay weakly in the sound of the chopper and made his thoughts stop altogether. Then he turned his face to the grey beyond the door and the clouds cracked suddenly and the South China Sea was beneath him and he gasped, soundless in the beat of the engines, but he gasped at the vanishing of the land. As he moved above the insubstantial sea he knew that for himself—and for Lanh, too, because she loved him—the escape was simply a more unpredictable danger.

He could not let himself drift like this. He had very little time. The chopper beat on, the clouds closed and broke, closed and broke, and a ship waited somewhere ahead. He had to have a plan before they landed. Cliff took Lanh's hand ahd her fingers fretted in fear.

He turned to her. The wind beat at her, and watching her long black hair thrashing about her face, he suddenly felt the wind on himself, clutching him. Until he looked at her he had not felt it. She was an extension of himself. After the years of love and fear in an alley room she had been grafted to him. He leaned to her, glanced at the Marines beyond her—they were oblivious, their eyes were closed, their heads drooped like water buffalo—he leaned nearer and shouted above the engines.

"Don't be afraid." His voice sounded tiny.

Her mouth moved, her eyes would not hold on his.

"What?" he shouted. "Talk louder."

Her eyes fixed on him sharply, as if she was angry. She was weeping and she glared at him and shouted, "We're lost. They'll arrest you on the ship. They'll send me back."

"No." He turned away. He could console her no more. Not till he had a plan. But her hand turned his face back to her. She strained toward him against her shoulder harness: He leaned to her and she kissed him. A kiss good-by.

"No," he shouted and he was angry at her—as angry as he knew she'd been at him making her shout her feelings.

He turned away again. Two alternatives, he thought. Two. The desertion had been four years ago. Four and a half. And from a place fifteen miles outside Saigon. It had been a long time ago, and as far as he knew, they'd never traced him to Saigon. The deserters he'd known about in the city had all been picked up or turned themselves in long before this. He still had his military intelligence cover ID card as a civilian technical advisor. But it had his real name on it. Two alternatives. Two. Two. The hammering of the chopper engines broke into his thoughts. He looked out at the sea. It had hardened. A vinyl sea. They crawled above it and the beat of the sound was pulping his thoughts. He turned to Lanh. Her eyes were closed, her face was still but for her hair—black flames raging from her head.

Two alternatives. There was no time. Two: keep the ID and try to pass himself off as a technical advisor or throw all his IDs into the sea and start again. The danger of the ID was his name. There would be time on the ship to radio ahead to check his identity if they wanted. His name. If he came in with nothing, he could claim to be anybody—a civilian, a journalist.

Martita Pell. He could see her striding toward him through the pocket park off Le Thanh Ton. A journalist. As he recalled her approach, the idea of claiming to be a journalist sharpened. He thought of the radical paper she'd instigated his writing for. *Free West*. A good paper at the time. National, getting attention. He saw her approach and her eyes were restless, as they'd been in all their meetings, as if she was the deserter. She took his article that day to pass along. It was the last one he wrote, for she broke off their meetings soon after. But *Free West* could be a hope now. To claim to be working for any of the other papers, the dailies, would be too risky. There could be a manifest somewhere with the straight reporters' names on it. There could be someone on ship—another journalist—to dispute his identity. Instead, he'd say he was a correspondent for *Free West*.

Cliff's mind paused briefly at this and his sight returned, the sea spread through him again, nagged at him. The sea was empty for a moment and then a sampan appeared

118

pitching in the waves, alone, its sail scything above the whitecaps. His plan seemed suddenly foolish. The sampan was tiny against the sea. Cliff's limbs felt leaden. He watched the boat fall away, overtaken, but just before the sampan disappeared he made out its deck, stuffed full of people. He could faintly see arms raised, waving, the deck was roiling like the sea. He turned away. He laid his head back against the seat and closed his eyes. He was a deserter dispossessed. Lanh was right. They were lost.

Free West. He didn't even know if the paper was still being published. But it was better than giving in. He did not flee Saigon, he did not let Lanh abandon her only home, to feed the wrath of the U.S. Army. He sat up straight. He looked into the chopper. The Marines were dozing or absorbed in themselves. Lanh was still, her eyes were closed. Cliff took out his wallet and removed the IDs. Army ID, military intelligence credentials, his intelligence cover ID. The same face, glazed with wallet grease, dim from wear, looked blankly out from each. This was a stranger. Cliff put his cover ID on top, paused to look at Clifford Wilkes. Clifford Wilkes, technical advisor, U.S. Agency for International Development, six feet, a hundred and sixty pounds, blond hair, blue eyes. Smaller than his thumb was the face. It was slightly gaunt but smooth, the hair cropped close. The face was general, to Cliff's eye, an artist's rendering of the robbery suspect. Cliff ran his free hand through his hair—an obscure impulse, as if, seeing that this face was alien to him, he wanted to know that he had one to take its place. He tugged at his throat just beneath his chin. He'd stayed smooth-shaven, he'd kept his hair trimmed—old habits—and it was well he had. He could pass. The clothes he wore—a tieless, Asian walking suit, almost paramilitary in its look, with flapped pockets, epaulets—these could be the clothes of a journalist. He looked once more at Clifford Wilkes, glanced quickly at the Marines, and then thrust his hand as far out the open side of the helicopter as he could, braced it against the flailing air, and he let the IDs go. But he felt them lift from his fingers and flutter. They swirled up before him and he dared not grab at them. One was gone, he saw it dip below the edge of the open door, but two IDs swirled just inside the door in the wind from the rotors. He saw the face of Clifford Wilkes dance before him. Cliff looked again at the Marines—he could not draw attention to himself—he would have to lunge to get the IDs—and the Marines would see. The face of Clifford Wilkes swirled just inside the door of the chopper and Cliff clenched his fists on his thighs and watched as his face, his stranger's face, spiraled before the South China Sea.

Then one card hit the door opening, pressed hard there for a moment and fell away beyond the chopper, gone. The last card—his Army ID—dropped to the floor at his feet. Cliff's hands loosened. He bent forward slowly and picked up the card. He looked at the wallet on his lap. Had he intended to keep the wallet? How would he explain having no identification but still having his wallet?

Cliff shook his head to clear it. There were details in all of this that he'd not considered. He had to stay logical. Figure out all the angles. He pulled his money from the wallet—the greenbacks he'd been able to accumulate from the black market through the years. Only a little over a hundred dollars, but it would be something to work with. He put his Army ID in the wallet, checked the Marines again, and then tossed the wallet out the door.

It was done. Clifford Wilkes was gone. Cliff folded the money tightly and put it in a front pants pocket. For a moment he expected a feeling of finality, but he felt nothing at all. He was empty. Then he turned to Lanh. He watched her profile—her long neck, her thin, almost Eurasian, nose—and he wanted to pull her to him, to press her against him. Her profile was etched against the hunched shoulders of the Marine just beyond her. She was tiny, he could see. He'd been with her in their alley room for so long that all outside contact had been lost. He saw her frailty now, her vulnerability. He felt his own vulnerability through her. Seeing her sitting there was as if he had been publicly stripped naked.

But they would have to split up for a time. Even in that moment, when he felt the most physically protective, he knew that for her own good they could not stay together through what was coming. There would be too many details to coordinate in his lie, if he included her. And if he was exposed, by whatever means, there was no sense jeopardizing Lanh. As a refugee who just clung to an available American to escape the communists, the U.S. could not refuse her. As an ex-prostitute who had lived for four years with an Army deserter, she might be cut loose as an undesirable.

Cliff leaned toward Lanh, reached for her hand. She turned at once to him—so quickly that Cliff could not be sure if she had responded to the very first moment of pressure from his hand on hers or if she had sensed him some other way just before his touch.

Her face made his chest pinch tight in fear. But it wasn't prompted by a recognition of fear in Lanh, though he did know somehow from her eyes, from her hands, little tremors that he could not place—that she was afraid. It was her strength that brought on his own fear. He loved her for that strength, the unwavering moments in her face. He knew what Lanh was, what she had gone through to keep him, to love him, to shelter him for four years. Now he had to protect her and no matter how strong she was, he knew how little she had to hold on to.

"We don't have much time," he shouted, leaning as close to her as he could.

"Time?" she shouted, not understanding. The hammer of the engines took away his voice—his mind worked, his mouth moved, his throat vibrated, but he made almost no sound.

"We don't have much time," he repeated slowly and he was conscious that he was wasting that time in expressing the thought.

She nodded and he glanced back over his shoulder. The sea was still empty.

"We have to split up on the ship," he said.

"What do you mean?"

"We have to act like we don't know each other on the ship." He'd rushed the words and she couldn't hear.

"What?"

"We have to act," Cliff began again, his face growing warm in frustration, "like we don't know each other on the ship."

"Why?"

"It's best. Trust me."

"Isn't there some way . . ."

Cliff could not hear the rest but he knew what she was asking.

"If I am exposed," he said, "you can still get into the U.S. safely."

Lanh strained toward Cliff. He turned his ear to her.

She shouted, "Do you think I give a fuck about that country without you?"

He looked at her. Her eyes were calm, but there was a hint in them of casual exasperation, as if they'd had this conversation a dozen times before and she'd been forced to repeat herself each time.

"I will go in as someone else," he shouted. "I will make up an identity as I go."

Her face tilted slightly upward to show she was opening her mind to his suggestion.

"There would be too many chances for mistakes if we both . . ."

She shook her head, pointed to her ear. She hadn't caught the words.

"There would be too many chances . . ." he shouted again and he coughed from the strain. He had so little time. There was so much to say. He felt himself growing frantic.

"Mistakes," he said and Lanh nodded, put her hand on his to stop him.

122

"I understand," she said. "Where do we meet again?"

"Put an ad in the *San Francisco Chronicle*."

"Where?"

"San Francisco . . ." he shouted and his throat felt squeezed dry, brittle. The engines beat on and his hands clenched and loosened, clenched and loosened. The shouting, the missed words, made the plan seem futile to him, foolish. He pressed at his forehead. He felt his hand trembling there.

Lanh pulled his hand from his head. Her eyes were steady.

"I love you," he shouted to her.

"What about San Francisco?"

"The newspaper there. The *Chronicle*. Put an advertisement in the want-ad section."

He paused and she nodded her understanding and she repeated "*Chronicle*," the word he did not translate into Vietnamese.

"Under the personal column," he said. "Do it when you are settled. When I can phone you."

"I will say 'Cliff' and a phone number," she said.

"Good. I'll tell them on the ship I'm a journalist." He felt the end of the sentence gust away.

"A what?"

"A journalist. I met you on the street. You were afraid. I brought you out with me. I don't know you."

She nodded again and waited. Cliff found himself unexpectedly out of plans. Was that all there was to it? He looked back to the sea again and he could not think. He repeated stupidly to himself only what he'd said already and he could press on no further.

"Cliff."

He heard the sound as faint but as clear as a thought. He turned to Lanh.

"What is the English for 'freedom'?"

He told her, shouting it three times till she repeated it correctly.

"I want to know," she said, "so I can tell them some fairy tale about why I came."

Her English was bad, Cliff suddenly realized. They'd spoken almost nothing but Vietnamese for as long as they'd been together and his fear began to stir again.

"And 'democracy'? What's the word?"

But they'd have many like Lanh. Surely. They'd have interpreters. He told her the word for "democracy."

"I will make a wonderful speech," she shouted and even above the engines he heard the irony in her voice. "If you'd heard my speech before you came to me," she said, "we would never have met." Her face moved in laughter, the sound beaten away utterly by the engines.

"What am I doing to you?" he said, but he knew it wasn't loud enough. Her laugh stopped and she motioned that she hadn't heard and he regretted saying anything to interrupt her. He gestured that it was not important. There was nothing else of his plans that he needed to say to Lanh. He wanted to take her hands and watch her until they landed. But Lanh wouldn't let him hide in affection at a time like this, he knew. And she was right. Besides, their touching had been inconspicuous so far, but with the Marines nearby and with their plan, they had to begin the separation now. He squeezed Lanh's hand once more and she looked at him and he knew she understood as he drew back and turned his face away.

He imagined himself lying glibly. My IDs were stolen by an ARVN soldier outside the hotel. He wanted to get out of the country. I told him I'd do nothing for him. I thought he'd kill me, but he just robbed me . . . Cliff jerked upright. The money. He clawed it out of his pocket. How could he explain the money, if he'd been robbed? He had to get rid of it. He couldn't give it to Lanh—it would be illegal for her to possess American currency. They'd likely confiscate it and certainly hold it against her. But he couldn't have the money on him when they landed. His hand groped around the frame below the seat, found a crevice, and he stuffed the money in.

He looked out at the sea and he was gasping. Clifford Wilkes was gone, had fluttered down into that sea. But he still had no real idea of what was left to him.

Ahead was the bullet-grey ship, homely, with the high central stacking of decks of a freighter. Cargo booms angled out and back in pairs like the posed gestures of Thai dancers. The chopper fell suddenly, banked, and Cliff saw landing craft stacked on the main deck, saw pods of 50-caliber guns. The fall, the weapons, made him close his eyes briefly, and the chopper leveled, hung, descended onto the pad at the stern.

The Marines began to move arms, rifles; bodies rose, Cliff fumbled at the seat straps. He felt trapped. He wanted to leap from the helicopter and run. Two Marine officers were walking slowly across the pad toward his side of the helicopter. I'm a fool. We're lost, he thought. He turned to Lanh. She had already removed her seat straps but she was smoothing them down, making them hang straight. Cliff turned back. He breathed deeply. He could not panic. At least not until Lanh was free of him.

He stepped from the chopper and found the Marine officers waiting for him.

Cliff smiled at them. "Good to be here, gentlemen," he shouted too loudly over the dying engines.

The face of one remained absolutely impassive. The other smiled vaguely. The engines were quiet now but Cliff's head pulsed on. The silence scooped him hollow. He tried not to stagger before the two men.

"We have to search you, sir," one of the Marines said. He was the larger of the two. That was all Cliff could tell about him. He could not focus on their faces. He looked at them but their features did not register.

He raised his arms and the larger Marine began to frisk him. Cliff felt a sound rise in his throat but he choked it back. They couldn't know who I am already, he told himself. This has to be standard.

125

"Is she with you?" the other one asked, motioning beyond him, to Lanh. Cliff did not look in her direction.

"Not really," Cliff said. "She came out with me, but I don't know her. She caught me in the street, said the communists would kill her. The guards at the embassy let me take her in. I figured it was okay to save her . . ."

Cliff's mouth felt awkward, his lips felt strangely twisted, as he spoke English. The Marine officers did not reply and he wanted to say more, to explain more, but he knew that impulse was dangerous.

"Don't you have any identification?" the larger Marine asked as he patted Cliff's pockets.

"No. I was robbed by an ARVN soldier . . . I've got nothing but my life . . ." Cliff said no more. These men, he decided, were the first line of security. They sought no fuller explanation and it could be suspicious to compulsively give them one. "The fuckers turned on us at the end," Cliff said, guessing at their prejudices.

"They weren't worth all this shit all along," the smaller Marine said suddenly in vehement agreement with Cliff.

The other Marine cuffed Cliff on the shoulder to indicate the search was done. "We do this to everybody, sir," he said.

The break in the tension chilled Cliff, made his eyes begin to tear. He pressed at his forehead so that he could wipe away the tears inconspicuously. He felt suddenly garrulous but he held it in. "Man, have I got a headache," he said low to cover his gesture. The sudden swings in his feelings scared him. He had to stay controlled or he would make a mistake.

"What's your name, sir?" the smaller Marine asked.

The clutching in Cliff's throat rushed back. He hadn't even figured out a name. "You got some aspirin?" Cliff said to gain a moment to think. He knew he had to use a name that would give the editor at *Free West* a signal in case Cliff needed him for verification.

"You're going from here to a medical exam. They'll give you some."

Martita Pell, Cliff thought. His link to *Free West*. And part of his own name. "Good," Cliff said. "I'm Clifford Pell. I'm a journalist."

A sailor led Cliff from the medical exam toward what he'd called an "interview." They moved briefly outside, high on the central decks on the aft side, and Cliff looked out toward the helicopter pad. A wind from the sea pressed his mind back into the gusts and shouts of the chopper ride. Those minutes seemed remote now and he felt something oddly like nostalgia about them. The last moments he'd had with Lanh. The two of them had been safe there, moving over the South China Sea. No longer. Cliff suddenly feared he would never see Lanh again. She was lost forever to him. He slowed. Far down on the pad men were using crowbars against the door hinges of a small helicopter, ripping the doors off. Cliff stopped. The sailor stopped, too, and they watched as the men tore off the second door and began pushing the chopper toward the edge of the ship. Other men came running to help. As they pushed, a helicopter swept in above them, hovered. Men broke off and motioned the hovering chopper to wait.

"What are they doing?" Cliff asked.

"Vietnamese Air Force pilots have been coming in all day with their families and friends. We have to push the equipment overboard. There's no place for it."

The helicopter went off the side, into the sea out of sight, and the men scattered as the other chopper dropped down quickly. People rushed from the doors, Vietnamese. Children huddled together and were herded off by sailors, the adults were rushed away, an old woman was carried bodily by a Vietnamese man. The helicopter rose again.

"He'll dump it in the sea and we'll get him in a launch," the sailor said.

Cliff watched the helicopter rise and he realized he was letting himself drift in the events. He pulled his mind back, began to prepare himself. He tried to remember every detail he could about *Free West*.

Off the starboard side of the ship the pilot leaped from the helicopter, his legs pedaling in the air, and his plane hung for a moment alone, empty, and then fell against the sea. It listed but remained on the surface, its rotors sweeping, breaking against the water.

"We have to go now," the sailor said.

Cliff nodded and followed the man into a dark hatchway filled with bodies. Vietnamese refugees crouched there, a woman rolled asleep in mosquito netting, an old man curled like a fetus. A woman grinned at Cliff as if she was a peddler on the street beginning a sales pitch. The chaos on the ship gave him a few moments of hope.

But the hope faded as they moved deeper into the ship through steel passageways that throbbed faintly from the engines.

The sailor stopped before a door, opened it for Cliff, and behind a steel desk sat a Marine lieutenant. Cliff had expected a naval officer this time and the Marine seemed a bad beginning to this. At least Lanh is safe now, he thought as the man rose. I'm fighting this only for myself.

"Mr. Pell is it?" the Marine said.

Cliff was at once aware of the ambiguity of the question but he knew he had to suppress reading things into the Marine's words or he'd be paralyzed. "Yes," he said and let it go at that.

"I'm Lieutenant Davis," he said offering his hand.

"Lieutenant."

"Have a seat."

Cliff sat down and he found the lieutenant still standing. Then the man sat down very slowly, his eyes fixed hard on Cliff.

Feeling intimidated, Cliff stammered, "There was a time this morning I didn't think I'd get out."

The lieutenant stared for a brief moment before answering. "You didn't make it by much."

"No . . . Listen, is there a way to get a message back to the States?"

"A message?"

"Yes. My editor must be thinking I'm lost by now. I was going to wire him for the past couple of days but things began to happen."

"You want us to get a message to your paper." The lieutenant's mouth moved but he was wax and wire. No, worse. Not just artificial, not just temperamentally stiff. There was something else.

"Yes," Cliff said, glad he'd taken the initiative. "His name is Sebastian French. Editor of *Free West*. Bolin Building. San Francisco." French was the prime mover of the paper when Cliff had been writing for it. Cliff recognized the risk that the man would be gone after a year and a half but this was the only convincing thing he could say to make his lie hold together.

The lieutenant's hand moved and his face tilted only slightly downward to write the name. "French," he repeated.

"Bolin Building."

"We'll get to him."

"Tell him I'm okay. Is there any way to file a story from here?"

"Not right now. We'll get back to you on it," the lieutenant said and his eyes, his face, his hand resumed their fixedness. Something was moving in the lieutenant's mind that he would not reveal, but Cliff sensed it shaping every inflection in the man's voice.

"Good. I blew my deadline."

"You were robbed, I understand."

"Yessir."

"Where?"

"Near the presidential palace. There were ARVN soldiers all over, looking for Americans."

"He took your identification?"

"He took everything. Like he was looting a store. Anything he could grab."

The man paused, his eyes did not move. Cliff readied himself for the man to leap up and declare this all a lie. Then it seemed to Cliff almost as if the man was listening to something far off. But there was no sound, there was no movement, and Cliff grew aware of his own hands gripping the arms of the chair as if he hung over a chasm.

"We have a form for you to fill out," the lieutenant finally said. "For our records. Who you are. Occupation. Next of kin. Routine."

"All right."

"Then the seaman who brought you will show you where the galley is. And he'll give you a bunk. Or a few hours of one. You'll be sleeping in shifts with the sailors and other Americans on board, I'm afraid."

"That's okay," Cliff said, thinking, Is this all of it? Is it over this easily?

"We'll get in touch with your Mr. French. He can vouch for you."

The last struck Cliff as ominous. The lieutenant still had a doubt. But of course he did.

"Here's the form. Why don't you take it down to the galley with you. Fill it out over a cup of coffee." The lieutenant's voice was strained.

"Is that all?"

"Yes."

Cliff rose and the lieutenant did not. The man's eyes did not even follow him now. Cliff turned his back to him, moved toward the door. He was unsettled by this encounter. It was too simple. They must know. But they couldn't for sure. If Sebastian French was still with *Free West*, if he would think quickly enough, be willing to take a chance, Cliff would have bought some time. If not, it was all over. He opened the door, paused, his hands were trembling again, trembling with the irresolution of all of this. He felt compelled to turn, to face the lieutenant for a moment more, to add another detail, force it further so he could fill up at least a bit of this sudden emptiness.

The Marine was turned to the side. He was tilted over a drawer and a bottle of Kaopectate was in his hand. He looked up, almost sadly, at Cliff, and Cliff stepped from the room and closed the door.

130

Cliff had had it all wrong. The man had been sick to his stomach through the interview.

Cliff had four hours in a sling bunk in a crew's quarters. He lay still and kept his eyes on the thicket of pipes in the dimness above him. He swung slowly there, from a clutch-in-the-chest fear of the authorities' contact with Sebastian French to something very strange to him—a perception of utter indifference by anyone on the ship as to who or what he was. It was as if what he'd done had made no difference whatsoever to anyone. They didn't give a shit. This feeling did not clutch at him but pressed against his face, pressed him numb. He preferred the fear. He found himself groping for scenes in his mind—the Marines come to him, drag him from the bunk, he breaks loose, runs onto the deck, commandeers a helicopter, he rises into the air, the 50-caliber cannon pump furiously at him. He would fight the Navy, fight the U.S., they'd come to blows at last—he'd wanted just to get away but they'd found him and he had no choice but to fight. This could stir him. This made some kind of sense to him. But the Marine lieutenant had not been focusing on Cliff, sensing some smell of a, murmur of a, twitch of a lie. He'd been trying to sit still so he could keep his cramping stomach calm. That was all.

Sleep. I have only four hours, Cliff told himself. Sleep. These thoughts are leading nowhere. Lanh. Think instead of Lanh. Crouching in a hatchway somewhere? But safe, safe no matter what was happening back in Saigon, now that the North had prevailed. All the rumors, her life with an American. His intelligence work. He was known by the VC. They would both have been lost back there. Wherever Lanh was on this night—crouching somewhere in a steel corridor riding through the South China Sea—she was better off. Stripped naked and paraded through the streets, then they vanished—that was the fate of the bargirls up-country. That was the tale told by the old women high on betel nuts in the alleys. Lanh hadn't worked the bars for several years, but there would have been informants.

Cliff grew weary of all this second-guessing. Bargirl. Yes, she'd been that. A prostitute. Why should that bother him now? He saw Lanh sitting in the piss stain of bare bulb light in their little room, sitting beside him on the bed, propped against the concrete wall, and she was staring at the picture of a GI in a Saigon newspaper. A sergeant who helped start a home for orphans.

—Someone you know? Cliff could not hold back the impulse to ask the question. She heard the edge to his voice.

—Are you finally asking me?

—What?

—Did I fuck this man? Are you asking me that? Lanh's voice was brittle with anger.

—No . . . I don't know.

—If I say yes, will you walk away from me?

—That's not possible, now is it?

—I've got you trapped. That's right.

—No.

—You get out of this taxi, GI, and you see what that meter says. You'll have to be a millionaire to pay me.

—I'm sorry, Lanh.

—How many half-hours in two years, GI?

—It makes no difference what you . . .

—I'm a good girl, Lanh said, her anger suddenly vanishing, her voice husky.

—I know.

—Then you know wrong, she said, suddenly sharp again, pulling away from his hands. I'm a bad girl. The worst. We'll stay up tonight and I'll tell you about all the men, all their requests.

—No.

—You love me? You said so. She was soft again, her hands tugged at his ears.

—Yes. Yes I do. That's why I get these twinges of jealousy.

—You've got good reason, she said, though her voice was still soft. Her hands dropped.

132

—I love you, he said. That's why . . .

—The quickest, meanest short-timer is jealous about the woman he's fucking. You know that? I don't understand it. I've seen men draw guns in the bar over a whore. They call her a cunt and make her lick their asses clean but they kill each other over her. I've seen it.

—Please.

Cliff wrenched his mind back from this memory. That was all done now. That all came from a place forever sealed off from them.

—You want to know the ones who fought with guns over my cunt?

—Stop it.

The voices would not fade. Cliff opened his eyes wide, tried to retreat into the pipes above. But he let her speak again. She was about to swing back once more. Her voice grew soft, she laid the palm of her hand against his cheek.

—I'm good, she said. We have no past in this room. You have no country to go back to. I have no memories. Don't ask me.

Cliff cut it off there. When they met again it would be without any memory. He heard a child crying somewhere, far off, faint and metallic.

He woke with a Marine officer's hand on his shoulder. Cliff started up.

"Hold it," the man said.

A Marine was here—not a sailor—to wake him. Something was wrong. Cliff looked about him quickly—a futile gesture, there was no way out.

"Time to go," the Marine said.

"Go?"

"This way. Bring all your things."

Cliff followed the man into the corridor and his legs barely held him, he felt weak, he had a strong sense that this was the end. French had denied him. But they didn't bring an armed guard and the Marine's manner was low-keyed. He seemed detached. That would fit, though. That would be how they'd do it. Take him, unsuspecting, some-where else on the ship to arrest him. They wouldn't want to fight it out in the sleeping quarters.

They were climbing—up into a hatchway—past sleeping refugees. These sleeping bodies—tattered, all their posses-sions rolled under their heads, heading for an alien world— these refugees were better off than himself, Cliff felt. He was heading for an Army prison. But he rejected the self-pity. His weakness veered into a frantic strength, his eyes began to grope for a turning, a hatchway to slip into and be gone. Foolish plan. But his limbs wanted to act, wanted him to flee.

They emerged onto the main deck, moved toward the helicopter pad. Cliff looked off to the edge of the deck. There was nowhere to run. His mind flailed about and he knew there was no plan to fix on and he saw Lieutenant Davis approaching.

The lieutenant carried a clipboard. He looked pale but there was no longer a stiffness to him.

"Pell."

"Yes?"

"We're taking you to the flagship. The *Blue Ridge*."

Cliff looked beyond Davis. A helicopter sat on the pad, its engines kicking over, the rotor beginning to move. There were American civilians inside.

"All the journalists are being moved there."

"Ah." Cliff held back an impulse to grin but his hands jumped.

"Mr. French said he would see you in San Francisco."

"Good. Yes. Good."

"You'll end up at Travis Air Force Base for your out-processing. It's near San Francisco."

"I know. Yes."

Lieutenant Davis jerked his head toward the helicopter and the other Marine officer led Cliff across the pad, beneath the rotor, and Cliff climbed in among the report-ers. The empty seat was in the middle of the chopper and after they lifted off Cliff was denied a last look at the ship where he'd left Lanh.

Cliff stood at the back edge of the milling crowd. A sailor rock band thumped and vibed through amplifiers and Cliff could smell the hamburgers broiling. He stood among sailors and reporters and embassy officials on the flight deck of the *Blue Ridge* in the South China Sea and a plastic bat thwacked a wiffle ball nearby and he could have let himself home back to a Sunday picnic anywhere in the U.S., a memory anyone could have no matter how neglectful the parents, but he didn't let himself go to it, he felt the grainy hardness of the flight deck beneath his feet, he shouted to himself who he was, what he'd done, and he wanted to shout it to these passing masks of contentment. It was all over for them. Make this deck a Sunday afternoon in Terre Haute and it was all finished. No one even suspected that a deserter would have been waiting in Saigon on April 30, 1975, would have fled Vietnam only when his own safety and the safety of the woman he loved were thrown into serious doubt. He was safe. Sebastian French had been unnecessary. Cliff felt as if he was a lamppost, a tree, standing there—no, a conning tower—he would not allow them the transformation of this place—he was a conning tower, part of the ship, safe as a light fixture. A Navy officer bumped Cliff's shoulder in passing and did not speak, did not look at him. Cliff smelled a park-table mix of food—the man balanced a paper plate of hamburger, baked beans, macaroni salad on his hand. He careened away and Cliff looked around to the averted faces. Bodies drifted, sprinted, milled past him and he stood absolutely still and tried to think of Lanh, tried to retreat with her to their room in a Saigon alley, tried to hold onto their time together before the fall. But he could not concentrate. The music juked around his head, found a way in, brought him back to this celebration of his safe escape, of his invisibility.

Cliff backed off, moved away from the crowd. He

135

began to edge around to go below, to find a bunk and force himself to sleep. He moved quickly past the backs of heads, the bodies turned away, the raised hamburgers. He saw a Vietnamese man moving in his direction walking a dog. He'd overheard an argument about the dog between two journalists who both wanted to use it in a lead for a story. It was a poodle named Nitnoi, Ambassador Martin's dog saved from the communists. As they approached, the Vietnamese man was looking away toward the band but the dog stopped. The animal bared its teeth, began to bark. It strained at its leash trying to get at Cliff and it barked and barked and would not stop as Cliff passed by. When Cliff had moved on and the barking finally ended, he paused and turned. The dog was still standing firm against the tug of the leash, not budging, watching Cliff. The animal barked again and Cliff waved and kissed the air at it.

He did not look out the window of the jet at landfall. Not until the jet was on the ground and he stood in the doorway did he see the United States again. The concrete, the whine of jets, linked him back to the air base at Guam where they'd taken off. But the palms and coconut trees were gone. Beyond the buildings, the trees, with their tiny leaves, blew in the wind, quivered in the wind as if insects were swarming there.

A gap opened before him in the file of people down the steps and Cliff felt others stacking behind him, about to speak, and he stepped forward. The afternoon was waning and he felt chilled suddenly—the very air felt strange to him now. He saw two Air Force officers with clipboards at the foot of the steps. They were separating the few Vietnamese passengers and the Americans were giving their last names as they passed. The officers pulled one American aside and Cliff was nearing them and he felt a rush of fear.

"Pell," he said to the officer.

"Mr. Pell, could you wait over here, please?"

Cliff moved out of the line and he began to shiver. The air felt cold to him. That was what he seized on—he could not bring himself to consider what he was doing there, separated from the others. He was chilled, though the officers were in short sleeves and obviously comfortable. He knew his body was different after his four years—he'd changed, and this wind was bitter to him, made his stomach tremble. Cliff knew he had to think about what to do next. He sensed another crisis coming but he couldn't focus his thoughts. The officers were casual, their sleeves flapped at their biceps, and the two men were calm. Cliff looked at his own arms—thin, prickled from the cold. Cold had never bothered him before. Never in his life. He looked at his arms as if they were a strange pair of shoes he'd found in the back of his closet—the wrong size, an odd color, he'd never seen them before. One more American was pulled out. Cliff wondered what they had in common. But he did not speak to the other two men. He turned away, looked out toward the runways, turned back toward the hangars, the barracks beyond, the camp streets. He knew something was going wrong. The end of the file was coming down the steps and Cliff knew he had to get away. There was no analysis, no logic, he just sensed that he could not go any further with his charade.

One of the Air Force officers took the group of Vietnamese off toward the processing building. The other officer came to the three Americans.

"Follow me, gentlemen," the officer said. He smiled. His tone was cordial.

"Why are we different, captain?" one of the Americans asked.

"You all three lost your passports. We'll process you through special."

The man who asked the question said, "More paperwork."

"I'm afraid so," the captain said. Then he smiled again and moved off. "Follow me, gentlemen."

The one who asked the question strode forward to walk with the captain and chat. The other man kept close behind. Cliff hung back a bit. He glanced quickly around. There were no visible security men. Some maintenance men were absorbed in tending to the jet. The last of the Vietnamese was moving into the building.

Cliff knew he was being taken to a more careful verification of his identity. Probably a fingerprinting. There were no serious suspicions about him at this point, but once inside, the process leading to his exposure would be inevitable. The great corrugated barn of a building neared. He could not let himself be trapped in there. This was the only moment for him. All backs were turned and Cliff broke off, angled away toward the far side of the building. He moved quickly but did not run. He watched the officer and the two Americans nearing the door. The building was packed; if they went straight in with no looking back there could be enough delay, confusion, before they realized that Cliff had bolted. Enough delay for what? Cliff began to run, sprinted past the edge of the building and toward the barracks. He was in open ground and he looked around as he ran. No one was near, no one was watching him and he made the barracks before finding the first clustering of people, three airmen on a barrack's steps. Cliff slowed and walked briskly, but with apparent calm, past them.

"The main road?" he asked the group as he passed. Two heads and a thumb pointed him in the direction he was walking and he faced down the row of barracks and moved quickly.

At a jog, he reached a street that curved on toward flagpoles and brick buildings in the distance. A car passed. He wouldn't be able to walk out of the base. He had only a few minutes, he guessed, before it would be impossible to get out the front gate by any means. The officer was backtracking even now, he sensed, looking through the crowd for him. Cliff could wait, hide someplace on base till dark, and then try to slip out somewhere around the perimeter. But with no food, no money, no real sense of terrain around the base, that seemed a difficult alternative. Another car passed and Cliff stuck out his thumb. The car went on and Cliff forced himself into a hitchhiker's casual backward stroll and waited. A car approached with a blue-numbered officer's sticker on it and Cliff let it pass. He stuck out his thumb to an enlisted man but the car was official and it went on by.

A panel truck approached. Filmtime Distributing Inc. Cliff stuck out his thumb and the truck stopped.

"Hop in," the driver said. He was a young man, with long hair pulled into a knot at the back of his head.

"Thanks."

The young man began to chatter—something about the post movie—supplying films—and Cliff watched the flagpoles come and go, the brick buildings, parked civilian cars, trees, the gate ahead.

"You're not a soldier."

"No," Cliff said and his voice sounded thin, tight. "A journalist."

They slowed at the gate. Cliff looked out toward the highway but watched the MP's face turn as they drew even with him. In the guard house another MP picked up a phone. Cliff turned his face away, watched the oncoming traffic as the panel truck stopped, waited for a semi to pass by. The back of Cliff's head, the back of his neck, began to tingle. He felt exposed. He rubbed at his legs as another car passed; the panel truck inched out. Cliff saw the MP in his mind, saw him slam the phone down, burst from the doorway, shout, Stop that truck—but there were no shouts, the truck whined out into the highway now, turned south.

"You headed for Frisco, right?" the young man said.

"Yes."

"You a newspaperman?"

"Yes." Cliff felt suddenly awkward with this young man. Cliff didn't want to speak to him, didn't want to acknowledge his presence. The young man's voice sounded flat, hard-edged, though his face bobbed smilingly toward Cliff at each question. Cliff wanted to lean his own face against the window and watch the blurred shoulder along the road. Cliff felt hollow now.

"You writing about the planes coming back from Nam or something?"

"I was on one of them."

"You just come back from over there?"

"Yes."

"Hey. Wow. No shit, man."

"I'm beat up, you know?"

"Oh sure."

"You mind if I doze?"

"No. Hey. Go ahead."

"I appreciate the lift."

"It's okay . . . Where you going, case you fall asleep?"

"Bolin Building."

"O'Farrell Street."

"I think so."

"I can drop you."

"Thanks." Cliff turned his face away, leaned his head against the window.

"Just got out of Vietnam," the young man said low. "I knew there was something different about you."

Lanh was strapped inside the helicopter and she turned her face to look out as the door was torn off by the sailors' hands and the men began to slide the chopper away. Lanh's body had disappeared in the darkness inside the machine but her face floated there, luminous, staring out at Cliff as the helicopter moved to the edge of the ship and then fell.

Cliff woke and immediately disputed to himself that he had been sleeping. The dream faded at once beyond recollection. He raised his head and the panel truck was coming out of the hills north of the bridge. To the right, near at hand, a hill-peak blocked Cliff's sight and he looked to the east. A haze hung over the hills where pastel houses mounted toward a pallid moon. The peak fell away and Cliff turned to look to the west bay and the ocean beyond. The haze, orange there, spread from a scab of sun and

Cliff looked out to the horizon where the sun would verge, would fall into the chasm of Asia.

"You must be real tired," the young man said.

Cliff put his head against the window. He could find no words to use to reply. He acknowledged now that he had dozed off before and he pressed himself down, clambered down into sleep.

"Welcome home," the young man said and Cliff just stared at him. But the young man did not seem to care. He smiled and waved and drove off and Cliff turned to face the Bolin Building.

It was a grey vault of a building with its name in art deco aluminum perched over the door. The street was growing very dim in the twilight and Cliff pushed through the revolving door into an empty lobby. If Sebastian French was gone, he'd have to sleep in a park overnight. But to get arrested even for vagrancy would finish him. Cliff fidgeted in the elevator to the fourth floor, rushed past frosted glass, stenciled names, down to the end of the hall. The *Free West* door was lit. Cliff entered.

The room was small, the blinds were closed, a man was sitting at one of four desks. Stacks of magazines, newspapers surrounded him. He was hunched over a typewriter and he did not look up right away. He remained hunched for a last long moment silently mouthing words over his story. Cliff wondered at the man's slowness to respond to the intrusion. He expected keener nerves from a radical.

The man's mouth finally stopped, tightened into a thin line, and he looked up without touching the typewriter. He was older than Cliff had expected—close to fifty—with a footprint of baldness surrounded by jawbone-length hair.

"Are you Sebastian French?"

"Yes."

"I'm Clifford Wilkes."

"Wilkes?"

"I wrote some pieces for you a couple of years ago. From Saigon"

"Oh yes," the man said rising.

"I'm the Clifford Pell who . . ."

"That was you." French strode across the room and Cliff expected him to clasp his hand vigorously but French pulled up for a brief beat of scrutiny and then shook Cliff's hand with an odd kind of reserve.

"My god," French said. "I see it all."

"Thanks for vouching for me."

"My god, you stayed till the last minute, didn't you."

"In Saigon? Yes."

"How'd you get here? Did the name thing work? Did I help?"

"You helped. Very much."

"The thing is crazy. I was writing about the liberation when you came in. It's like an obituary. That whole thing is finished for all of us now."

"I threw away my IDs and said I was a journalist."

"Of course, it's been finished for some time, really."

"Working for you."

French wagged his head once again in wonder at Cliff. "You okay?"

"I'm okay, I guess. I'm tired. I'm on the run."

"They get onto you finally?"

"They were about to."

"How'd you get away?"

"I ran. At Travis."

"They follow you?"

"No."

"Sit down. Sit down. I've got questions . . ."

"You won't write a story."

"No. Of course not." French paused and the animation faded from his face. He stacked his hands at rest in his lap. "I wouldn't jeopardize you, Cliff," he said almost gently. "I've been feeling the old spark writing this story about the liberation, but I know things won't be the same. Hell, I don't understand Africa. You know? *Free West* is going after local politicians now. Writing for junkies and queers. The voice of oppressed creeps everywhere. You know?

142

Then you walk in here and it's like you're the Ghost of Christmas past. Damn if you aren't.''

"I'm no ghost."

"A woolly mammoth then."

Cliff watched the man's hands leap again from his lap, his face tilt upward in a laugh.

"From my youth in the Ice Age," he said.

"This whole thing may be over for you now," Cliff said, and the stupor he'd felt since he'd left Travis fell away. "But it's not for me."

French jerked his head toward Cliff as if in surprise.

Cliff jumped up from his chair. "Before you put your necktie on and get on the press bus to follow the mayor around you better deal with me, you goddam dilettante." He felt like grabbing French by the throat.

The man rose and put his hand on Cliff's shoulder, gently pressed him back into the chair. "I'm sorry," French said. "What do you need?"

"I've got no IDs, no money, no idea what the hell I'm doing here."

French pursed his lips, folded his hands in his lap again. "I can give you some money. Some kind of ID, maybe. I used to have good contacts in the city. I helped a dozen fighters go underground. It's been awhile, though. I'm out of the center of things now, Cliff. I'm down to a couple people here. I'm monthly now, see. I'm taking personal ads even. Well-hung males looking for a fix or a butt fuck—those are becoming my readers. The world changes. Right? But I'll see what I can do."

Cliff felt suddenly weary. His head grew nearly too heavy to hold erect. "I'm sorry," he said, though he wasn't quite sure for what.

"It's okay," French said, obviously assuming Cliff was referring to his outburst a few moments ago. "You need a place to sleep."

"Yes."

"I'll make a call." French picked up a phone and Cliff turned his face away. He rose and went to the window.

His hand lingered at the closed venetian blinds and then he raised one of the slats.

What had he expected to see, that his strength should drain away now before an unspecified but unmistakable contrast? The building surrounded by MPs? A stunning sweep of lights—San Francisco and the bay? Instead, he looked down on a dark street, pale lamplight, the top of a station wagon glinting faintly, the facade of a warehouse.

The young woman leaned forward toward him—he sitting on a couch that smelled of rutting cats, she sitting on a footstool pulled before him—and he thought of the dun-colored cat at the top of the stairway a few minutes before. The cat had looked down at Cliff, hissed, and disappeared. The young woman, though—she'd said her name was Mindy—drew nearer still.

"We don't have much time to talk," she said.

"Oh?" Cliff didn't understand her intensity, didn't even really understand the meaning of her words.

"I'm glad Sebastian turned to us to help you."

Cliff waited, thinking he should find some other place for himself. French had given him some money. This woman seemed mad to him. Mindy was young—early twenties—and he knew she was pretty, though he was conscious that this reaction was an intellectual one now—the American women he'd seen on the streets in the past few hours, and now this one leaning very near to him, all seemed outsized, rough-skinned, all fist and jaw.

"Scoop'll be home sometime soon and then I can't talk very much to you, see. He gets crazy like that. He'll be your friend, though, don't worry. I just can't say anything to you for more'n a couple seconds unless he works me into the conversation, you see. But he'll take good care of you till Sebastian can find you somewhere to go or whatever it is he's doin'. You on the run? You come over from Nam? That what Sebastian said?"

"Yes."

"Can I ask you about things?"

144

Cliff looked at her for a moment and tried to understand what he was feeling. He wanted to talk, yes, he wanted to explain all his choices to somebody and have the person stamp around a room in respect or rage. But at the same time he wanted to get away from questions, he felt awkward, as if he was being fulsomely praised by someone he despised.

"You were a deserter?" she asked.

"Yes."

"Over there? You actually deserted while you were over there?"

"Yes."

"You really didn't expect ever to come back here?"

"I guess not."

"Why did you, then? They'd have made a hero out of you."

"Who?"

"The Liberation Army."

"I don't think so."

"Oh sure . . ." and Mindy began explaining the politics of the situation and the words were meaningless to Cliff—they'd always been meaningless—this choice had never been political—and he knew too much about the Vietnamese people to believe that deep down they really acted on political grounds either. Not the Southerners, not the Northerners even. He would have never been a hero to anybody over there.

"Why'd you come back then? You going to continue the fight?"

"Fight?"

"Go underground?"

"I don't know." Cliff balked at this, felt torn again, as he might if a pimp were to press a woman on him tonight.

"Why'd you go over the hill, anyway?" Mindy asked.

"Desert?"

"Yes."

"I was in military intelligence. I was involved in an interrogation that killed a prisoner."

145

Mindy gasped.

Cliff waited for images to rush back—but they did not. He'd had them all out already. The long last night in Saigon had ended, and he was in another country.

"Not just that," he said. "I was alone. Cut off. I have no one in the States, really. Wasn't all that much."

"Just your country."

It was an odd phrase to hear from a programmed, twenty-three-year-old revolutionary groupie. Cliff found himself holding his breath at it, found the flow of his thought cut off.

"That would be easy to give up," she said and though Cliff could see now how she'd meant the phrase, its first effect—as elusive as it was—remained.

"I liked Vietnam," he said, though he was distracted, he looked around the room—the television set was big-screened, a pizza carton was on the floor, cat toys. The room suddenly seemed familiar to him. *Playboy* magazines stacked by an arm chair, a hand-held hair drier nearby, the strong-jawed face with the wide mouth, wide-set eyes moved before him. She laid her hand heavily on his.

"You want to make it with me?" she said. "We got enough time."

Cliff did not let the words in for a moment. He was snagged still on the feeling that he knew the room.

"You've got quite a story," she said and she pressed his hand.

On the coffee table was a spiral notebook with the University of San Francisco logo stamped on the cover. He said nothing, let his head fall back against the couch. The streets and cars and buildings of the past five hours swarmed in his head.

"You've been through a lot," she said and she rose from the footstool and knelt before him. He said nothing, closed his eyes briefly to stop his mind.

"You look tired," she said. "I understand."

He still said nothing. Said nothing as the woman reached forward and opened his pants, pulled them from him,

146

sucked him erect, rose and stripped, crouched upon him on the couch and held his face in her two strong hard hands as she barked his name and the room filled with her smell.

Burning—rope and metal—a burning smell as the cable car gripped its way down the hill. Ahead, the dark water was littered with lights and Cliff watched the bay windows passing—TV screens flickering, lamps and chairs, half-drained glasses, parts of bodies—the side of a face, shoulder, arm; a back; legs propped. Cliff thought of the woman easing herself onto his penis the night before. He was a stranger to her. Once, that was his dream of heaven, like every other American man's: a pretty woman throwing herself in passion upon him within minutes of meeting. He was struck by how odd he felt. It had never clearly happened before to him, but only a few hours after his return from Vietnam, it did. His years of exile had changed him. They had made him into a man who could move this woman at once, and they had also stripped that male American dream from him—it had not been the pursuit of that fantasy that had let him take Mindy onto himself.

The woman's passion was understandable enough to him. From Scoop's long conversation—Mindy sitting quietly nearby—Cliff knew that she'd been with him since she was seventeen. He'd gotten her off the streets, a runaway from Minnesota, and taken care of her. Her eyes widened at Scoop's stories about others he'd aided underground. Some of the names were familiar, even to Cliff, and he knew that Mindy's attraction to him had been based on the same things—the celebrity of the fugitive, the excitement of his views, his jeopardy.

In those ways she had seen Cliff as similar to the others. He was another outsider with the scent of doom about him, the power of defiance. How distorted that was as a definition of himself, he thought. But in this country, on this night, what else was he? He turned away from the question. He still felt the woman crouching on him, clamping him inside her, he felt his own passiveness before her, sensed the height, breadth of her body over him, smelled the cats and stale pizza and her. At that moment he had begun to sense something vaguely familiar about her, something he was then ready to experience. Her body was familiar to him as he closed his eyes but as the second neared when his mind would begin to pump itself with his semen into her, he wanted to withdraw, wanted to flee again. He did not. He was afraid to find anything in her that he could recognize, and still he could not withdraw. He remained inside her, he did not move, and as he began to empty himself he tried to force his mind away to Lanh, to see her face; but Lanh was battered away by Mindy's cries, the hands pressed hard at his face, a head fell against his chest. Coarse hair. His hand touched the hair. He was a stranger to this woman and she to him.

He was alone on the cable car as it came off the hill and turned parallel to the shore. He got down and walked past couples clinching and spinning and leaning together. No one looked up at his passing, though he came near to them. He walked a tiny slip of a beach covered with dog tracks.

It took a glance away from the bay to the word "Ghiradelli" in high bright letters to move Cliff toward Francine. When he'd left Vietnam and met her on leave in this city, before Carmel, they talked about their divorce. Not directly, though. Cliff stopped walking. Odd, he thought—he'd returned to San Francisco now after these years, had even mentioned his former wife to someone, had had sex with an American woman, and his first independent thought of Francine did not occur until he saw the sign. An elegant shopping center. They had poked about the shops set into the hill there, him hanging back, watching his wife, her long model's body angled over a rack of silk blouses, a shelf of potteryware, a case of gold pendants. They didn't speak. She'd already made herself clear in the letter. It had been a persuasive letter, he felt now. After all this time, he could see the letter with the objectivity that a criminal in a courtroom might have as he sits

148

passively listening to all these people talking about him. Yes, this testimony sounds plausible. That man with my name sitting in this space with me must be guilty.

—It's a shame, she said out of all context. They were up there in Ghiradelli at a white wrought iron table, drinking coffee.

—What? he said. They hadn't spoken for a long time and he was startled to realize that her mind had been working all this time.

—We talk well together.

—Not this trip we haven't.

—We're good companions, really.

Cliff tried to remember now how this had been true. Art, music, literature, the quirks of old friends from school— the subject areas suggested themselves to him but he could hear no words, he felt no connection to Francine because of their good conversations. It was like trying to remember a specific cup of coffee he'd drunk and enjoyed.

—I don't feel guilty about any of this, she said.

—Ah.

—What does that mean?

—I have no idea.

—It makes no difference anyway.

—I'm glad you don't feel guilty.

—Not even for my letter.

—Would it hurt you to know that I wasn't devastated by it?

—No. Of course not.

—I was only a few months into a year in Vietnam. A war, you know. I was in danger, really.

—You *were* hurt. You do blame me. You must have shocked your friends to tell them you had a wife who could write a letter like that to a GI.

—You get brittle when you're in pain, Francine.

She began to answer this but she stopped. She would neither confirm nor deny her pain.

—It's my own damn fault, she said at last. I'm just one

of those women who can't be locked up in the tiny room of marriage.

—The house of Francine has many rooms.

—Don't get slyly theological on me. I know it's not sincere.

—It was a cheap shot. I grant you.

—I've always enjoyed our arguments.

—You sloppy sentimental fool you.

—You don't understand what I need, do you.

—Frankly?

—Yes.

—I think I don't care anymore.

The argument from that night flowed fiercely in his mind—this he could remember but he could not recall her tastes even in music—vaguely Baroque, he thought—art, whatever it was that had been good between them. He turned his face out to the bay. Far off, lights clustered on a dark vertical plane of the night—they looked like a city seen from a banking jet, from a great height, and Cliff shivered at the open space—he turned around on the beach, he began to gyre there with no object, no person near him. Where was Lanh tonight? The question rushed upon him and he stopped still on the beach. Foolish—his concern for her resolved itself at once into a curse at not turning around at the Marine's words on the ship. When the man asked Cliff if the woman was with him, he could have turned then and no harm would have been done. Then he'd have a last clear image of her. Last? No. He would see her again. This was foolish sentimentality—she'd mock him for it—yet he cursed again, wanted to see her standing on that deck, her hands composed before her, her profile sharp against the sky. But even that imagined view of her turned bad. It was the sky beyond her that was the problem, just as the night sky now was sucking the strength from Cliff. He turned, he staggered on the sand but he moved away, up the beach, fast, toward the confines of the cable car.

*　　　*　　　*

150

The *Chronicle* had nothing in it, though after only a few days he hadn't expected anything. But he kept the paper, folded it and held it tight, jammed it up into his armpit. He would go over the ads once more that night, just in case. He climbed the stairs with his face down, so when he got to the top and Sebastian French was standing there filling the open door, he reared back.

"It's okay," French said. "Come in."

Cliff followed him in. Scoop was sitting on the floor, his knees pulled up to his chin, smoking a joint. Cliff felt the room tilt slightly, right itself, threaten to tilt again—it was the ropy rich smell of the pot. And it was French's sudden appearance.

"What's okay?" Cliff asked.

"I meant there's nothing to get nervous about."

"You startled me, is all."

"It was just a routine call." French's mind was flowing in some other channel.

"What call?"

"The dudes you dumped at Travis."

"They called?"

"Wanted to know about Clifford Pell. I said you worked for me. They said you disappeared before you got checked in. They said they could help you get your passport. Big favor, see."

Scoop laughed, a vague, floating laugh, as if he was blowing a smoke ring. He was a small man, small-boned but with biceps that stood out, at rest, like his calves.

"But they were really wondering what the hell happened," French said, "You could hear it in their voices. I said you hadn't shown up yet. You were a good reporter but kind of spooky. Didn't like crowds. I laid it on like that."

"This man knows all the ropes," Scoop said to his knees. French knelt beside Scoop and waited for a drag on the joint.

"It won't stop at that," Cliff said.

"Maybe. Maybe not," French said, though he was

151

watching Scoop take another drag without passing the joint.

Cliff turned his eyes away from the two men crouching in a stratus of spent pot. Mindy was staring hard at him from the kitchen. Cliff started. Nerves again, he thought. I've got to keep control. He looked back at French.

"There are crazy anomalies," the man said. "I've heard of deserters working in their own home towns under their own names living six blocks from their parents and going on like that for years. Others get hounded down into the back alleys of nowhere. No damn pattern to it."

"You're getting me an ID?"

"I'm working on it. Yes. I still know some people," French said, finally getting the joint.

"Knows them all," Scoop said and his hands came together at his knees, his biceps flexed, bulged, his face disappeared into his thighs. French twisted around, sat straight-legged on the floor. He was snorting the smoke deep in, holding it till there was nothing to exhale.

Cliff wanted to turn and walk out the door and away from here. But he didn't want to go outside. He went to the couch, sat down, and let the two men do their chatty fade across the room. Mindy looked at Scoop, then at Cliff, shrugged her shoulders, and disappeared into the bedroom. Cliff stayed where he was. He laid his head against the back of the couch and focused on the ceiling. He drew it down with his eyes, he let the walls nudge in tighter around him.

Cliff counted the days by editions of the *Chronicle*. Three papers later, he lay in the dark waiting for sleep, holding back from Lanh, from Francine, from the country beyond this house. Someone moved through the room. Cliff turned his head—he was lying on the couch—and saw Scoop opening the door. It was the first time the man had gone out for several days. He and Cliff had stopped talking long ago. Cliff stayed in the living room and Scoop stayed in the bedroom while Mindy prowled the perimeter of both rooms alternately staring at Cliff and giggling, out of sight, with Scoop.

But Scoop went out now and after his steps had faded away Mindy appeared. Cliff turned his face away but he heard her faintly padding across the floor, felt the air move as she knelt beside him. Her hand fell softly on the nape of his neck.

"He's gone out," she said.

"I'm tired," Cliff said, though he was already throbbing erect, just at the play of her fingers.

"Come on. He'll be out a long time."

"I'm sorry," Cliff said scrunching his neck to push her fingers away. He heard her suck air in abruptly. He was hard now and he hoped she wouldn't touch his penis or he would end up screwing her and releasing himself to feelings he feared. And what were those feelings? He didn't know. He would not let himself consider the question but even if he did he knew he wouldn't be able to say what they were. It was a fear like some of the grunts he'd known in Saigon said they'd felt on patrol. Just before the first rounds of an ambush, before a twig snapped even, there was a thickening of the air, something, and they knew to be afraid. Cliff waited for her touch but she just hung, still holding her breath.

"You son of a bitch," she whispered and he felt the air move again as she drew back; the padding was faster across the floor.

The room settled, the air buzzed with silence, Cliff focused on the dark of his closed eyes and the front door flew open, banged against the wall. Cliff leaped up, turned waiting for gunshots, waiting to be cut down. But there in the doorway stood Scoop. The man glared at Cliff, looked toward the bedroom.

"That you, hon?" Mindy called and Cliff heard how shaky the voice was from the near miss.

Cliff said nothing to Scoop but began to lie slowly back onto the couch. His arms trembled for the brief moment

153

that they propped him up on the way down. He lay flat and turned his face from the door.

The phone rang about noon the next day and Scoop answered it. The man immediately shifted his gaze to Cliff and watched him all through the call. Cliff got no inkling of the caller from Scoop's grunts of affirmation.

"French," Scoop said hanging up.

"What did he want?"

"He wants to see you."

"Okay."

"Union Square. Sometime between two and three."

"Why there?"

"Precautions, man. What do you think's goin' on here?"

"I really don't know," Cliff said with a vehemence that surprised himself.

"You been over the big pond too long . . . The man's got to make sure he isn't followed. You want to watch your own tail gettin' there too."

The possibility that something was going wrong nipped at Cliff but he didn't want to talk any further with Scoop. Instead, Cliff turned away, left the house.

The street was deserted. He walked a long way round, tracing a slow maze-path west then north. He didn't cut directly toward Powell Street until he passed a bar with a marquee sign that said, "Bring back the nooner. Take a hooker to lunch." A few blocks up, a string trio of music students was playing a Baroque set, for quarters pitched into a violin case. Cliff paused. The piece was familiar. Cars honked in the street, the woman playing the violin was heavy but her hair was a familiar darkish blond, the music attached itself to Francine and he turned away.

It was nearly two and he walked quickly on, entered Union Square, made one quick circuit without seeing French and sat down on the end of an empty three-abreast bench.

French strolled up nonchalantly almost at once and sat at the other end.

"Where'd you come from?" Cliff asked.

154

"I followed you into the park," French said while looking casually about, taking in everything except Cliff. Though the day was warm, he was wearing a watch cap pulled down low to the tops of his ears. "You ought to be more careful," he said.

"What's going on?"

"Your friends came to the office today."

"The military?"

"Oh, they had their ties and coats on but they made no secret of it to me. They asked about Clifford Pell again."

Cliff turned his face from French, who still had not looked at him. I'll be one of the ones hounded down into the alleys of nowhere, he thought. "They don't have anything to connect Clifford Pell to Clifford Wilkes," Cliff answered himself aloud.

"Not from me, they don't," French said. "I set them off the scent. Said I didn't know anything much about you, really . . . I gave them some bullshit about free-lance journalists." French paused as if he expected Cliff to say something. But Cliff remained silent, trying to think of ways that they could figure out the person calling himself Clifford Pell was really an Army deserter of four and a half years earlier.

"Don't worry. They didn't follow me," French said. "I wasn't wearing these clothes an hour ago. I left the office bare-headed. Wearing a different shirt. I went to a friend's house, changed into this and sneaked out the back way . . ."

Cliff turned to French. The man was talking to a spot in the air at an angle slightly off center, away from Cliff. Cliff couldn't see French's eyes. The man was clearly trying to keep his mouth from moving too much but every few words the sounds would become muffled and he'd temporarily abandon the effort. Cliff had a vision of Scoop and French sitting in their apartment watching some spy series on TV and taking notes for just such a situation as this. The more French explained the precautions he took, the clever story he told the investigators, the more nervous Cliff became.

155

"Do you think they're watching us now?" Cliff cut in.
"No."

"Then why don't you look at me?"

French did not answer for a moment, keeping his eyes where they were, then he turned his face to Cliff. "Damned if I know," he said. "I'm probably just making a fool of myself."

"They could have tried to follow you," Cliff said, feeling the impulse to soften it for French, though he didn't know why. "They're overgrown kids. I was part of all that in the Army, you know. They love to play at that game."

"Almost as much as I do. Right?" French pulled the watch cap from his head. "Oh, this all meant something once, I guess. But I think those two candy-asses today were just for the record. They really didn't pay any attention to what they were doing."

"If I could only move on."

"You should."

"There's a complication," Cliff said, more to himself than to French.

"I've taken care of that," the man said, thinking he understood the reference. French pulled a card from his shirt pocket. "I've got your ID. It's a New York State driver's license."

"New York?"

"It's all my contact had. But it's good for three years. It'll do you wherever you are."

Cliff took the faint blue rectangular card from French as the man said, "It's classed so you can drive a cab. In case you want to go straight for a while and starve."

Cliff looked at the face of the card. Clifford M. Smith, it said.

"What the hell is this?" Cliff said.

"What?"

"Clifford Smith."

"We figured you wouldn't want to use the name Pell again because you bolted under it."

156

"But Smith, for god's sake."

"So my friend doesn't have much of an imagination."

Cliff felt his stomach twisting in anger. He couldn't understand why. "Shit, French, couldn't you even ask me what name I wanted?"

"It was done at the last minute and under difficult circumstances . . ."

"Goddamit. Smith." Cliff wondered at himself. He felt hemmed in by the name. He was standing now, watching his own anger as if it belonged to someone else.

"What's the matter, Cliff?"

"Smith."

"Sit down."

"If I'm going to get a new name . . . It's me, after all . . ." Cliff's mind thrashed around for a few moments more and the anger was draining from him and he sat down thinking, What fucking difference does it make, but feeling there was some difference.

"You okay?" French said, putting a hand on Cliff's shoulder. "I'm sorry I couldn't ask you . . . You're under a lot of pressure . . . It's easy for me . . . You called me a dilettante . . . Maybe you're right. But I want to do what I can to help you. Things have passed us by, you and me. We have a lot in common. Passed us both by." French dug into his pocket and pulled out an envelope. "Take this."

Cliff opened the flap and saw money. "I'm into you for fifty dollars already. I've got most of it still."

"Keep it all. You'll need it. Get on away from here now. That's the best thing for you."

Cliff made a vague motion with the envelope to say, I shouldn't take this.

French said, "First bank you rob, send me a cut." The man rose crisply.

Cliff suddenly didn't know how to read the man—the money was a gift out of personal sympathy for a bad situation or it was payment to get out of town, out of

French's life already. Cliff didn't know which. He rose and shook the man's hand.

"Good luck," French said. "Don't worry about your cover at this end. Wilkes and Pell are both dead." And the man strode away across the park.

Cliff looked down at the blue rectangle in his hand. Wilkes and Pell are dead, he thought. But who is Clifford Smith?

Cliff, it said, the type tiny but wiping away the rest of the page. And a phone number, area 312. He stopped on the street corner, people bumped and flowed around him.

In spite of the waiting he'd gone through, he stood in suspension as if this had been entirely unexpected. And it had been abrupt, inevitably so—for a long time the words had not been there, then suddenly they were, and just as suddenly this part of his ordeal—the worst part, he felt—was over. She was far away. He knew area 312 from his college days—greater Chicago. The farther the better, he thought. I'll get to her—and then we'll be safe, deep in the continent.

He began to walk, began to trot. There was a bank on the next corner. He was jogging, slowly into a sideways sidle past clumps of strolling people, then jogging again, running for a handful of change.

He stood in the back of a dime store near the sizzle of hamburgers, a bin-full of bras, and he fed the phone quarters and at the other end it rang.

"First Presbyterian Church," a woman's voice answered.

Cliff didn't speak for a moment, then repeated the phone number to the woman.

"You have the right number. This is the First Presbyterian Church of Speedway. Can I help you?"

"Do you have a Vietnamese woman there named . . ."

"Oh Lanh." She pre-empted him, pronouncing the name with a flat, hard, foreign vowel-sound—foreign, that was his impression of the sound, he realized.

"Yes, Lanh," he said, pronouncing the name correctly. "May I speak to her?"

"She's around somewhere here. Yes. Hold on . . . Who's calling her?"

"Tell her Cliff."

"Hold on now."

The phone was silent for a long while and Cliff leaned his head against the metal frame of the phone stall. He felt the skittering of his pulse in his throat.

"Hello?" Lanh said.

Cliff jerked upright. "I love you," he said. "You're okay . . . Where are you?"

"Cliff," she said and her voice was trembling. "Come to me quickly," she said in Vietnamese.

Cliff realized that he had first spoken—instinctively spoken—to her in English. He wondered at this—his instinct with Lanh had always been—always—to speak Vietnamese. How could it be changed so quickly?

"I will," he said in Vietnamese.

"Please," she said. "I shake all the time. I want you here with me. I can't talk to these people."

Her voice clawed at him. He'd never heard her like this. "Yes," he shouted into the phone. "I'll be there . . . Are you treated badly?"

"No. They're good people here. I'm just afraid. I don't know enough English. They talk and motion to me like the GIs used to—not insulting, but like I'm a child or a fool. But I can't understand. I *am* a child here. Please come quickly."

"You're at . . . a church?"

"They sponsored me. All the refugees needed sponsors to leave the camp. I was lucky to get out so quickly. Come to me. I'm at the First Presbyterian Church in Speedway, Illinois."

"I'll be there as fast as I can. Please be strong. We're safe now."

"They didn't arrest you."

"I'm okay."

159

The operator cut in with a time warning.

"I'll hang up now," Cliff said. "I'll walk away from the phone and not stop moving until I get to you."

"Cliff, they're so big, these people. Everybody is. They scare me. I don't understand what's happening."

"Let's hang up now," he said. He was anxious to get started but also he knew he could not bear hearing her like this much longer.

"Cliff."

"Yes?"

"What's the word for 'privacy'?"

He told her.

"And 'understand.' "

He told her.

"And 'intelligent.' "

He told her.

"Come quickly."

"I love you," he said and it wasn't until the phone was down that he realized that he'd said it in English.

Cliff stood on a blacktop, on a plain, no cars for a long time, a fallow black field before him, its furrows slicing to the horizon as straight and as quick as Cliff wished he could move now. A shadow slipped across the road and then fluttered along the furrows. Cliff looked up and three gliders were circling there, bone-white, slim, they circled and did not move away, like waiting birds. The circles were tight and the gliders were high over Cliff and he had no depth perception watching them. As their paths crossed, the gliders seemed to merge, to pass into each other's taut skins, then separate and merge again. One swooped up and, tail-on, disappeared for a moment against the blue, then flashed again, looping out of the climb—a gesture, it seemed to Cliff, in the silence there, in the hot sun, of extraordinary leisure, nonchalance. Cliff wondered who they were, moving with this calmness that mocked his sweat, his aching knees, his fragmented flight to protect Lanh. Rich farmers, he decided. Cliff cursed softly at the sky.

*　　*　　*

From the edge of Speedway—marked by two separate welcome signs, one from the Elks and one from the Eagles; a Hamburger Castle with whitewashed turrets; and a grove of century-old bur oaks—Cliff could see Chicago far off to the east. The big-city haze made the buildings rise darkly from across the stretch of flatland like the warrior braves were supposed to rise in a boy's fantasy on an Indian summer night.

Cliff turned and got one more hitch, with a quiet old man in a pickup, over a bridge in the center of town spanning the Fox river, and out to the First Presbyterian Church. The church was a large A-frame building with a fake fieldstone exterior. A wooden cross in the front yard was angled sharply from the vertical and enclosed beneath it the church marquee. Reverend Paul Potter welcomes all visitors, it said, and below, the weekly homily: The only woman a man should dictate to nowadays is his stenographer.

Cliff went to a side extension on the church, long and low, and he opened a glass door. Inside he stopped. The church office was up at the end of the dim, slick hall but he stopped and stood for a long moment, held by the smell of linoleum and floor wax and cinder block—smells of primary schools—the faint whine of a metal water fountain—his own childhood in a grade school somewhere in these plains—he had no specific recollection, he allowed himself no specific recollection, no faces, no voices, no hallways other than this one he stood in, which was not a school, after all, but the smell stopped him, made him feel intensely awkward, made him feel like ducking his head. He pulled his arm to his face. He smelled the dust and the sweat, wiped his face with his forearm. He moved forward toward the office.

"Yes?" The woman rose from behind a desk. She had rhinestones in the frames of her glasses and her hair was pouffed into a tight little helmet.

"I would like to see Lanh."

"She's not here right now . . . Who are you, please?"

161

"My name is Clifford . . . Smith. I'm a friend of her."

"Are you the man who called her a few days ago?"

"Yes."

"My. She was in a terrible state after that. She was crying."

"She was happy to hear from me. I'm an old friend."

"I see . . . But she seemed very agitated . . ."

"Didn't she tell you about me?"

"She said something. She does know you, I understand."

Cliff's hands came tightly together before him. He couldn't understand what this woman was doing, though he did realize that Lanh's poor English probably confused the explanation of her state after the call.

"I'd like to see Lanh," Cliff said, trying to keep his voice calm.

"She'll be in tomorrow. You can drop around at noon and see her in this office."

Cliff realized that he must have gestured or grimaced or something, because the woman recoiled, her eyes widened slightly. But he had no independent awareness of having done anything threatening, in spite of his growing sense of distress at this woman's attitude.

"She was crying because she misses me," Cliff said very slowly. "I am a close friend. I am a Vietnam veteran who cares about Lanh and I want to see her."

"I think you better speak to Reverend Potter. Please wait here."

Cliff said nothing, did not nod, and the woman edged away from behind the desk and went to a closed door in the far wall without taking her eyes off him. She knocked once, a man's voice sounded from inside, and the woman disappeared into the room, closing the door behind her.

Cliff waited, blowing out air, trying not to let the anger sweep up and out of him. Then Reverend Paul Potter burst from his office—a big man with a long crew cut and a sport shirt open at the neck. He advanced on Cliff with a broad smile and his hand extended.

"Mr. Smith, is it?"

"Yes."

Cliff didn't have a chance to clasp the man's hand at the crotch of the thumb and Potter squeezed Cliff's fingers in a firm shake that both hurt him and put him at a psychological disadvantage. The man reminded Cliff of a CIA case officer he'd met in Bien Hoa.

"Come in," the man said, nodding toward his office. The woman edged past and Potter said, "It's okay, Dottie. I won't take any calls for a few minutes."

In the office, the man said, "Have a seat, Mr. Smith."

Cliff sat but Potter did not; he perched instead on the edge of his desk, keeping himself above Cliff. For a moment Cliff considered standing back up but he decided to wait.

"So you're a friend of Miss Lanh," Potter said.

"Yes. I knew her in Vietnam."

"I can understand your concern for her, of course. She's been through a difficult ordeal."

Cliff wanted to say something—about how he shared her ordeal, helped her, how he was linked to her, loved her—these were the things that brought him to this room, but he realized that he could not say them. He was Clifford Smith now and he did not know what to invent for Smith's claim on Lanh.

"We are happy," Potter said, "to help one of the unfortunates from that troubled land. Speedway First Presbyterian is known widely for its compassion. We are heavily into charitable-type work."

"I appreciate that," Cliff said. "You're . . . very enlightened, I'm sure."

Potter cocked his head at Cliff. He seemed to like the word but was checking Cliff's sincerity. Cliff sensed a line to pursue and made his voice as smooth and steady as he could to say, "I just hope there are more people like you to help the rest of those refugees leave the camps. Lanh was lucky to find you."

Potter was nodding now.

"Their long struggle against communism has finally ended in tragedy," Cliff added, looking for still another opening.

"Yes. Yes," Potter said. "Enlightened. I like to think of ourselves here in that way." Potter's voice slowed, throbbed low, then stiffened suddenly with an elongated "However . . ." Cliff figured Potter used the same technique every Sunday in sermons, the exact spot marked on his text with a red pen. ". . . we have, in our enlightenment," Potter went on, "a responsibility. We are Miss Lanh's family, as it were. It's our duty to protect her."

"Do you want to keep her away from friends?"

"Not at all. But we are concerned here with . . . ethical . . . considerations . . . As a church, we . . ."

"How long do you expect the church to be able to help support Lanh?"

Potter stopped his groping for phrases, pursed his lips. He inclined his head at Cliff as if in acknowledgement of an unspoken, broader understanding.

"I'm sure the community is proud of what you've done so far," Cliff said, playing a hunch, suggesting to the man that he had already gotten all the real mileage out of Lanh that he was going to get.

Potter's mouth fell open briefly but then closed as he considered something that Cliff could only guess at. Cliff felt he was close to Potter's true feelings on the matter because the man's histrionics had disappeared.

"I speak fluent Vietnamese," Cliff said. "Language can be an extraordinary barrier."

"That's true," Potter said. "There were so many things we couldn't get through to her."

"That's terribly frustrating—particularly for a man, such as yourself, with a great command of words."

"Language is a fascinating thing. Man's fall from the tower . . ."

"Lanh is twenty-eight, you know."

"You saw the cross in front of the church, Mr. Smith?"

"Yes."

164

"Did you wonder why it is so strikingly different? The angle of it? Its look?"

"Well, I . . ."

"It's a symbol, Mr. Smith. A symbol of modern theology. This is a modern church, Mr. Smith. Active, concerned. I like to think we're in the vanguard of modern theology."

"I'm sure you are."

"Now, I understand the arrangements—the sincere arrangements—of young people these days. Especially when a young man is interested in a woman of a different . . . ethnic background . . . and they are placed in extreme circumstances . . ."

"I'd like to go to Lanh now," Cliff said rising, trying to keep his hands at his sides, trying not to pull Potter by his throat off his perch on the desk and slam him against a wall.

"She's in a rooming house," Potter said. "It's the least we could do . . . She has a job here at the church helping around the grounds, for which she is paid. That's in addition to her room . . ."

"We can discuss all that later," Cliff said. "I want to see Lanh now."

"Dottie will give you the address."

Cliff turned stiffly, did not look at Potter again until he'd gotten the address in the outer office. Then, at the door, Cliff shook Potter's outstretched hand by jamming the crotch of his thumb onto the central joint of Potter's forefinger, enfolding the hand, and squeezing firmly. Cliff watched Potter hide his wince in a broad smile.

The old woman barred his way, but gently. The four-family flat was a rooming house and allowed no visitors. I'll tell her to come down though, the old woman said. He turned from her, stepped onto the front porch to wait. The street was lined with elms, was quiet; down the street a boy with a baseball glove was throwing a rubber ball against his front stoop and fielding grounders.

The street seemed odd to Cliff in its silence. A street in a city could not be this silent. That was his first response. His years in Saigon with its monsoons of sound—no, not monsoons, for the Saigon sounds came, every day, every season, and lasted as long as the sunlight and then deep into the night, lasted until the curfew, when the silence finally came—and the silence always came with Lanh naked beside him, in the dark. That was the oddness of this silence—there was sunlight here, he was alone on the porch, though he listened for her footsteps from inside. As the moment persisted, as Lanh did not come, he felt a shift in himself—somewhere inside the front of his head— suddenly the silence of the street seemed vaguely familiar. He felt as if he were peering closer and closer at a face in a dim snapshot—someone he knew. This silence was familiar, yes. Back beyond Saigon, beyond Vietnam even, beyond the Army. Francine—though the silence began to lurk about behind Francine's voice—back earlier, unspecifiable, strong behind the echoes of a dim hallway like the one at the church. He knew this sound was from his past life—his life as what? An American. The idea of himself as that—his mind's approach to the phrase—my life as an American—cast out the sense of the silence, filled him with a jumble of catchwords, half-political phrases, issues. He brushed them away like burrs from his pant legs. They meant nothing to him. Never had. He listened to the silence of the street, the whup of the ball on the stoop, he felt the sequence again—odd, the silence, unlike Saigon; natural, the silence, like his past in this country—and he felt the striations of his feelings, of his mind—eons cast in layers in the land. But there was no land except in the layers.

Footsteps inside. Rushing. Cliff turned and Lanh was flickering in shadow in the foyer, her eyes wide, no smile on her face. She was through the doorway and Cliff held out his arms to her but close together, palms down, to take her hands. He jerked his head up and motioned with his eyes toward the old woman to tell Lanh why he was being formal. But Lanh pressed between his arms and embraced him, turning her head to lay it against his chest.

"I don't care what she thinks," Lanh said in Vietnamese.

Cliff put his hand on her hair—slick as an otter's, her hair—he touched her hair, let his hand flow long down it, long down her back—but his head remained upright; he watched the old woman watching them. The woman was heavy, her face was pale and variegated as a doily. She stared without expression, as she might watch dogs humping in the street, Cliff thought. The rubber ball whupped and skittered faintly, a slap of leather. Cliff clutched at Lanh, pressed her tight against him. He closed his eyes and he felt a rush of something that he took at first to be desire—he was half erect now—but then the sound again of the ball, the silence following, the stare of the woman that he felt beyond his closed eyes—he could picture her face clearly, a familiar face—and he knew that what he felt was fear.

"We have to go someplace where we can be alone," Lanh said.

Cliff fumbled with the key at the motel room door. They'd spoken hardly at all since they'd left the porch. Instead, they'd held onto each other and waited. Now Cliff was trembling from anticipation of the words they'd speak—from that fully as much as from the physical desire he had for her.

He pushed open the door, turned on the light. It was a small room and that pleased him. They could pull the room about them as they'd done in Saigon. But after the first moment of ease at the room's intimacy, the place asserted itself—the big-screen TV, the smell of fire-proofed drapes, the velour painting of two cats—Cliff felt sharply that there was nothing of their former life here. But Lanh denied it with a quick movement beside him. She flicked off the light and pushed the door closed. The room was nearly dark. They stood silent for a moment and Cliff heard her breathing—fast, a faint pant—and the room was tight about them—yes, they were held safe here. For the moment there was nothing beyond the door.

"You want to fuck, GI?" she said in English.

"Don't," Cliff said in Vietnamese.

"You like me plenty, GI?" she said in English coming to him, clasping her arms about his neck.

"Why are you talking like this?" Cliff said.

"I'm sorry," she said, speaking Vietnamese now. "I want us to start over again. From the beginning."

"That's not how we started," he said and he drew her to him.

"No," she said. "We were so serious from the first."

"I was on the run."

"Now we both are."

Her face was turned up to him. Her eyes were very dark in the dim light. Dark and very large. Her eyes sucked him into her smell, her feel—these eyes were what he wished to enter—no orifice at all—they were opaque now in spite of the illusion of their depth—when he came he would have her open her eyes so he could transfer the feeling of release to her eyes—and before that he would touch her there—as they moved to suck at each other he would touch her there, on the eyelids—he'd feel on the head of his penis her eyes move under the lids—Lanh's eyes—looking at him in the dark of their alley room—very early—their first night together? Perhaps.

—What are you looking at? he had asked.

—Why do GIs always ask questions they know the answers to?

—What's the answer?

—You can see my eyes.

—All right, he said. What are you thinking? That's what I was trying to ask.

—You're worse than the Vietnamese, talking around things.

—You're Vietnamese.

—Yes.

168

—You still haven't answered me. Who is it, of the two of us, that's talking around?

—I'm thinking another question.

—Yes?

—How long will you stay with me here?

—How long do you have?

Cliff and Lanh now fell back on the motel bed.

"Let's not speak," Lanh said.

Cliff kissed her and let her speak in his mind.

—How long do you have? he asked her.

—Much too long.

—What do you mean?

—If I was an old woman I could see me filling my life. But I'm not old. There are too many years before me. They frighten me.

This was the wrong memory for this moment, Cliff realized with a rush. His tongue lolled at her nipples abstractedly now—he and Lanh would clutch tightly together tonight—over and over—they would grow wet and sink deep together in their bodies and when they woke in the morning they should be old—by rights they should be ready to die together—but they would be young in the morning and it frightened Cliff now—Lanh had been right.

She seemed to sense his distraction. She tugged at him gently by the ears, pulled his face up to hers and kissed him deeply. They started again and Cliff spread his thoughts thinly over the surface of his skin and he remained there with the pulse and thrash of her body except for one brief image as he slid inside her tight loins: he saw a glider loop up against the sky—invisible briefly—then flash again in the sun, bone-white.

"We used to lie now and listen to the bombs far off," she said.

The room was dark; they lay flank to flank, their hands entwined, resting on her hip.

"You told me once you didn't care about them."

"I said I didn't care if anyone was being killed by them."

"Yes." He thought: I tried to say it softer than it was, but she never spares herself.

"I wasn't thinking of that now," Lanh said. "I was just thinking of the times after we made love in Saigon."

"I used to listen for a dog to bark."

"When it was quiet . . . I heard them too."

"In the alleys they sounded as far away as the bombs."

"I feel very calm," Lanh said. "Here. Right now."

They lay in silence for a time. There were footsteps outside, the pecking of a key at a lock up the way, then the silence resumed, complete except for the faint buzz of the quiet room.

"There are no bombs to listen to in America," Lanh said.

"That's good. The war is over."

"I just have to find something new."

They were quiet for a moment more.

"I can hear you breathing," she said.

"I can't."

"That will be our new moment. We make love and then I listen to your breath."

"You miss the bombs falling?" Cliff said.

Lanh turned on her side, laid her leg across Cliff, letting her calf fall gently into his crotch. "The sound," she said. "It's the sound I miss. But I have a new one."

"Can you actually hear me breathing right now?"

"And it's you. Nothing from outside."

"You can't hear me breathing," he said. "I'm too calm at the moment. I can't even hear myself."

"You always laugh at me when I don't let you make things up."

"I laugh because I like that in you. No bullshit, right?"

"I guess you had to pick that up from me sometime," she said.

"Did you really hear me breathing? Maybe you did."

170

"Don't take it back," she said. "Don't let me get away with it."

"We'll find another sound."

"Okay."

Lanh withdrew her leg, lay flat beside him as before. Cliff at once began to pant loudly.

"I can hear the lizards moving on the ceiling," she said.

"There are no lizards on ceilings in America."

"I thought I heard something."

Cliff began breathing loudly again, gasping, panting.

She said, "I can hear the monsoon clouds gathering together out in the next province."

"There are no monsoons in America."

He liked the tiny lizards prowling the ceilings, snapping at invisible foes, chewing with their mouths open. He liked the monsoons mounting in the afternoons, pressing in, the great rush of the warm rain, then the clouds pressing on. He stopped his joke, stopped breathing audibly. The two lay in the silence. There was no sound in the room, just the silence humming itself. They lay with their hands linked again for a long moment and then Lanh rose from the bed. She went into the bathroom and switched on the light, pulled the door to.

After a few moments Cliff heard water running and the vague sadness that had come to him in the past few moments faded as Lanh linked them back to their life together with her routine. He saw her rising after making love in their alley room, going to their tiny, tubless bathroom, and he could hear her running water, filling a large plastic bowl. He rose from that bed in Saigon, moved to the bathroom door, looked in. Lanh was crouched on the floor. The sleek angle of her naked body folded there tugged at his penis. She looked up and smiled at him beneath the coil of her hair, she sponged water from the plastic tub onto her breasts. Her nakedness filled the tiny room; her smile, the beads of water, plucked at him. He crouched beside her.

171

He listened to the water running now in the motel bathroom and he lay in ease, letting his limbs disappear, withdrawing all his senses into his face, into his ears, listening. The water ran on and on—a long time—then stopped. He thought of water beading on Lanh's breasts and he rose from the bed. He went to the bathroom door and opened it.

He sagged against the doorframe. Lanh looked up at him from beneath the coil of her hair. But she did not smile. She was lying in the tub. She was tiny there, tiny in the great glinting white trough, tiny and soluble, soluble in the wide deep scoop of porcelain. The water collared her neck and spread away, cutting her body off in a slick sheen, twisting its image, the breasts, each darkly nipped, her arms pulled to her sides, the pinch of the lips of her cunt, her legs close together, and the image of her wavered as the water surface rippled, the image shrank tinier still, and he was afraid she would disappear before his eyes.

The next day Cliff found an apartment for them—one main room, small eat-in kitchen, a bathroom. They were rooms over an antique shop near the geographical center of the main drag through Speedway. For two blocks in one direction and two and a half blocks in the other, the two-story red brick buildings stretched, unbroken except at the cross-streets. The lower floors were store-front windows, splayed goods; the upper floors were russeted blinds, frayed curtains.

Cliff was aware that he had tried to find a tiny room in a city-noisy place. But after paying the week's rent in advance, he stood in the room that would be their home and he was struck by a whirring sound. The refrigerator motor. From the start there had been no way to reproduce Saigon here, he told himself. The refrigerator would be convenient.

Cliff found Lanh crouched at the side of the church building, gardening gloves making each of her hands as large as her head. The fingers seemed paralyzed, moving only from the bottom joint, as she picked at weed sprouts in the strip of naked earth along the wall. Lanh was thrust forward awkwardly as she tried to keep her face in the narrow ribbon of shade near the building. Cliff approached her. She looked up at him without a smile.

"Why are you sitting like that?" Cliff asked, though he knew the answer. Vietnamese women hated the sun—tanned skin was the sign of the peasant.

"I have to get a hat," she said.

"You're in America now. Women here crave tans. It's a 'democracy.' " He said the last word in English, gently mocking her pronunciation of it from the helicopter.

Lanh did not respond to the joke. She turned her face away, leaned into the shade, poked at the dirt.

"I found us a place," Cliff said, crouching beside her.

Lanh smiled and briefly put her forehead against his shoulder. "Good," she said. "Can we go there tonight?"

"Yes . . . The money I brought from San Francisco is nearly gone."

"They'll let me keep this job," Lanh said. "That will help."

"I'll find some kind of work. They've got a day-laborer temporary agency down the street from us."

"Won't they?"

"We're right on the main street."

"Won't they let me keep it?"

"Who?"

"The church. The job. Will they take the job away if I move out from the rooming house?"

"I don't know." Cliff looked up and saw Potter across the grounds. The man was walking with his side turned to them, his hands thrust into his pockets, his head angled slightly up—a dramatic pose of inner-directed thoughtfulness. Cliff assumed from this that Potter had been watching them.

"We have to have money," Lanh said and her voice was tight. She laid her gloved hand on his arm and he recoiled from it slightly—the texture of the canvas—slick with soil—it was like the paw of a dragon. He blinked against the foolish image, pulled Lanh's gloves from her, pressed her hands.

"I'll talk to Potter," Cliff said motioning slightly toward the man with his head. Lanh followed the gesture and rose at the sight of him.

"Let's talk to him now," she said.

Potter turned with a smile at their approach but he did not extend his hand to Cliff.

"Mr. Smith," he said.

"Mr. Potter."

"Mister Revered Potter," Lanh said in English.

"Reverend," Cliff corrected, but Lanh did not hear. She was agitated, Cliff could see. She was concentrating hard on speaking to the man.

"I come here," she said. "I be . . . lone . . . ly. Lonely by self."

"Lanh wants . . ." Cliff began.

But Lanh overrode him. "Lone and you help big much . . ."

Cliff felt awkward suddenly, faintly embarrassed at Lanh's inarticulateness. But he looked at her eyes fixed firmly on Potter. He knew that her strength—the very strength he had always loved in her—was what drove her to speak for herself.

"You give jog . . ."

"Job," Cliff said firmly.

Lanh's face turned quickly to him. Her eyes were more tentative now, he saw. "Job," he repeated.

She turned back to Potter. "Job," she said. "You give job to me . . . Make money . . . This one, I find good friend . . ." She put her hand on Cliff's arm. It was a gesture that fit what she was trying to say but Cliff could feel her grabbing on to him for support as well. Lanh dragged the back of her other hand across her forehead.

"Please let me say it," Cliff said to her in Vietnamese.

"Yes," she said and her voice was faint, her hand left his arm.

"What Lanh is trying to ask comes down to this . . ." Cliff began.

Potter turned the same, sincere face upon Cliff that he'd held before Lanh as she'd struggled with the English words.

"Your kindness," Cliff said, "in keeping Lanh at the rooming house at church expense is no longer necessary. But Lanh would like to keep her paid job here for a time longer."

"Of course," Potter said. "She can work here as long as she needs."

"To-ma-toes."

Cliff heard the woman's voice coming from the back of the store.

"No squeezie," the woman said loud, slow.

Cliff moved quickly toward the sound, thinking it had been a mistake to bring Lanh in here. He'd told her they had a refrigerator, they should stop to get some food. They'd passed this little grocery store near their apartment but Lanh had wanted to go straight home.

"To-ma-to bruise," the woman was saying. Cliff could see her—stout, with a bib apron on, waving a tomato before Lanh's face. The woman was not harsh. She was talking as if to a favorite grandchild. As Cliff approached, she was patting Lanh's hand.

"I find you good ones," she shouted smiling.

"I no hurt . . . vedgebles . . . I . . ." Lanh was stammering. Her tone was neutral but Cliff could sense it was only from the pull of strong contrary feelings—her anger at the woman's tone balancing her anger at her own awkwardness with the language.

"It's all right," Cliff said to Lanh. "I'm sorry I brought you here."

The storekeeper stopped choosing tomatoes and turned in surprise at hearing Cliff speak Vietnamese.

"I want to go to our place," Lanh said. "I don't want this kind of trouble even before I can see our place."

"I'm sorry," Cliff said.

175

"People are looking at us."

"Forget them."

"Get me out of here."

"We'll come back some other time," Cliff said to the woman.

"It's okay," the woman said to Cliff. "She no understand. I'm not mad." The woman was speaking loudly, slowly to Cliff, overarticulating.

"We'll come back some other time," Cliff said and he took Lanh by the elbow and guided her toward the front of the store.

As they neared the door a man's voice said, "Can I apologize for Winnie?"

Cliff stopped, turned to a man whose eyes at first seemed to bug at Cliff but then held steady—the eyes were magnified by thick glasses—the first impression of their aggressiveness became now the opposite—a seeming timidity. But the eyes were the only thing timid about the man. He was Cliff's age, around 30, and Cliff's height, but he was thump-chested, thigh-armed, in a University of Chicago tee-shirt.

"I'm sorry Winnie insulted you and your wife," the man said, advancing to Cliff with his shopping cart, smiling at Lanh briefly, then addressing Cliff again. "Did you notice," the man said, "that she talked to you the same way? You spoke the language—Vietnamese was it?—and then in spite of your appearance to the contrary she treated you like a foreigner too."

"I noticed," Cliff said.

The man turned to Lanh and said, "So you see? It was nothing personal. Winnie will probably give you the tomatoes free tomorrow after a sleepless night worrying about the offense she's caused."

Lanh nipped her fingers at Cliff's arm, out of sight of the man.

"Thank you," Cliff said.

"We're not all of us, in Speedway, what you might jump to conclude from that little misunderstanding."

176

"I appreciate that," Cliff said and he turned away from the man—with a slight pang of reluctance—he felt once more a feeling of familiarity—this time a clearly pleasant familiarity—but he turned away and guided Lanh out into the street and he felt her wanting to bolt. He felt her straining toward the place where they could shut out all of these people.

He heard thunder in the distance and rose from the bed. Lanh had just gone into the bathroom. The room was dark. He heard the faint crackle and thump once more, only moments before the water began to run in the other room. It struck Cliff that he'd known immediately it was thunder. Plains thunder. Early-summer thunder. In spite of Lanh having just risen in the dark room, their lovemaking done, in spite of the night lying before them to sleep entwined in a tiny room. The sound of the bombs falling on the horizon in Vietnam had always suggested this sound of thunder but now there was no link back the other way for Cliff.

He rose and approached the bathroom. His hand paused at the door—the image of Lanh in the motel tub rushed back upon him—the tub in this room was just as big—but he opened the door.

Lanh was crouched on the floor beside the tub. She had just turned off the water which she'd used to fill a large kitchen pot. She looked up at him and smiled and she lifted the pot out of the tub and placed it on the floor.

Cliff smiled at Lanh pulled tight before the pot of water while the tub gaped empty and large beside her. "Come in and lie down with me for a moment," he said.

"I want to wash first."

"Come with me now. I have a sound for you."

She uncoiled, rose, slipped past him into the dark room. They lay on the bed, he pulled her close and a moment later the thunder undulated, louder than the bombs had been, harder-edged. There would be no suggestion of the bombs for Lanh either, Cliff knew.

"Thunder," she said.

"Yes."

"It's nice," she said.

Cliff heard a disappointment in her tone. He wondered if he should make her express it—as she would have him do. But he waited. The refrigerator motor kicked on. A hot rod bratted past in the street.

"You don't think it's all that nice," Cliff said.

"What?"

"The sound of the thunder."

"It rains everywhere, I guess."

Cliff didn't know how to answer the sadness in her voice. He touched her cheek. He bent his head, slid his tongue from the bottom of her breast up her side and along the rim of her armpit.

"Yes," she said, as if he'd answered a question. She fanned her fingers at the back of his neck. "*You* are nowhere but here," she said.

He buried his face against her neck and lay still, in wonder, at her kinship with his thoughts. She was right— that was why he'd run his tongue along her side, to tell her that—but he hadn't fully realized the reason until she said it. He drew one deep breath at the strength of their kinship, but as he exhaled, his mind snagged at its mystery. He didn't know how they had attuned themselves so well to each other, he didn't know how they came to know things about each other, and so he didn't know how these things could be preserved. He didn't even know how fragile they might be.

They lay for a time without speaking. The refrigerator motor kicked off and Cliff knew in the sudden silence that he had no idea what he wanted to do next in his life.

"Tomorrow . . ." he began, thinking aloud, having nothing in mind to finish the sentence. But he needed nothing, for Lanh moaned faintly and turned her head away. Cliff said, "What is it?"

"I was thinking of today, at the church."

"Don't worry. The language will come. You'll be fluent in . . ."

"Not that. I was scared this afternoon about money. I always have been. You understand."

"Yes," he said. He knew she'd been orphaned, ignored by cousins; the bars had been easy compared to her fears. "I know all that." He said the words mechanically, to drive out any intrusion of that part of her past.

"But I'm afraid of something different now," she said. "Stronger. Tomorrow . . . I don't want to leave this room."

"It'll get easier."

"We feel awkward in this room, a little bit, like the motel. But it's not that far from what we had."

"And you won't have to work for long," Cliff said.

"Out there are things I can't handle. The people scare me."

"Potter . . ."

"Not just him. Everyone. *Every*one."

"They're just like me," he said. It was the obvious argument to make.

"My god. You don't believe that?" Lanh said, rising on her elbow.

"You'll get along . . ."

"I said do you believe they're like you?"

"You're not sleeping with them. You don't love them. They don't speak Vietnamese. But except for the language, that doesn't make you different."

"What did you desert for if you felt they were like you?"

"I killed a man."

"That's a lie."

"I was part of his killing."

"And these people've never had a hand in killing? That doesn't make you different."

"I had no one here . . . Why do you want me to go over this?"

"What are we doing here? Yes. Go over it. Are you so fragile? More fragile than me?"

179

"My father was dead."

"Mine too. It's not so unusual. That doesn't make you different."

"My mother was . . . I don't know where she was, exactly. Not in my life."

"Mine was dead. My cousins, my grandfather—they were Vietnamese even, and they vanished too . . . That doesn't make you different." She was crouching over Cliff now, bending into his face. He raised himself up, lay back against the wall.

"What do you want?" he said.

"Are you them out there? Why did you desert?"

"Everybody I cared about deserted me . . . My parents. My friends at school. My wife, even, really . . . What do you want, Lanh? You're my life now."

"I was your life in Saigon. You had nothing else."

"I still have nothing else."

"Not if they're just like you."

"*That's* what's bothering you."

"Why did you stay in Vietnam?"

"I saw enough fragments of you in other people that I knew you must exist."

"Pretty words." It was an epithet. She was on her knees, leaning into his face again, shouting. They'd both been shouting, he realized.

"True," he said, defying her reaction to the words. "I love you."

"And I'm like them?"

"Who?"

"Out there. Americans."

"I love you."

"Am I like them? You found what . . . fragments of me? What the hell does that mean? You found somebody with my slanted eyes and said Lanh must exist? My flat chest? My tininess? You weren't finding a nice American girl over there."

"No."

"I'm not like them?"

180

"No. No."

"Then how can I leave this room tomorrow? I'm scared. Please . . ."

Lanh fell against him sobbing. He stroked her hair and she stopped crying very quickly. He continued to stroke her hair for a long time. He and Lanh were slick with sweat against each other, as if they'd just made love. He found it difficult to breathe. The thunder had stopped. There had been no rain. The night had merely thickened, like a head cold.

Cliff sat at a wooden desk filled with carved initials and he glanced down the form. Laborpool Inc; the education question was "grade completed"—should he put 16?; "church preference"—Cliff shook his head and smiled. He would put "gothic." He started at the top, printed the name "Clifford M. Smith," and then he put his pen down with a quick throb in his temples. "Social security number," it said. Should he use his own? The government—if it was smart—would have its computers monitoring the social security numbers of fugitives. He had to think all of this through. He folded the form, nodded and smiled at the girl at the reception desk, and left the storefront office of Laborpool.

He walked twice around the block trying to decide what to do. His mind drifted away, back to the morning. Lanh had gotten up without a word, had gotten dressed, had left for her yard-job at the church. If she could face that, how could he let himself be paralyzed by a thing like this? Was he getting paranoid? No. He had to use a different number. There was no doubt about that. He could make one up, but if it turned out to be a bogus number, a dead man, someone about to retire, whatever, he could have troubles.

He wandered on up the street, past the antique store beneath his apartment. He paused. He needed a number that was plausible, one that he could monitor. With all the social security numbers clogging the government computers, surely the number he used would never be called into

181

question as long as it was valid to start with and no claims were made against it. He entered the shop and he recognized a plausible number at once.

"Hello, Mr. Smith. How's the apartment?" The owner of the store, who owned the apartment as well, was a friendly man, early forties, robust in health. He was even a man of some leisure—he could readily have other jobs. That kind of detail was unnecessary, but it comforted Cliff.

"Doing fine, Mr. Pickett. Thanks . . . And you?"

"Same as always."

"Say, Mr. Pickett, I've still got a New York driver's license. How long do they give you in Illinois to change over, I wonder."

"Don't rightly know."

"Think it says something about requirements on the Illinois license itself?" It wasn't a strong ploy, Cliff realized, but the conversation was casual.

"Might could," Pickett said, though he was clearly dubious.

"Let me see what mine looks like," Cliff said digging out his wallet. It occurred to him as he opened his wallet that there might already be some kind of social security number on his phony New York license. He was assuming the Illinois license would have one.

"I'll see," Pickett said pulling his own wallet out. "But thinking about it, it doesn't seem right. If you got the license to look at, there wouldn't be any reason to find out what you're after."

Cliff turned the New York license over twice in his hands. No social security number.

"Don't see anything," Pickett said.

"Can I see?" Cliff asked.

Pickett gave his license to Cliff and said, "Easiest thing'd be just to call Motor Vehicles."

Cliff held Pickett's license—a blue wash, name, address, driver's number printed across the state capitol building, the spreading lawn. Then he saw to the right, slipping across just under the capitol dome, a social security number. Pickett was talking about where the office was located and Cliff blocked out the words, concentrated hard on the number, got it firmly in mind.

"Maybe I'll go over there now," Cliff said and he exchanged good-bys with Pickett all the while mumbling the man's security number at the back of his mind.

I'm becoming fragments of people myself, Cliff thought. For a while at least I'll be working for Mr. Pickett's old age.

Whatever apprehensions Cliff had, he put aside. He'd made his application, he'd tried to cope with the dangers; that was enough. He stood on the walk before the side staircase of the antique store. He stood in a patch of sun and felt an instinctive calm, a calm that immediately caused him to be vaguely alarmed. The patch of sun, the brick storefront, the sugar maples fluttering at their tops along the street, the faces passing that he'd never seen before but that were, nevertheless, intensely familiar to him—all this set him between conflicting pulls of feeling. He was calm and that made him nervous. He felt safe and that scared him. A man passed—no one in particular, a middle-aged man in a sport shirt, closely cropped grey mustache—and Cliff's eyes followed him. The man looked toward Cliff and smiled the brief nodding hello of one stranger to another—but the natural hello of strangers who recognize that they have much in common. Perhaps everything in common. Cliff thought of the wide-eyed, vigorous, whooping hellos from strangers in Vietnam—they would hear Cliff's automatic greeting in Vietnamese and they would dip and float and flap about in response. But the passing of this man on this street had rubbed a tenseness out of Cliff's temples, made his shoulders sag a bit, comfortably. It's a sham, Cliff told himself. If the man knew what I am, where I've been, what I've done, even if he knew who lived with me now, I would be a stranger to him with no common ground—the language that we share,

183

the options for small talk, the twenty-odd years of history we share, the similar bulk and form of our bodies, would mean nothing. They would isolate us from each other all the more profoundly. I am a stranger here, irrevocably, Cliff thought. But though he moved these ideas through his mind with force, conviction, at the same time he pulled back a bit from them, wondered if they were true.

"You posing for a sculptor?"

The voice drilled through Cliff's thoughts, turned him to the magnified eyes, the man from the grocery store.

"No," Cliff said, feeling inarticulate before this man's vigor.

"There's an Indian carved into a bluff upriver a ways from here that has that same expression."

"Ah." Cliff wondered if the man always arranged what he said so that no reasonable, articulate response was possible. But the forms of his expression were not unknown to Cliff—he'd had friends in college, good friends, who talked like this, and Cliff had held his own.

"I hope I didn't speak out of turn yesterday," the man said.

"Not at all."

"Was your wife terribly hurt?"

It struck Cliff that the man just assumed that Lanh and he were married. Or perhaps it was a matter of semantic tact. "She's tougher than that," Cliff said.

"Good. Yes. Of course."

"Not necessarily 'of course,' " Cliff said, some of the old mind-set coming back—rhetorical shoulder rapping. "Your first assumption was probably more appropriate. The Vietnamese don't take condescension and rudeness as a matter of course."

"Ah," the man said. "Just so . . . My name is Quentin Forbes."

"I'm Clifford Smith." They shook hands, Forbes waiting for Cliff to get his hand set properly and then the two of them mutually establishing a firm, equal clasp.

"You just move into Speedway?" Forbes asked.

"Fifteen feet above your head."

Forbes smiled wryly, accepting the riddle, and looked up.

"Over the antique store," Cliff said.

"Mr. Pickett's. We're practically neighbors. We—my wife June and I—live just a few blocks over . . . You're from this part of the country once, though. Am I right?"

"A long time ago."

"Your speech is clean—the good root strain of the Midwest."

"From long before college even."

"Where'd you go?"

"College? Northwestern."

"No kidding. I'm . . ."

"U of C."

"Right. How . . ."

"Tee-shirt yesterday."

"Of course . . . Say, Cliff. Wouldn't you and your wife come over some night for dinner? We'd be glad to have you."

Cliff wavered a bit at the ease of all this. But it was natural. He knew it was natural for two contemporaries, college graduates, in a little Illinois exurban city, to get together over just that much of a connection. It was natural, and still he felt the great chasm of his experience, the passage of time, the changes that he'd passed through. Didn't these things show? Didn't they show in his face, in his voice? Couldn't this man see these things about Cliff?

"I'll check with Lanh," Cliff said.

"Lanh's her name?"

"Yes . . ." Cliff might well have said no to the offer at once. But he was reluctant to reject the man's friendship. Why? he asked himself. Friendships were the last thing he returned to this country for. But if he rejected a friendship, then what was he planning for Lanh and himself? They could not reproduce their Saigon alley room in this country. He hadn't thought all this through, but that much now, suddenly, seemed clear to him.

185

"I understand that she might be reluctant," Forbes said. "But please try to persuade her."

"I'll do what I can."

Cliff presented Forbes' request to Lanh in the dark as they lay down to sleep. He asked it flat, no preferences implied in his voice, and Lanh did not answer right away. She made no sound.

"Did you hear?"

"Yes," she said and she sat up in the bed. But she didn't turn to Cliff. She sat bent forward—the streetlight slipping beneath the window shade modeled the curve of her back. As the silence persisted he guessed the reason for her silence.

"Forget it," he said. "You're right."

"I haven't said anything yet."

"You're thinking, 'Who needs this? They're strangers.' "

"That's not what I'm thinking."

The denial was a sincere one, Cliff knew. He was surprised he was wrong. "What is it, then?"

"I don't know. Not that."

"You're afraid."

"Of course I am."

"We can't . . ."

"We can't hide here," she finished.

That could be true enough, but it wasn't what he was going to say. "We can't live in fear all the time," he said.

"We always have."

"Yes."

"But this is different now. This kind of fear."

"How?"

"I'm not sure," she said.

"What are we trying to do? Have a social life in this country? I'm sorry I didn't refuse him right away."

"Don't say that," she said, and though her voice was firm, the curve of her back did not move. He wanted to touch it, lay his hand on her back, but he did not.

"We'll stay here," he said.

"Stop it." She twisted around to him. She sounded angry.

"I don't want to put you through . . ."

"Shut up," she said. "Please."

"Why are you angry at me?"

"You turn so stupid when I get scared."

"So I'm trying to take away the source of your fear. Forget the invitation."

"You're not helping at all. Don't you know that? If I try to keep us locked in this room, I'm going to lose you. That's what I'm scared of."

"No," he said rising toward her. She brushed his hand to the side.

"You'll come to hate me if I try to keep us shut away."

"I don't understand that."

"I don't either. But I think it's true."

"These people mean nothing to us."

"Please just stop talking," she said sharply. "We should visit these people."

"Why not have a normal life together at last. Yes." This notion rushed on Cliff unexpectedly.

"Don't talk," she said, lying down, turning her back, pulling the sheet over her shoulders.

Cliff lay back and stared into the dark above him. His feelings surprised him again. They opened to the sidewalk before the antique shop, the afternoon, him standing in the sunlight feeling that worrisome calm. Why worrisome? Maybe this feeling of his was related somehow to Lanh's clearly contradictory feelings about going to the Forbeses'? Cliff couldn't make the connection, but the moment from the afternoon grew once more inside him. He was part of this place, clearly so, the people passing in the street recognized it. But at the same time, he insisted, he was separated—forever separated, perhaps—from this country, its people. The woman in the grocery store had known this as soon as he'd spoken to Lanh. He and Lanh were strangers here.

Odd, he felt, the twists inside him, as he watched his

thoughts flow back to an American who was a stranger in Vietnam. He saw Martita Pell opening her notebook to him. It was at a time when she was making the assumption most readily that Cliff thought exactly as she did. She was puzzled over an exchange she'd had with a former ARVN infantry lieutenant who was then an amputee panhandling in the parks.

—Don't you hate the Americans now? she had asked him.

—I have no feelings about them.

—No feelings?

—I hate the Northerners.

—The North Vietnamese?

—Yes.

—But why? They are your brothers, she had told him.

—No.

—They are Vietnamese.

—They look like me, yes. We understand each other's words. I hate them the more for that.

—Why?

—I see much better how different they are. They are strangers. I see how much I hate them.

—I don't understand.

—The leg they cut off me was not mine. I came to hate the leg.

Cliff felt certain Martita never resolved her puzzlement over the exchange, had never used the man's words in a story. But Cliff believed he understood now, understood well enough that he realized he was not the lieutenant who hated the strangers that looked and talked like him. Cliff told himself: I am, instead, the hated stranger. I am the amputated leg.

Quentin Forbes rose up with the wine bottle and Cliff could see the man's napkin tucked in at his belt. He leaned over the table and refilled Cliff's and Lanh's glasses. June Forbes laid her palm over her wine glass to stop her husband.

"June doesn't like to let her mind get even a little bit fuzzy," Quentin said settling back into his chair.

June closed her eyes at this with a faint smile, as if before a sudden fresh breeze. She was Quentin's physical counterpart—big-boned, weak-eyed, but there was no slackness about her—her body was taut, she was pretty in a square-jawed way.

"Somebody's got to keep the roast from burning," she said.

"And somebody's got to keep our footnotes in order," Quentin said. "She's a better scholar than I am."

"He has a tendency to mix his cultures," she said.

They were interested in pre-Columbian American Indians. Cliff and Lanh had barely entered the house before their hosts had shown them half a dozen prehistoric stone ax heads, fragments of pottery, the detritus of long-since dispossessed cultures.

"We sound foolish talking like this," Quentin said.

"It's so easy to assume others share your enthusiasms," his wife said. "We must sound particularly foolish to Lanh."

"Yes," Quentin said and both of them turned their attention to Lanh. She had hardly spoken so far. Cliff had been watching her try to smile, to nod at the broad gestures of the two Americans, but he had seen, once, tears begin to fill her eyes even as she smiled. She held the tears back but her smile weakened and now she sat, her arms pressed in against her breasts, her hands in her lap, her head inclined slightly downward, her face impassive. She glanced up at the sudden attention. Cliff knew she hadn't been understanding a word. Cliff had sensed from the start Quentin and June trying very hard to treat Lanh absolutely normally. Cliff had seen not even a trace of patronization in them and he liked them for that—but he knew that Lanh had been able to coast with this attitude, she had turned off their voices.

June seemed to have some sketchy notion of the situation, for she said, "We talk a lot, Lanh. I'm sorry if we seem to ignore you."

189

Cliff felt a curious shift in his identification as he heard June speak. For a moment he felt included in June's "we." He sat opposite Quentin, mirroring, he could see in his periphery, the very angle of Quentin's head, its sympathetic tilt toward Lanh; June's words moved through the portal between his and Quentin's heads; and Lanh sat alone, tiny, different. For that moment Cliff felt a trickle of comfort—he felt connected to these two people. He was their size. They talked pedantically, perhaps, at times, but they talked in cadences, in genres of interest, that he could understand, that he had even once shared. The long night as Saigon fell—the undulation of memories—had shown him that he'd always wanted to connect like this—he'd always been—what?—susceptible to this impulse. Susceptible, he thought. He used that word to disengage himself, for he had grown fearful. His awareness groped its way across the linen tablecloth to Lanh, embraced her, clung to her—like a mast before sirens? She had not understood even these words that June had spoken.

"Perhaps," Quentin said gently, "the interest is not so foreign to her. Her own land is filled with the kind of history that interests us so much. Am I right, Lanh?"

"He wants to know," Cliff said to Lanh in Vietnamese, "about history in Vietnam."

"History," Lanh said to Cliff. She sounded thick-tongued, drugged.

Cliff turned to Quentin and June and said, "Lanh doesn't speak English all that well. I should have made that clearer to you. I'm sorry." He turned back to Lanh and said, "Tell them about how they bury farmers in the fields. The old tombs." He could see she didn't understand what this was all about but she understood his suggestion and it must have seemed the safest alternative.

Lanh sighed before the language and said, "Farmers my country . . . die in . . ." She stopped.

Cliff thought she had sensed something wrong with what she had said so far. "Buried . . ." he began to correct.

"Die in buried . . ." she said.

190

"No," Cliff said and he felt flushed. "Buried in the fields."

"Buried in . . ." Lanh had not caught the word.

"Fields," Cliff said firmly.

Lanh took a deep breath and said, "Farmers my country buried in fields."

Cliff waited, watching Lanh. But Lanh sat back. She was finished. Cliff felt a twist of anger at her. "You know more than that," he said to her sharply in Vietnamese.

"But I can't say it," she said. She did not return his sharpness. She sounded beaten down. This was so unlike her that it shocked Cliff into realizing what had just happened. He had been genuinely angry at Lanh for her awkwardness, for her seeming stupidity. He felt ashamed of his anger. He turned to Quentin and June. "She wants to say that when the farmers in Vietnam die they are buried in the fields where they worked. The Vietnamese build little tombs to them and many of them are quite old . . . I think . . . She thought . . . Well, you see how it might interest you—the burial sites of the Indians are your most fruitful sources of information. These farmers are resting in the earth they grew up on, lived off of."

"I see, yes," Quentin said. "That's the very attraction of this kind of history."

"Quentin is such a lover of history," June said, "that when we traveled in Europe by train he always sat in a seat facing the rear—so he could see where we'd been." Her voice was a bit shaky and she squeezed a laugh from her throat. Cliff turned to look at her. He knew exactly her feelings—and Quentin's. Her irrelevant little joke about Quentin—she was intensely uncomfortable now, nervous about Lanh's not being able to understand. Cliff saw the same feeling in Quentin's great bulging eyes.

"We were very interested in the farmers, Lanh," June said and she had begun to overarticulate.

"Yes," Quentin said and Cliff could see the man's hand wanting to pat at Lanh's. But Lanh kept her hands in her lap.

191

"I not talk good," Lanh said. "Talk talk GIs long time but Cliff talk talk Vietnam."

Cliff felt another twinge of anger. The doubling of words was a coy bargirl affectation. That was how it struck him—she knew better than to speak like that.

"You know," June said, "there are other Vietnamese in town. A family came in only a few weeks ago."

Cliff saw Lanh straighten up, her eyes widen into life.

"Isn't that so?" June asked Quentin. As he chatted in confirmation with her, Lanh leaned toward Cliff.

"Did she say something about other Vietnamese?" Her voice rippled with eagerness.

"Yes. Apparently there's a refugee family in town."

"Find out where." Her hand clawed its way across the tablecloth toward him.

Cliff withdrew his hand, did not let her touch him. He was angry at her sudden animation. He pressed his fingers against his forehead, tried to push away these feelings. He'd never been angry with Lanh in such an irrational, compulsive way. It scared him. He forced himself to turn to June, to say evenly, "Do you know where the family lives?"

"Quentin can find out for you."

"I'll be happy to," the man said.

June went off to get the roast out of the oven and she returned and the dinner went on for a long while in near silence. The clink of silverware on china, pass the horse-radish please, the pleasant masticating smiles beamed back and forth from the Forbeses while Lanh pecked about in her food, the fork awkward in her hand, her eyes averted. Cliff felt separate from all of them. He found it difficult to swallow. His throat was tight, he felt as if he was collapsing in on himself.

"I don't even know what you do for a living," Cliff said to Quentin. "You're not an archeologist?"

"No," Quentin said. "That was the road not taken. I'm the national sales manager for a small . . ."

"Medium-sized," June said.

"Well, a getting-to-be-medium-sized electronics company . . . Does that surprise you?"

"Not particularly." After he said the words, Cliff found them to be true. He had no feelings at all about Quentin's being a businessman.

"He doesn't have the slightest regret," June said.

"Hardly," Quentin said.

"Of course," she said, "then you shouldn't even ask if it surprises anyone."

"That's probably true," Quentin said. "But I understand how you might have some negative feelings about business, Cliff. Many of our contemporaries do, you understand. I don't know what your experience was in Vietnam—but you've seen the world in a way I haven't and it might make what I'm doing seem . . . what? . . . old-fashioned . . ."

"I really don't think anything about it."

"As a matter of fact, I see a connection between my two interests. There's a splendid burial mound just south of Speedway, on a bluff overlooking the Fox River. From the . . . Hopewell?" Quentin turned to June.

"Hopewell culture. Yes," she said.

"She's more certain of that than some of the archeologists out there," he said smiling. "Could be the very beginnings of the Mississippian culture, but we're still talking about the thirteenth century, early fourteenth at the latest. Still, it might as well have been the fifth century or earlier as far as the basic way of life is concerned. But the mound was excavated by the University of Wisconsin and they found the grave of some early tribal king of these parts. He was buried on a cape of shells—shells that aren't found in the Fox River or anywhere near. Never were. They're from the Gulf of Mexico. These were traders, see. That's something the archeologists know for sure. There was a lively commerce throughout the midwest. The center of it was the ancient city of Cahokia on the Illinois side of the Mississippi River around St. Louis. That was the hub. But the Indians sold their goods to each other down to the

Gulf, on up to the upper Great Lakes, out deep into what's now the Dakotas, down to territory that's Oklahoma. Commerce has been going on out here in the plains from the beginning. Me, I'm just moving in ancient forms, you see, playing out a primal destiny."

Quentin laughed to conclude his tale, laughed with just the right measure of self-mockery to pull Cliff once more into a moment of keen, connected comfort. June joined the laugh and Cliff found himself laughing and he remembered Francine—remembered with the side of his face, with his shoulder, remembered her presence at moments like this—the easy, thoughtful, crackling companionship of two young couples.

"Tell me this, though," Cliff said in mock-seriousness—the rhythm of all those past evenings of companionship, long lost, was coming back to him. "What if the Indians were right about death and afterlife? Doesn't the king need those ax heads? What if tonight while we're eating our pot roast he's stalking through the Great Spirit Forest and a grizzly rises before him and he reaches for his ax. But it's not there. It's in a glass case at the University of Wisconsin."

The three laughed and June said, laughing, maybe we shouldn't laugh and Quentin said, laughing, there *is* a serious point there, one worth considering, and Cliff, laughing, knew he had absolutely no feelings about the point he'd made, he'd made the point simply to move their minds together, to allow their minds to caper with each other, to connect them all in a way that was familiar to him, pleasing. But this time he knew the sense of Francine at his side was a sham and he looked at Lanh whose eyes were raised now, who watched the three laughing people with wonder, with a hint of fear, with absolute incomprehension.

Cliff's laugh evaporated even as he raised his chin to laugh once more, he gaped at Lanh, his sight turned inward and he gaped at himself. It struck him: he was Clifford Wilkes behind this charade—he'd become Clifford Smith to free Clifford Wilkes. Surely that's what he'd done. He'd put it to himself in the wrong way on the helicopter. He'd turned away from all this—this easy laughter, these people at a table, forks in hand, trifling with issues, tribal in their isolation, ready to cut each other loose at the turn of an idea, at the baring of a breast. Cliff's mind flailed about, he knew he should be as wide-eyed and alone as Lanh in the presence of these two people. These two didn't see what he was, they were blind to him like the Marines, like the people passing on the street. They were cutting him loose, even now, cutting him loose in a subtle way—by not letting him keep his place apart. They cut him off from his own past, his own decisions, and isolated him in their vapid companionship. But they had a claim on his past, as well, his mind answered. They were reclaiming Clifford Wilkes, too. There was a Clifford Wilkes before Vietnam. Cliff's face wheeled away from Lanh, away from Quentin, June.

"Are you all right?" Quentin asked.

Cliff turned to the man, met the bulging eyes—the eyes were magnified, the man was seeing out the other end of the scope, I must be tiny before these eyes, Cliff thought. Cliff wanted to tell him. Tell him now: I'm not Clifford Smith. I'm Clifford Wilkes. I'm a deserter from the U.S. Army. I'm a fugitive. Fugitive? With no one in pursuit? With the whole country oblivious to me, reading only my surface, accepting me, cutting me off from what I chose to be, cutting me off from Lanh, too? He feared that the most.

"You looked ill for a moment," Quentin said.

"I . . ." Cliff began. Should he tell him? Should he rise and say what he was? For what? So he could run from this town too? So he could go to prison and leave Lanh alone in a place that terrified her? These questions drove him back from the words that were forming in his throat. Clifford Smith can remain with Lanh. Clifford Smith— Smith—Mr. Smith—my god, why did that tired old pimp of a radical give me the name of Smith and make me cousin to half the goddam country?

"I'm okay," Cliff said. "I'm tired, I guess. Tired."

Quentin and June both spoke sympathetically to the announcement and in their first pause Cliff turned to Lanh and said in Vietnamese, "We'll go soon."

He would have said more to her, would have apologized, agreed with her sense of disaffection, but the moment had passed. He did feel tired. Drained. His attachment to the Forbeses had been severed, but the sense of his displacement had slackened too. For the moment he felt nothing.

Cliff and Lanh did not speak while walking the few blocks home. But Lanh's voice was still clear in Cliff's mind. So long, she had said at the door, Lanh eat good food your house, talk talk nice.

They climbed the steps, Cliff opened the door with "Lanh eat good food, talk talk" running unwanted over and over in his head, like a commercial jingle.

In the center of the dark room Lanh's voice said in Vietnamese, "I would have felt more comfortable stripped naked and marched through the streets of Saigon before a VC bayonet."

Cliff turned to the figure beside him. The woman on the stair, the one who walked home with him, the one connected to that good-by, to the dinner talk—she was gone and there was another woman in her place. This notion was understandable enough but Cliff realized that for a moment it was this woman—the woman in the dark with the clear, cool, vigorous mind, speaking Vietnamese—who was the stranger. He felt his breath jerked away. She was no stranger, he cried to himself. No. She was Lanh. This was Lanh, beside him here, this was the sensibility he knew in Saigon working as it always had. But he could not stop that rush of fear. He put his hands gently on her shoulders and he found himself going back to the Lanh who stumbled in English—his irritation with her over that had a closer link to his love than this feeling of strangeness about the woman he'd known in Saigon. And he sensed

196

where the dangers were. For a moment he knew that if he could turn her into an American, even a foolish-sounding one, it would be easier for them both. He lowered his hands and he was afraid, he knew, so afraid that he grew harsh. "I didn't know your English was so bad," he said.

"Yes."

"It's terrible."

"I didn't know it was so bad either."

"Just terrible."

"I've not spoken it for four years."

"You sound . . ." he hesitated, his face burned as he thought how terrible she sounded speaking English.

"And before that," Lanh said, "all I knew was what I picked up in the bar, really."

"You sound like a bargirl."

"I'm not surprised." She said it matter-of-factly. Cliff was stirred by her—she knew how bad she sounded, she knew the difficulty she would have in this country speaking as she did—but she acknowledged it coolly, without panic. And this made him love her; it wasn't strange now, his Lanh's strength, his Lanh's probing mind, his Lanh. He pulled her to him and she was trembling and then he knew the statement was not cool from courage, it was cool from despair.

"I'll teach you," he said.

She did not reply, she pressed hard against him, put her face into his chest.

"I said I'll teach you," he said.

"Not tonight."

Cliff felt angry at this. It was late, they were tired, of course it was impractical to teach anything now, but it angered him that her only response would be to put it off. He drew back from her. Her eyes rose to him and he could see them in the dim light; wide, they were, but they did not arouse him. He saw them widen at the dinner table at the mention of the Vietnamese family.

"You only came alive once this evening," he said. "Once. When the Vietnamese family was mentioned."

197

"I was alive other times. I tried to talk."

"You were going through the motions."

"No."

"Using all your bargirl affectations."

Lanh turned her face away sharply at this. The hurt she showed lanced Cliff's anger. He pulled her close again. "I'm sorry," he said.

"I *was* dead. It's true."

"You lit up at the thought of seeing other Vietnamese. But in Saigon you avoided them. You talked as little as possible with the old women. You and I were enough."

"I know."

"You come to this place . . ."

"I don't understand it myself," she said. "I did not feel Vietnamese in Vietnam. I felt part of you and that was all . . . But now, even this moment, speaking of the Vietnamese family makes my heart flutter. I don't understand." She clung tight to him.

"I was just as bad," Cliff said.

"You and those two laughing. I don't know what it was all about, but those two were strangers to me and you seemed so natural with them. I felt for a while I didn't know you."

Cliff shuddered at the words, he pressed her head against him. He had strong feelings that were incomprehensible to him and he sensed himself swerve away from them, transform them—his penis moved. He bent to Lanh, kissed her throat, lifted her—she was light as an empty mind—and he took her to the darkness of the bed.

She slept and Cliff lay awake for a time, at first listening to a trickle of water somewhere in the walls and then to the refrigerator motor when it kicked on. He was too tired to sleep; the dinner party, his intermittent anger at Lanh, had roiled his feelings and they were settling only gradually. With Lanh quiet beside him, with his semen spent, with the faint smell of earth and grain sifting through the window, he heard the laughter of Quentin and June again and he joined it in his memory and the laughter was passed back voice to voice, back through half a dozen couples in college, in Army schools, and he paused with one couple, the husband a fellow Vietnamese language school student. Cutler, their name was, Nate and . . . he couldn't remember the wife's name but he saw them clearly. She had heavy eyelids, eyes the color of a switched-off TV screen; he had a mustache trimmed back only barely from the brink of military insubordination, and a pocked face that Cliff always thought must have subliminally stirred the man's interest—for he was most of the way toward a PhD in geography. The topographical implications of his complexion was the only observation that Cliff hesitated to make to the man, for they were close in school, the two couples were close, and Cliff could see them all sitting on the Cutlers' little garden apartment plot of grass in Arlington, Virginia, eating dinner on TV trays and folding chairs while the sky turned slate at sunset. Cliff heard their laughter. The conversation had faded from the recollection like a color tone in an old oil painting but the scene remained, and the laughter. Then he did hear a voice—Francine's.

She was talking about a children's TV show she'd seen that morning. The show had had a group of puppets that had delighted her. I saw at once, she said, from these Muppets, they were called, what the art of puppetry involves. Every art cuts away whole areas of human experience to focus your attention on a selected few elements. Then you can see those elements as you never have before. Painting cuts away sound and words so you can see better, music cuts away words and vision so you can hear better. Well, these Muppets showed me that puppets cut away the human qualities that they do so that you can experience as you never did before how heads or bodies or hands move. They had incredibly expressive hands. And also so that you can hear the inflections of voices better than ever before. These Muppets are the high art of gesture and inflection.

Cliff remembered how they all laughed in appreciation and they talked about puppets and childhood; Kukla, Fran, and Ollie—the words faded away again in Cliff's mind but the feeling remained and the closeness they all had, the childhood they'd shared, the way their voices moved in the gathering dusk, the way their bodies fit on that little patch of grass, the play of their minds.

Cliff felt chilled now, his arms prickled, his face turned toward the wall and he felt an unmistakable regret. He saw Francine opening her robe. The light on the night stand was on. She never wanted to make love in the dark. She opened her robe to him and he rose up on his elbow on the bed so that his face was opposite the triangle of soft, matted hair streaked with her blondness.

Cliff sensed a danger in this memory. He sat up, bent forward, hooked his hand on the window sill, sucked in the air. Francine receded but the identity of the night remained—the rustle of trees outside, a distant train whistle, the smell of the land were American. He wrenched himself away from this feeling and he realized he'd been doing that often in the past few weeks—he'd been making himself go numb, making himself, his face averted, beat away the fears that he knew were rising in him. But if he couldn't let himself fear, then all his other feelings would wither away too: that was his deepest fear now. And what couldn't he face? he demanded of himself. That he saw Francine naked and he desired her again? That he had felt a kinship once to people in this country—and he feared he still did? Why should that scare him? Because it was a lie, he felt, a sham, because he would be building a false hope that this whole thing was going to work out that way. Lanh. Lanh was what he loved. She was his nationality. And he could not split his allegiance. He looked around at the room in anger. He felt angry at these dim walls, the shapes of furniture. Why couldn't this room hold them like the last room? The room in Saigon made life possible. Now he felt cut off from his life.

He lay down. He forced out the fear once more. There

was no other way. He couldn't face it. Couldn't. He drew himself near to Lanh. He strained to hear the light slip of her breath.

Quentin honked Cliff's weary attention into the street. The man had stopped his car and had twisted his torso down and to the side to face Cliff across the front seat.

"Got a few minutes?" Quentin asked.

Though Cliff had vacillated radically in his feelings about Forbes in the several days since the dinner, confronted with the man he had no inclination to spurn him. He got into the car and found, indeed, that he felt at ease.

"You getting off work?" Quentin asked.

"Yes."

"You put in a full day?"

"First one."

"Day laborer work?"

"Gutting some discount store that went bust."

"Say, if you've got fifteen minutes or so," Quentin said, "I'd like to show you what kind of thing I get so excited about."

"What's that?"

"There's an Indian mound site just out of town. You like to see it?"

Lanh wouldn't be home for a short time yet and Cliff nodded.

Quentin drove through the main street and turned onto a state highway that ran in four lanes along the Fox River, angled away past a stock car track, a stretch of gas stations and motels, and then cut back toward the river as two lanes. It left the ragged commercial edge of Speedway and slit off fields of soybean and alfalfa from a gently rising wooded margin along the river.

Quentin turned into the woods and followed a state park macadam through oak and hickory, out to a clearing. The two men got out of the car and Quentin hung back a bit like a father who'd led his child to the Christmas tree. Even though Cliff was conscious that the man was watching him, expecting a reaction, he instinctively liked the spot. In the center of the close-cropped clearing was a rising of the earth into a flat-topped mound large enough to set a small house on. Beyond, Cliff recognized a stand of sugar maples—he'd known the oak and hickory, too, knew all these trees at once, like the faces of old school-mates. At the edge of the clearing, the land fell away and he could see the river, narrow here, moving before a low, grey, bluff face. The river struck him as odd in some way he couldn't identify. A rhythm here, something; at the sight of the river the ambivalence rose in him, the same feeling he'd had before in this town—a sense of the familiar and the alien bound intimately together. But Quentin's voice deflected Cliff's thoughts.

"It's called a platform mound," the man said. "They found some burials here, caches of arrowheads from all over the Midwest. Basketloads of mica. They liked to buy and sell their shiny things."

Cliff expected an extensive re-creation of the past from Quentin, but they moved forward and poked about the mound, stood in the clearing and listened to the chittering of birds, the swish of cars out on the highway, and Quentin said nothing. Cliff began to automatically fill in the scene for himself. He began to sense, by their utter absence, the makers of this mound. This land did indeed have ghosts—Indian summer ghosts—he'd been open to them once, he knew. But he did not pursue them. He thought, instead, that Quentin was shrewd—he knew, for the sake of his own purpose, not·to speak at this time.

Then Quentin said, "My father thinks I'm nuts."

"What?"

"My father. He owns the company I work for . . . I don't think I mentioned that."

"No."

"He thinks I'm nuts—my interest in archeology."

"That's not so unusual as an interest."

"That's not what really gets him. It's when I tell him

about how he himself is working in the tradition of these Indians that he gets very uncomfortable.''

''I'm not surprised at that.'' The two of them wagged their heads and grinned.

''You planning on being a labor temporary for long?'' Quentin asked.

''I don't know. I hadn't thought of it.''

''That surprises me, you know.''

''I can see that.''

''You just making some money till you find a good job?''

Cliff didn't know what to say. Once more, he found something he hadn't thought through adequately for Clifford Smith. The real answer, of course, was that he hadn't thought about the subject because he'd only just—and maybe only temporarily—escaped from prosecution. He didn't know how to shape the lies that would let him try to get a better job. If he wanted one at all. Cliff almost said these things. His impulse to confess—no, not ''confess,'' to declare himself—rose again. But he simply answered, ''Yes. That's it.''

''You're a bright guy,'' Quentin said.

Cliff shrugged.

''As national sales manager I hire all the salesmen. I'm good at that because I've learned to trust my guts . . . Hell, anybody can learn about the things we sell. They're simple components and you don't have to be an engineer to pick up what you need to sell the damn things. A bright guy, with the right instincts, is the kind of guy I look for.''

Quentin paused and Cliff could only nod and grunt for he saw what Quentin was leading up to. Cliff held back his own reaction until the man actually said it.

''Anyway,'' Quentin went on, ''I think you'd make a strong member of our sales team, Cliff. I mean that sincerely.''

Quentin had planted himself in the clearing, one arm akimbo, an open, placid expression on his face. Cliff waited for a feeling—revulsion, hilarity, relief, something. But he felt very little. Only a faint bemusement that he was faced over and over with decisions he'd never dreamed of having to make but which he knew, as soon as he confronted them, were only natural.

"You don't know much about me," Cliff said and in spite of the words he felt no impulse at the moment to tell Quentin what he was.

"As I say, I hire by my guts. On personal qualities . . . I must care about the bottom line from my people." Quentin paused briefly and laughed. "If it doesn't work out, I can always fire you."

In spite of the man's laughter, Cliff knew Quentin was coldly serious about his remedial option. There was no real risk for Quentin; Cliff himself knew that he had qualities that were probably useful in sales—the offbeat plausibility of the suggestion held away the extreme reactions that Cliff might otherwise have expected.

"I'll think about it," Cliff said.

As Cliff got out of the car, Quentin stopped him. "I almost forgot," the man said. "I've got some information on that Vietnamese family. The Elks sponsored them. I called the Elks and they gave me this address."

Quentin handed Cliff a piece of memo paper with the address written on it.

"Think about my offer. I've got a hunch about you," Quentin said and he drove away.

Upstairs, Cliff found Lanh lying on the bed, awake, motionless except for her eyes which seized at him as he entered the room and followed him as he approached. Cliff thought to tell her of Quentin's offer, of the Vietnamese family's address, but he could bring himself to say neither for the moment. He watched Lanh's face—she did not smile, did not frown, but there was no placidity there either, it was a face he'd seen in interrogations.

He sat beside her on the bed. "Are you all right?" he asked.

She looked at him for a moment in silence and then her hand rose to him. "I'm all right," she said. The flatness of her tone was out of phase with the circling of her fingers on his cheek and it filled the gesture with despair. Cliff felt suddenly helpless.

"Let's work on your English now," he said.

"Now?"

"You've put it off too long."

"You just came home," she said.

"You have to begin," he said in English.

"Go to hell, GI," she said in English, turning her face away.

"Listen to me," he said slowly, in English. "You have to work at the language or you will never be able to leave this room."

"I don't want to leave the room," she said in Vietnamese.

"Say that in English."

"I no want go room. GI talk talk too many."

He flinched before this sound. But he had to face it in order to eliminate it. He sensed how important this was. "Much," he said.

"Much?"

"Say, 'you talk too much.' "

"GI talk talk too much."

"Don't say 'talk talk.' "

"What should I say?" she asked in Vietnamese, her voice weary.

"Say 'talk' only once," he said in English. Then with a rush: "That's one of your worst habits. I can't stand it."

"GI talk talk too fast this time."

He jumped up from the bed. " 'Talk,' dammit. Not 'talk talk.' And stop calling me 'GI.' "

"Please," Lanh said in Vietnamese, rising to him. "Don't make me do this now. Not now. I can't adjust to everything at once."

"Say that in English."

"No. Didn't you hear me? Doesn't that make any sense to you? You can be glib about all this—you grew up in this country. Don't you understand there's too much for me to take in, to worry about the language right now?"

205

The flash of Lanh's mind soothed Cliff. "I'm just worried about you," he said low. "Having to communicate outside of this room."

"That won't be a worry for a while," she said and she averted her eyes.

"What do you mean?"

"I quit the job at the church."

Cliff didn't say anything. He felt vaguely relieved, though his mind told him this should worry him. But it was easier for Cliff too, to have her simply avoid problems.

"You're working," she said.

"Not steadily," Cliff said.

"I'm sorry," Lanh said. "I just can't do it anymore."

Cliff turned Lanh's face to him. Again he had some abstract sense of danger, but he had an impulsive feeling of satisfaction as he pulled the slip of memo paper from his pocket and said, "I've got something for you."

She read the address of the Vietnamese family and she smiled a faint, peaceful smile and she moved to him, held him, put her head on his chest. After a moment she kissed him, deep, and then she knelt on the floor before him and began to open his pants.

Cliff laid his hands gently on the top of her head and watched for a moment as she took him into her mouth. She had not done this in this way since they'd come to America, had not impulsively knelt before him, let him join at her face. Why now? The address of a Vietnamese family? Her refusal to speak English? Instead of English words, she filled her mouth with him. She articulated him, spoke him, her tongue shaping at him, speaking him. She had felt keenly Vietnamese at this moment, he knew, and she had crouched to suck him. To suck out what he'd been secreting in his body, to suck out the seeds of his Americanism, wasted seeds, the crust of an old fuck on a bedspread. He felt the shadows of so many moments like this—all in the fish air and lute tongue of Saigon. He looked down on the top of her head, the straight white parting of her hair. But he knew this was another room and

206

he grew tighter inside her, his fear tightened again in his chest—this was not Saigon, Saigon was ten thousand miles and a millenium ago. There was no Saigon. It was a planet in a solar system beyond the life span of a man away. The light he saw now from its star had begun its travel before he was born. He dared not have sucked out of him anything that could help the two of them connect to this new place. But though this planet held the forms of a civilization he once knew—the buildings still stood, the roads still tracked through the countryside—the atmosphere had long ago burned away. There was nothing here but wreckage. How could he come back, become again what he once was? Lanh was pulling it from him—sucking out of him everything that he wanted to shun anyway. He pressed his hands tighter on her head. He wanted to hold her there for as long as he could—she protected him, he was safe inside her. He denied his fear. There was still a chance for them. She was happy, she held him in her, they were together, safe, they could be what they'd always been.

Mr. Binh, his wife, and six children lived on the top floor of an old five-story walk-up apartment building that faced the Fox River. Cliff and Lanh climbed the stairs, Lanh holding tight onto the bannister, Cliff rising in the central foot-worn trough of the steps. He expected the stairwells to smell of piss, but they did not. The place was seedy but scrubbed. As they neared the top, they were both breathing hard from the climb but Cliff read excitement into Lanh's panting. She'd been almost ebullient in the past twenty-four hours when they'd talked about dropping in on these people. Cliff had found himself getting very quiet—he knew he'd seemed almost morose—the more excited Lanh had become. But she'd hardly noticed. He knew his mood was insignificant to her, compared to this chance for a link back to Vietnam. And why shouldn't he feel just as good about this as she? he asked himself now. He had loved Vietnam, after all. That's what he'd understood of himself—and that feeling had never wavered while he was there. He had expected to be a stranger in America—and he often felt that way, as he'd anticipated—but this growing, retrospective alienation with Vietnam was something he hadn't expected.

They stood before the door and he shut down his mind. He wanted to be open to these people. They were at home. He could hear the laughter of children. Lanh pressed Cliff's hand with hers and knocked.

Mr. Binh opened the door. His cheeks looked sucked in, his instinctive smile seemed that of one of the old alley women. He was in his mid-fifties, sinewy.

Cliff thought to speak, but Lanh's voice seized the man. "Are you Mr. Binh?" she said.

"Yes." He opened the door wide, his joy at seeing another Vietnamese had opened his smile to its broadest possible extension, was making his arms rise without purpose from his sides.

"I'm sorry to come to you like this," Lanh said. "But the times are unusual. When we heard you were in town we had to come."

"Yes. Yes," he said. "Please come in. Please." His hands fluttered before him, he bounced up and down on his toes as Cliff passed him and he closed the door.

The children flocked in, all the boys with wild shocks of upstanding hair. The oldest girl—perhaps 16—was wearing an ao dai. The oldest boy—in his early twenties, clearly a young man—stood slouched against the bedroom door-frame and was the only one whose smile was faint. Cliff could see the oldest son in a bush cap riding a Honda in Saigon, swiping GIs' watches. Emerging from the kitchen was Binh's wife—a tiny, plain woman with wire-rimmed glasses.

Lanh introduced herself and Cliff; and Binh recited the names of all his children ending with the baby, a two-year-old that had climbed into its mother's arms. The woman waited and let her husband tell her name—Mai.

Cliff looked at Lanh and saw her eyes clutching eagerly at the people around her. Binh was making extravagant

208

declarations of welcome and Lanh was devouring the faces. Then Cliff could see words beginning to well up in her—she wanted very much to talk but she waited for Binh to stop. Binh turned to Cliff and said in heavily accented but confident English, "I'm sorry we've been talking so much in Vietnamese."

"You've just been talking here and there," Cliff said in Vietnamese, using a popular Saigon idiom.

Binh raised his eyebrows and smiled in surprise. Binh's was a common gesture but Cliff saw in his periphery Mai's hand clutching at the air toward him. He knew at once that she didn't speak English at all.

"You speak Vietnamese," Binh said. "You speak it very well."

"Well but not very well," Cliff said, using another idiom.

All of Binh's family hooted in delight and Cliff felt a surge of pleasure—he thought for a moment that he'd had an instant remission of his alienation—he felt an intimate connection to this group of people—this group of simple, intensely friendly, loyal people. But Binh said something quickly that Cliff did not catch and he found himself thinking in English about the sounds he'd just heard. A momentary crossover of languages—a minor thing, a common thing—but it pulled him back and the connection he'd felt in this room was broken. The people around him continued to flap about in admiration of his Vietnamese—he found himself automatically responding to questions—using other idioms, tricks, phrasings—he was putting on a linguistic show and these people were an audience. He was on a stage, alone. He heard the friendly squabble of sound that had filled the streets of Saigon and the sound was foreign to him. So quickly? How can this be? He wanted—desperately wanted—to connect again to these sounds, to these people, but he sat in the chair they offered him, and in the core of himself, away from the conversation he was conducting, he felt numb.

He was glad when Lanh's words could no longer be

held in, when she came into the center of the conversation and began to talk with Binh and Mai about fish sauce and chilly nights, grocery stores and English, Saigon neighborhoods and the refugee camp. The oldest son sat on the floor near Lanh, the children huddled around, Mai and Binh pulled chairs next to Lanh, and Cliff looked away to the window. He watched a slip of the Fox River flaked with the sun. Now that he'd stopped talking, his numbness gave way to a prickling that made him blink at the sunlight on the water and then to a full and unmistakable sadness, a sadness filled with the kinds of sounds, faces, that had delighted him just weeks ago. He looked at his hands in his lap and began to grope his way back to the origins of this sadness. The dinner with the Forbeses? The ridicule of an old woman in a grocery store? The pathetic games of an old radical? Landfall? Back. Further back. The seeds of his sadness lay in the wet soil of Vietnam. floated like motes there in the stark sunlight. No, back further. He felt light-headed, faint. Back. In the life he'd lived in America long ago and relived in the alley room as Saigon fell. Back further still, beyond his recollection. And he plunged through that blankness and ended up in the future. He'd pressed back until he'd found that these feelings had no beginning and would have no end. He was indulging himself now, he cried. He could not let go to these feelings—these were night fears, as distorted as waking in the middle of the night, sweating from a bad dream, and fearing, as real, the worst things his imagination could shape. Those things were impossible. This was impossible. He looked out to the Fox River once more, to the quaking light. He sought his numbness again and turned it into repose.

"I'm sorry we seemed to talk around you at dinner," Binh said in Vietnamese. He and Cliff stepped from the apartment house. The sun was squatting in the elm trees beyond the river.

"I didn't mind," Cliff said. He and Lanh had stayed for dinner and Binh's family had made much over his

Vietnamese for a brief time, had asked him about America; but he'd been laconic, evasive, and that wasn't their real interest then anyway. The onus of speech had been extremely unpleasant for Cliff. That had been a new sensation for him—he'd always delighted in banter with the Vietnamese—but when they'd ignored him after a while, he'd been glad, for it fit his sense of isolation.

"We were all . . . lonely," Binh said. "Vietnamese can be lonely for familiar voices. We've only seen one other Vietnamese since coming to this town."

"There's another?"

"Yes . . . I suppose I should be thankful at that. I don't know what I expected . . . There is one other at least. I hear there may be several. The authorities tried to cluster us, when they sent us from the camp. I understand some towns—one in Arkansas?—have very large numbers of us."

They crossed the street, entered a thin strip of a city park along the Fox River.

"So it was good to see you and your wife at our door," Binh said.

Cliff nodded. "Yes, she was lonely too."

"I'm sure she's not . . ." Binh said quickly.

"You didn't offend me, mentioning the loneliness, Mr. Binh. Of course she's lonely . . . You saw how eager she was . . . how she talked. She hasn't been that animated for . . . as long as we've been here."

"I . . . You . . ." Binh began to stammer, apparently not accustomed to someone addressing so forthrightly what he'd feared was an offense given. He would have preferred to repair things by indirections, Cliff sensed. It struck Cliff that Lanh perhaps was not typical of other Vietnamese in her directness. That notion gave him a moment's ease.

"You understand it's difficult for all of us," Binh said. "I can see she loves you very much. You are a good man."

"It's all right, Mr. Binh. I do understand."

Binh's glib assertion of Lanh's love wiped away Cliff's

211

feeling of ease. It made him feel awkward, it let him go back and begin to fear that Lanh's directness was not a special link between the two of them but had simply grown from her prostitution. He turned sharply away from the fear by kicking at a stone on the path, picking up another stone and throwing it out into the middle of the Fox River. The stone was swallowed up without a sound, with only a momentary pucker in the water's surface.

"I hope you don't mind my speaking Vietnamese to you," Binh said.

"Not at all." Cliff hadn't minded until Binh drew his attention to it. After that, he did feel a peculiar vexation, which he dismissed as the power of suggestion.

Binh laughed. "I'm beginning to forget how to speak. In any language. As an accountant at your embassy in Saigon I spoke English each day all day long for twenty years. Now I sit around the house all day and I speak nothing and I'm forgetting everything. Even my own mother tongue." He laughed again, but it sounded forced. "I don't speak much with my wife and I am forgetting even Vietnamese."

Binh fell silent for a time and Cliff saw the man's instinctive smile fade. Cliff thought: his silence with his wife—he is sad at that. How long have they been like this with each other?

But Binh said, "It's very difficult sitting around. Work is so important to me. To any man, don't you think?"

The question was rhetorical. Cliff realized his misinterpretation of Binh's sadness. Cliff thought, briefly, of his ambivalence about work. He'd done very little during his years in Saigon and he'd had surprisingly little problem with that. But Binh's words stirred a vague anxiety in him now.

Binh said, "How can my family and I fight our way onto an airplane, people shouting, rockets falling on the city, and fly across the ocean in order to sit idle, staring at each other?" He said this with a series of comically broad shrugs and with his easy laughter. Cliff did not laugh with him, though he knew Binh was inviting it, knew that he would have laughed with him in a comparable conversation only a month or two ago, in another country.

"An amusing thing," Binh said, regretting, Cliff thought, the somber turn he'd let their conversation take. "When we were at the refugee camp, the Army base nearby shot off a cannon at sunset, when they lowered the flag. This always made me homesick." Binh laughed long at this, without even a trace of bitterness. "We'd come to that— gunfire made me homesick," he said laughing. It was the delighted laughter of a child, Cliff thought. No, not a child, he told himself. Cliff would not patronize him. Though the man's impulse to joy was basic and strong, it was not simple. All the Vietnamese he'd known had had that impulse. Even Lanh, though she showed it differently. This man's laughter chilled Cliff now—he knew from it how sad Lanh had grown. Cliff forced himself to join Binh's laughter, forced his mind away again. I'm avoiding something basic, Cliff told himself but he kept on laughing with Binh until the man watched him laughing and led the two of them to a stop.

Binh sighed and wagged his head afterwards. The gesture could have been the aftermath of the laughter but Cliff knew it was relief. He knew Binh was relieved at making the conversation light again. And he knew Binh was being harsh with himself for putting his problems onto Cliff.

They both looked away to the river. It had turned the color of steel in the twilight. They walked on, along the manicured banks, beneath horse chestnuts that smelled like the water.

After a long silence, Binh said, "I can't get over the emptiness of your rivers. It seems like such a waste. In a city, our rivers are full of people. Fishing there, living there, traveling there. Why don't the people here use such a wonderful thing as a river?"

Cliff had no answer but he suddenly realized that he'd felt this very thing—it was the oddness about the Fox River that he couldn't identify out at the mound site—it

213

was this emptiness. Cliff became conscious of the perception only now as Binh articulated it. He waited to feel close to the man, waited for Binh's perception to link them. That was a natural thing to expect, but it did not occur. The man's face in the dim light had grown as placid and shrunken as a cadaver's. The language he had used to articulate their shared insight sang a perceptibly foreign song in this little American park by this little American river. Cliff could identify both park and song, could see their incongruity, and his breath caught, he nearly cried out. He saw that he belonged to neither, he had nowhere to stand, he had no voice.

Cliff and Lanh were quiet that night. In spite of her great outpouring of words at Binh's, Lanh was quiet.

Cliff lay in the dark and knew Lanh was awake—they lay together blinking into the darkness—and as the minutes passed, Cliff grew increasingly agitated. He resented her silence with him, after her chatter of the evening.

Finally he found himself angry and he said, "You paying me back tonight for the dinner at the Forbeses? Is that it?"

"I think I missed something," she said. "You're talking crazy."

"You had plenty to chatter about tonight to your countrymen."

Lanh did not answer.

"And with me you can't think of anything to say."

Lanh still said nothing, but Cliff's anger was spent. He felt weak. He said, "I'm sorry."

"At least you knew what we were saying." Her voice was hard.

"I said I'm sorry."

"I wasn't paying you back. No."

"I'm glad you found friends."

"I don't want to resent you."

"How do you feel?"

"I'm talked out, I guess."

214

"Sure," Cliff said, beginning to wish she was silent again.

"Except I don't think it's as simple as that," she said.

"It's okay. You don't have to talk now."

"I know you don't understand what I did tonight. You've never seen me like that with anyone . . . Tonight was like a memory to me—a hazy one, one I can't place. It was like something from a long time ago in my life. The way we talked—it's the way of people out in the countryside. I had a childhood once too. I can go back for one night, can't I?"

Lanh was weeping softly. Cliff put his arm around her, pulled her against him, but the gesture felt stiff to him, automatic, even though he understood what she was saying. His sympathy for her was so reflexive now that he felt detached from her. He knew her regret at being in this country, but he felt no guilt at bringing her here.

"If we'd stayed on in Vietnam," he said, "you weren't going back to that life anyway."

"I know that," she said. "I understand why we came here."

She did understand. They understood each other. The correspondence of their thoughts and feelings, the expression of them—all this seemed still to be alive long after their uprooting. The moment persisted and Cliff was holding Lanh and it occurred to him that they should make love now. There was a pitch to their minds, a peaking of their feelings that had, for all their life together, always called for a resolution through their bodies. But this occurred abstractly to Cliff, he did not feel the compulsion in his groin. He lay still and Lanh did not move either. She had never hesitated to begin their lovemaking, but she lay still now. We're tired, he told himself.

Then he thought of Binh. Cliff had known Binh's feelings in their brief time together. He'd known after their laughter why the man had sighed and shook his head, had known that the man was angry with himself for Cliff's sake; he had shared precisely Binh's impression of the river. Surely those perceptions of each other would have inevitably led to some recognizable intimacy, a friendship, a bonding. But they hadn't. Cliff hadn't felt close to the man. And moments like these with Lanh—their life together had been full of them—moments like these with anyone in his past life—were they only outward signs? No matter how compelling or penetrating the insights about each other, were those insights, those correspondences, only outward forms of something else, forms without any power in and of themselves to connect people? Forms of what else? Historical moment? Novelty of body? Linkage of souls? Race? Confinement? God? Glands? Whatever it was, Cliff felt he had no control over it. He felt only weary at this moment, with a body curled against him, a tiny body, a child's body—supple-smooth, small-breasted, almost hairless, moved by enthusiasms he could not feel part of. He heard Lanh's babble in Binh's apartment, felt mystified and then vexed, and then he recognized her need for a link back to her past, something stable. He and Lanh were drifting. They'd hidden from the Americans in Vietnam, and that had given them something clear to do. They'd run, and that had been clear. But what wasn't clear was how they were to live a life in America.

"Quentin Forbes offered me a job."

"What?"

"A job. He offered me a job selling for his company."

"Would it mean much money?"

"It could mean some money. Steady, certainly." He waited for Lanh to say something about the offer. She did not speak.

"What are you thinking?" he asked.

"Nothing."

"Should I try the job?"

"I have no thoughts."

They lay in silence once more, though he still held her against him. He tried to stir himself to touch her. But he felt abstracted. And weary. She pulled away from him,

216

turned on her back and they blinked into the dark until their eyes grew heavy and they slept.

He had four more hours' work the next morning through Laborpool. When he climbed the stairs toward the apartment at noon, he heard Mr. Pickett's voice briefly, the end of a sentence. Then he heard Lanh.

"I no have money. My . . . one . . . mister have for you . . ."

Cliff darted up the last few steps in twos. Pickett, standing in their doorway, turned to him.

"Mr. Smith," he said, turning. "You people are a little behind in your rent. I was asking your wife."

"She doesn't speak English very well, Mr. Pickett." Cliff was angry with this man for provoking Lanh into speech. Her words staggered back and forth in Cliff, lurched like a drunkard at him, numbing his sympathy.

"I thought you'd be here," Pickett said. Then he changed his tone, made it gently chiding. "You often are, during the day."

"It's the temporary job," Cliff said. "I'll have your money in a day or two if you'll just have a bit more patience with us . . ." Cliff wanted to beat the jagged sounds of Lanh's voice from his mind. She must never be made to speak English again, he thought. And suddenly he found he'd made a decision—he said, "I've got a good job now, Mr. Pickett. I'll be starting soon."

"Where's that?" Pickett said, not suspiciously but with what struck Cliff as a genuine interest.

"With Quentin Forbes' company."

"Quentin. I know Quentin. Fine. Yes. I'm glad for you, Mr. Smith . . . You get things together. I can wait."

"Thanks," Cliff said and he felt a vague pulse of liking for the man.

Pickett left, Cliff closed the door of the apartment. He could see that Lanh had not followed his conversation with their landlord enough to have any inkling at all of his decision to take the job.

"I couldn't think," she said, her hand at her face. The hand seemed a gesture of anguish but then Cliff could see her trying to hide a smile.

"I couldn't think what to call you," she said. "I couldn't think of the English for 'husband' . . . At first I could only think of 'short-timer.' " She turned her face, her voice filled with suppressed laughter. Cliff felt as if his arms were pumping up tight with hot, sticky air.

"Then I thought of 'boyfriend,' " she said, growling to hold back the laughter. "That still wouldn't do." And she laughed. Her hand fell and she laughed openly, uncontrollably, she shook with laughter. "Can you see me," she gasped. " 'Sorry. No can talk. My short-timer not home.' "

She came to him, fell against him in laughter. He dared not raise his arms to hold her. He made himself go blank but he knew his arms still raged at her. He kept his arms at his side. But already Lanh's laughter was changing. The breathless quaking turned within the space of a few beats into weeping.

"I'm just a goddam whore in English," she said.

"You are a very fortunate man," Binh said.

Cliff didn't answer. They sat on a park bench near a pedestrian bridge that arced over the Fox River.

"To have a good job," Binh said.

Cliff couldn't remember a Vietnamese coming this close to self-pity with him before. But the man's tone was light. Perhaps Binh was just genuinely happy for him.

"This week of training has been . . ." Cliff couldn't think of the Vietnamese word for "bizarre." He settled for "unusual."

"Do you understand this electronic thing you will sell?"

"Not the thing itself. That I don't need, they tell me. I understand why people will buy it. Its function."

"That's very American."

"Is it?"

"I believe so. I would make my own mind work like that, but it's balky."

218

"It's strange. I can't think of things as 'American.' I don't think I could identify one thing, really."

"That's why I never did more at the embassy than be a middle-level accountant. I only had three people working for me."

"The clichés, I could name," Cliff said.

"What's that?"

"What's 'American'?"

"Winters, I'm afraid."

"Yes," Cliff said.

"Will the river freeze?"

"Oh yes."

Binh shook his head sadly.

Now that the subject had come up again, Cliff felt compelled to say, "Binh, I agree about rivers, their emptiness here." But they were just words. He still had no feeling for the man.

"That will be something to see," Binh said.

"What?"

"The river frozen over."

They fell silent for a time.

"Shall we walk across?" Cliff asked, nipping his chin toward the pedestrian bridge.

"No please," Binh said. "I'm afraid of heights."

"Then how did you make it onto that plane in Saigon?"

"I held my mind on my family living by an American river and me sitting beside it talking with an American friend."

What had come out of Cliff as an astringent rhetorical question—he could not hold back from the compulsion—had been returned to him as a plea for closeness. Cliff could not bring himself to look at Binh—he could not face himself either, in his inability to accept Binh's sentiment. Cliff looked away toward the bridge, closed his eyes, hoped that the man would say no more.

Silent again. This second visit to Binh's made them lie in bed once more with nothing to say. Cliff leaned to the night table, picked up his watch and angled its face into a

219

ribbon of light from the street. It was not yet ten o'clock. They'd been going to bed earlier each night. They'd been sleeping long, just as they had in the days before Saigon's fall.

Cliff put the watch on the table and lay back down. He knew things were beginning to go bad. He saw Lanh down a sunless street. The drone of helicopters, Vietnamese crouching on the sidewalk, weeping. She was a shape only, far down the street, but he knew it was Lanh. She'd disappeared from the gate of the embassy. He'd followed her. He would not leave without her and now she was far down a street, stopping. Running then, toward him, they ran and spun once more. They spun slowly, soundlessly, and Cliff knew what was happening. Even before their spinning began to lead him to another spin—on a campus beach, in the dark, with Francine. He cut off these thoughts for he knew he was starting a night like the one he'd spent as the communists began to sweep into Saigon. He wouldn't allow it. He squeezed himself shut. There was no crisis here. The day had gone badly but it was still the newness of it, the displacement, whatever. And he knew more: he knew that the times in Saigon, Lanh, the escape, had already turned into finalized recollections. This was intolerable to him. And untrue. Yesterday, even this morning, ten minutes ago, would come to him in the same way—this fear was childish, he told himself. But these moments of fear swept upon him more often now; even in Saigon, even as a hunted man in Saigon, they didn't come quite like this.

He saw Lanh again—he could not keep this out, he had to deal with it—he saw her running toward him, they both ran and spun in that street near the embassy. Then he heard her say, What if I change in America? No, he cried to himself now. He knew Lanh was awake beside him but he held everything in. He would not alarm her. He grew stiff. What if she was changing? Even if they couldn't be comfortable with others they were still who they'd always been when they were alone together, he answered. But he lay in the dark and he could not control these fears when they chose to come to him. Things had changed, even here, even alone together. But if all this was going bad, he told himself, he and Lanh would be flaring, crying out, ranting at each other. Not just growing quieter and quieter.

He turned to her. She was almost invisible in the shadows, she gave off no sense of substance there, just a shaping of the dark. She seemed to him to have been silent for so long in this room that he could place no memory of her voice here. His body moved, knowing what the moment called for, his body dragged his feelings behind. He touched her breasts, heavily, his hands seemed stiff. Lanh did not move. He turned on his side and his penis lolled against her. It was slack. He was startled by this. His hands moved on her breasts and she remained passive, she seemed to be waiting. He knew she felt his limpness curled against her leg 'and he rose to his knees. He was blind in the shadows, he could see only random spots of her body. Her silence, her motionlessness, split his mind further away from his moving hands. She's watching me, he thought. She's judging me. He felt his penis dangling in the dark like a hanged criminal. He ducked his head and tried to concentrate on Lanh's body. He tried to picture her in the Saigon alley room standing naked by the window, her body splashed with hazy sunlight. But his penis did not move, was still slack when her hand suddenly touched him there, briefly, then recoiled.

"These are my breasts," she said low, hard.

He could not answer, did not understand. His hands stopped.

"You're touching them," she said. "You'll never be able to convince yourself they're June Forbes'."

Cliff pulled back, shook his head to try to make her words parse.

"Or that blond woman's in the park." Lanh's voice rasped at him, filled him with the sound of scuttling insects.

"What blond? My god, what have you been doing?"

221

"It's my own fault," Lanh said, her voice suddenly faint. "My breasts are tiny. You can't be blamed. These women are more beautiful than I can ever be."

"That's not true," he said and he felt his mind moving in old ways—he'd assured her of this many times in Saigon—but now he said these words, felt the rhetoric of reassurance rising in him, and he felt weary before it all, he had no patience for all this again.

He bent to kiss her breast. He placed his lips against her nipple and felt it poke up at his touch. But it did not stir him. He felt cut off from her in spite of knowing her needs at this moment. His penis dangled forward in its stupidity and he knew that if he did not make love to her now, she could do nothing but take it as affirmation of her fears. He licked at her and he tried to think of Lanh, Lanh the woman he'd loved so strongly for nearly five years and he heard her voice saying, Lanh eat good food, talk talk.

Lanh pushed his head away from her breast. "No," she said. "Not tonight."

"I love you," he said faintly.

"I'm tired," she said. "It's late."

Cliff lay down on the motel bed, his tie still clamping his neck, his shoes still on, and he closed his eyes. His mind vibrated like a muscle clenched tight too long. He'd sat through a day of electronics seminars in the motel meeting room and after a time the words had all run together and he'd started thinking in Vietnamese. He smiled faintly at the irony—he'd actually begun to think in Vietnamese, all at once, and the seminar leader suddenly had become a foreigner speaking an utterly incomprehensible tongue.

Cliff breathed deep, blew out the air, tugged his tie loose. He turned his face toward the window. The shades were open and he could see an iron railing, a fringe of treetops, and a large panel of grey. If he rose up he could see the Minneapolis skyline in the distance, but he stared at the grey and lay still. As his body settled he became aware of the silence of the room. He thought of Lanh. This had become their element—a silence in a closed room—he had felt an unmistakable relief when Quentin told him to come up to this seminar—and now he was lying in a room, his mind emptied, and he was beginning to think of Lanh in this silence. He knew she was with Binh's family, talking—was her talk with them becoming more and more desperate? or was she lapsing into silence with them, too? Cliff pried his shoes off, let them thunk to the floor to break this silence. He'd expected Lanh to be terrified at his leaving on this trip, but she had said nothing. He began to feel the burden of that worry lift from him but he suddenly realized that she wouldn't necessarily share her terror with him anymore. He knew that was so, though he didn't understand why. His face turned from the window, he closed his eyes. He heard the sound of a truck passing far out on the freeway. Then the silence returned and Cliff made a sound in his throat—he could not bear the silence but he could not rise from the bed. He linked back to the bed in the apartment over the antique store—he swallowed and it felt as if there was something jagged caught deep in his throat. The bed in Saigon, he tried to connect instead back to that bed, and it was night there, Lanh was sleeping beside him and he could hear the rockets falling in the distance, the sound of the helicopters rising from the embassy roof. He felt as distant from Lanh at this moment as he would have if he'd left her in Saigon. More distant, he thought. If I'd left her there, I could at least see her now in my mind as the woman I love. What would have happened to her if I'd left her? The question pulled him back to that bed—back to the groping of his mind as Saigon fell. He couldn't go through all of that again.

He lifted his head, wanted to rise, but he lay back. A bed in Carmel. A darkness in the room as he woke and he knew he was alone there. Earlier, listening to Francine's breath beside him—had he heard it? He could remember it;

223

could remember the smell of her on his finger—that moment passing an alley—rock dust, sour wood, and Francine's smell gently crusting on his hand, seeming to stretch at his skin. If she'd stayed, if that bed had not been empty when he'd opened the drapes, if she'd stayed and they had gone on . . . He felt closer to Francine now than he had before. Not emotionally closer, for the suspension of his feelings had not been altered since that motel room in Carmel, but physically closer. Being in this country had at last given him a reference point that was meaningful. He was some number of thousands of miles closer to Francine. Where was she? What was her life after these years?

About eighty miles south of this motel, in Rochester, Minnesota, Francine's parents lived. Or did. They would know. Cliff saw Francine's mother—a slender, sandy-haired woman, oddly bejowled despite her thinness. She had always liked Cliff in an arched-eyebrow, wry-smile kind of way. Cliff yanked his mind from this path but there was nothing beyond it except the silence of the room—the ticking of the furniture, the faint swish of a car out on the expressway.

Cliff rose up, swung his feet off the bed, picked up the phone. He dialed the old number—his index finger remembered what his mind hesitated over—and the phone beeped. Cliff dug his key from his pocket and gave his room number to the operator. That pause nearly stopped him. In the practical moment of finding out his room number the idea of calling Francine's parents seemed absurd. But before he could hang up, the phone was ringing, and then he heard Francine's mother answer.

"Hello?"

"Hello?" Cliff thought to hang up. But he hesitated.

"Yes?"

"Is . . . Francine there?"

"Francine?" The voice twisted to say without words—she's been gone for years, but there's something familiar in your voice.

Cliff heard that note of recognition and nearly hung up again. But instead, he stayed on, speechless. "Yes, Francine," he finally said.

"Why, she doesn't live here . . . Is that you, Clifford?"

He was in this deep already, and hearing the mother's voice brought back associations that pushed him forward—a winter night in the downstairs game room, the Minnesota snow mounting in swooping drifts outside, his penis locked inside Francine, the lights off this time so that her parents wouldn't realize where they were, Francine's face clear, though, in the dark.

"That's you, isn't it Clifford?"

"Yes."

"My god."

"Where's Francine?"

"What . . ." The voice tottered. "Evanston . . ." she said, almost absent-mindedly.

Cliff sensed the moment's advantage. "What address," he pressed.

"Clifford, I can't believe . . ."

"What street," he said firmly.

"Street? . . . Hinman . . . She's . . . Wait now. Clifford, what are you doing? Where are you? Didn't you desert from the Army?"

Cliff felt a rush of satisfaction that surprised him. Someone knew. At last. Someone said, You are a deserter. "Yes," he said. "Yes, I'm a deserter."

"There were military police here on and off for six months . . . More . . . Where are you?"

"I'm in . . ." Cliff pulled up, as she had done. "I'm back in the U.S."

"Are you pardoned?"

"No," he said quickly, firmly.

There was a long pause on the other end of the phone.

"What's she doing?" Cliff asked.

"She's an assistant curator at the Chicago Art Institute." The woman's voice was suddenly stiff.

225

Cliff tightened his hand on the phone, his face lifted and his eyes closed in a moment's excitement. She was close, in Chicago. And with a job in the city she'd gone to Evanston to live—the place where they'd gone to school together. He cursed his own foolishness at trying to read a sentimental gesture into that. He lowered his head, loosened his grip on the phone. But he asked, "Is she married?"

Francine's mother paused and then said, "No."

Cliff didn't know what else to say. His hands were trembling, though he didn't know from what, and he knew this was all foolish. "And how are you?" he found himself asking.

"All right." The voice was growing stiffer with each response.

Cliff hung up without another word. He sat shaking before the phone for a time, his feelings thrashing about, finally calming.

He stood up. He was hungry. The panel of grey out the window had darkened. Cliff's hand rose to his tie and paused between slipping the knot tighter and pulling the tie off completely. He stood like that for a moment, a moment more, the time stretched on and he felt as if he was going mad. A deserter in Saigon, a desperate flight, domesticity with Lanh in Speedway, Illinois, a family of refugees living by an empty river, his former mother-in-law, his ex-wife, electronic components, a tie, wing-tip shoes, madness. "I am a deserter," he whispered into the silence. His hand fell and the tie stayed as it was, askew.

He slipped on his shoes, stepped out of the motel room into the muggy twilight. He walked along the second-floor balcony. Ahead, a room door stood open and Cliff looked in as he passed. A bald man in his early fifties, wide crescents of sweat under the arms of his light blue dress shirt, was stacking Creamaster Ice Cream cartons into a display on one of the twin beds in his room.

The man looked up at Cliff as he passed and winked and said, "Hi. How's it going?"

*   *   *

Cliff felt heavy in the head and in the sides of his neck. He was passing through a long corridor leading from the motel dining room. Muzak tinkled and hummed at him as he padded along the thick carpet. Just past the check room was a couch and he sat down. A newspaper was folded in quarters, abandoned at the other end of the couch, and Cliff sat for a moment to let the heaviness pass—it was the steak, he decided.

He stretched to the newspaper, brought it to him and opened it. In a boxed-off story in the center of the front page was a photo of young Vietnamese women in a dais standing on a curbstone as if watching a parade and holding North Vietnamese flags. "The Blood bath Fails to Come to the South," a sub-head read, and Cliff snapped the paper closed, choked back any thoughts. He dropped the paper onto the floor beside the couch, out of sight.

A man passed and Cliff looked up at him, tried to concentrate on the man, tried to wipe his mind clean. The man was in his early forties, wore a dark suit, had a sharp part in his hair just over his ear, the long arc of hair obviously covering a bald spot. This man is a salesman, Cliff decided. The place is full of them.

The man peered into the check room, went past, turned snapping his fingers, passed the check room with another look, drifted away down the corridor; his shoulders heaved, he turned and came back and approached the check room.

"Hi," he said to someone inside.

"Hi." It was a young woman's voice.

"Not many coats."

"No."

"No."

There was a long pause as the man leaned on the counter and smiled into the check room, one foot flung back onto its toes and flapping side to side.

"I'm closing up soon," the woman said and the tone

227

was flat, a little hard—she was telling him to leave, not wait.

But the man tried to take it the wrong way. "That's a good idea," he said tentatively. There was another pause. "I can give you a ride," he said.

"I have to go home and study."

"I can help you study."

"Sorry," she said.

Cliff leaned his head back into the soft pile of the couch. He closed his eyes. The Muzak jittered about in his head. He opened his eyes and the man was moving slowly down the corridor. Cliff shut his eyes once more, but this was no better than his room.

On his way back along the second-floor balcony, Cliff saw a rhomboid of light before a room. The door was open. Cliff looked in as he passed and the ice cream salesman was sitting in a chair, his hands folded in his lap, the pyramid of off-brand ice cream rising beside him, and the man's face was sagging, his eyes were fixed in space before him and they did not turn even at Cliff's passing.

Cliff paused at the door to his own room. He turned to face the chirruping, pasty-black Minnesota night. He clutched at the iron railing, squeezed it hard. He was a stranger here, an alien, he knew. This was madness, this life he was trying to make. He pulled at the railing, pulled hard, wished he had the strength to yank the railing up by its iron roots and fling it down on the car tops below. But he could only pull at the railing until his hands began to cramp.

It was sundown when Cliff landed in Chicago. He sat in the front of the airport bus and it moved up a ramp and onto an overpass crossing an east-west freeway.

Cliff saw the full moon low on the horizon. It was large as the sun, faintly orange, like the sun burnt cold. The west-bound lane of the freeway was clogged with cars and Cliff had a vision of the end of the world—the sun going cold and people fleeing the city, senselessly, fleeing the city when the trouble was in the sky and there was nowhere to run.

Cliff went straight to Binh's, expecting Lanh to be there. Binh seemed subdued as he stepped back and opened the door wide. Cliff entered, bracing himself for the sound of Lanh chattering away with Mai. But Lanh wasn't in sight. There was a sound from the kitchen that Cliff did not identify before he turned around in the living room. Two of the smaller children were there and bowed at him. The oldest son looked blankly at Cliff from the bedroom doorway and then turned away.

"Lanh's gone home," Binh said.

Cliff wondered if this was a hopeful sign. Was she bored by these people at last?

Crying. That was the sound from the kitchen. Crying snubbed into near silence then squeezed out again. Cliff turned his face toward the sound.

"It's a man we know from the refugee camp. He's living in Speedway, too." Binh sounded faintly embarrassed, to Cliff's ear. The man in the kitchen was weeping uncontrollably now.

Cliff automatically took a few steps toward the kitchen and a corner of the table came into sight, the man was bent forward into the crook of his arm. Cliff stopped, kept the man framed in the proscenium of the kitchen door. The man was quivering furiously, sobbing. A hand—Mai's, Cliff presumed—entered the frame, touched the man's arm.

"His family was left behind," Binh said low, in English.

Cliff knew he would once have gone into that room, tried to comfort the man. But Cliff balked, he could not move forward through the proscenium, he could think of no words to say, he didn't want to consider these things now.

"Lanh is home?" he asked and he felt crusty.

229

"Yes. I think so. She was going there."

Cliff nodded, said nothing, picked up his travel bag and moved toward the door.

"He'll be okay," Binh said in English, as if Cliff had expressed concern.

"No he won't," Cliff said and he found himself suddenly very sad for the stranger in the kitchen. "He won't."

Cliff unlocked the apartment door and he paused. His face grew warm—in fear, he realized—in fear of what his feelings would be, in fear of Lanh's feelings. No. He denied this fear—he couldn't begin to be afraid or they were lost. But he was afraid, he was still afraid even as he tried to deny it, and his body moved forward without any of this being resolved.

He opened the door and the air was thick and sickly sweet. Lanh was crouched in the middle of the room, her back to him, and before her was a footstool with bowls of flowers. Curling up from beside her head was a wisp of smoke—incense—the smell filled him and he staggered before its sweet stink. And he saw her again—the first vision of her, the first moments ever in her presence when she turned around, the incense palmed in her hands before her, the smoke sinuous extensions of her fingertips.

She did not turn to him now. And the memory held no life. He stood in this room in Speedway, Illinois, this silent room, and a tiny creature was crouched there—an animal happened on in the dark. Lanh was connected to this makeshift Buddhist alter, breathing an atmosphere that soured Cliff's stomach, that made the room wobble about him. His body still felt compelled to go forward, he stepped closer, he could see her cheek, her hands moving up and down, quietly lashing the thin whip of smoke. Her eyes were closed but he knew she sensed him there. He groped back to the first moments. Start it once more, some part of him cried. Start it once more—what did you say that first time? I'm a friend. Cliff's mouth

230

shaped the words but he did not speak. The movement of Lanh's hands were gentle, graceful, but they were foreign to his eye, they were the dipping of a sail on the South China Sea, a palm frond in a hot wind, far off, alien, a memory.

"Please stop," he said.

Her hands continued to move, her head did not turn, but her eyes opened. He could see tears glistening there. He wanted to touch her face, close her eyes again with his fingertips, as he would a dead man's. Her face blurred. He found his own eyes filling with tears. Why? he asked himself, fearing the answer, knowing the answer. He was a stranger standing in this room and he had to go.

"I'm praying," she said.

"What is it you're praying for?"

"I don't know."

Cliff stood for a moment more and then backed away, quietly, his eyes on the floor. He turned at the door and closed it behind him with a faint click so she would know he was gone.

Francine was in the book. She'd kept Cliff's name and there she was in the North Suburban phone book—F. Wilkes, and her street address on Hinman in Evanston.

Cliff let the phone book drop back into the metal-sheathed bank of books and he turned to face the terminal waiting room. It struck him that everything he'd done in the past few hours had at heart been secretly leading him to this piece of information. The impulse he'd had moments ago to see if he could find out Francine's address was the inevitable conclusion of his silent withdrawal—travel bag in hand—from the apartment in Speedway, his impulse to come to Chicago at once, the bus, this terminal. He had the address now. And she'd kept his name—that made his groin crawl—or was it fear? for at that moment a policeman strolled into the terminal. But the man moved idly, this was part of his normal rounds, and he went out again. Cliff had felt a quickening in himself in the past few hours. The impulse to leave Speedway immediately had been sharpened by the alternative he'd considered for the night—sleeping under the pedestrian bridge over the Fox River. He saw himself being arrested for vagrancy and that leading to his identity being revealed. It had struck him suddenly then, forcefully, that he had to avoid even the most minor of encounters with the police. This thought animated him—even weary, leaning against the bank of phone books—Cliff felt his blood quicken, his mind cast out the silence it had absorbed in the past weeks.

Lanh. She filled him briefly, wrenched him, he straightened, his hands flew up and pushed through his hair once, twice, his fingertips dug at his skull. I've left her. I've left her. He turned away from the terminal, bent over the phone books as he felt his eyes fill with tears. She's gone. Dead. I've deserted her at last and she's been taken away by the VC, dragged from the alley room and taken away and raped for a week by tiny jaundice-skinned men and then killed. No. She's at Binh's. Right now. He could see her there, sitting in a chair surrounded by the family. They would keep her with them. They'd begun already to knit her into their little community. Lanh would know what to say to the man weeping in the kitchen. Perhaps he would know what to say to her. But this rendering dissolved in Cliff's mind. He remembered her in a sudden agitation of his skin down his chest, his abdomen, into his groin. Then he flushed hot in embarrassment—Lanh's voice stammering in English—he could not think of her now or he would start sobbing audibly, start talking to himself, start stomping around in this public place and he'd draw attention to himself, dangerous attention.

He turned his mind to Francine. He knew her address. And she filled him and it felt very different, the scale changed, the sounds and smells and sights that had grated at him in these past weeks suddenly were transformed, their sharp edges were smoothed. He had to act. It was late. Not tonight. Tomorrow he could see her at the Art

232

Institute, but he didn't want other people around. He could call her. No. Given time to think, she could become angry, become scared. He would see her at her apartment tomorrow after work.

With that resolved, he grew immediately calm. The moment surprised him, he closed his eyes before it briefly. He considered the night ahead and with the calmness came a clarity—he realized he had money. His hand jumped to an inner coat pocket and felt the folded envelope. He had a good deal of travel money from the Minneapolis trip and he smiled faintly at his first thought in Speedway, that he was alone, naked, resourceless in the landscape, that he would have to sleep in the open. And this moment of clarity persisted—he could acknowledge even his own feelings. He knew he could not check into a hotel room tonight. The confinement of a room, its silence, would drag him back into confusion, despair. Cliff knew he was in control for now. He straightened his tie for the sake of the police and went to an end seat in the terminal where he could lay his head against the wall.

The large old trees vaulted the street and they held the new night beneath them in spite of a blue stain remaining in the sky, a golden crust remaining on the tops of the apartment buildings. Cliff found Francine's foyer doorway in the back of a courtyard. Her full name was on the box within—Francine Wilkes. He held back the urge to bound up the steps. He climbed deliberately and stood before her door.

At his knock there was a stirring inside, the sound drew near. "Yes?" Francine's voice took his breath away briefly. "Who is it?" she asked.

"Francine?" he said.

The door began to open immediately. In that moment, as the door moved quickly at the first sound of his voice, a wild, thrashing hope rushed through him like a naked woman clutching in passion. But following at once—as if the naked woman had moved in strobe light and this was her after-image pressing back into her—a fear came, a fear of the face, the words, a sense that something was very wrong.

Francine's face was before him—her eyes leaped deep into him and ignored everything that it saw. That was the feeling he had of her look—he hadn't recalled it before in his memories of her, but she had always looked at him that way. Her hair fell long across her cheek, the color of hazy sunlight. The faint lines about her eyes, her mouth, made his breath catch—she was beautiful to him, of course, and her eyes drilled on, ignoring him. Her mouth moved.

"My god," she said. "I couldn't believe what mother had told me."

Chilled, he felt, chilled by the flatness of her voice. He was like a newspaper headline to her, her mother had told her about something she'd heard on the radio and now Francine was merely reading it in a newspaper headline.

Cliff wanted to speak but he could not find words, he could not sort out what it was he was feeling. He gaped.

"What do you want with me?" Francine said, and her voice had softened but her eyes darted away, past Cliff, back to the stairs.

"I wanted to see you once more," Cliff said. That was true, that was a beginning, he could go no further, though.

"Please," she said and she seemed agitated. "There's nothing for us to say anymore. I've thought this out carefully since mother said you might come here."

Cliff found himself without words because he was suddenly without any feeling. His desire for Francine had flared and died in these few moments—an exploded star sucked back in now into a white dwarf, he felt his density increase.

Francine said, "Don't you know you meant something to me once?"

Cliff said nothing, did not move.

"That sounds like a contradiction, doesn't it," she said, mocking her own mind, a gesture he did not remember in her but which he appreciated now in an abstract way.

"It's not though," she said. "You meant something to me that I've turned away from. All we did to each other can't be undone. It's shaped us."

She paused. Again, she looked past him. Her hand fretted at the door that she clutched against her.

"I can't go back," she said. She'd gone brittle. She was waiting impatiently for him to agree.

Cliff thought: I do agree. She's said what I feel. Again someone knows my heart and I know theirs and it means nothing between us. We're strangers.

"I . . ." he began with no idea what he was going to say. Then he heard a sound in the foyer below. Someone entering. He had a sudden fear and Francine apparently read it.

"Come in quick," she said, flinging open the door and grabbing him. She closed the door behind him and Cliff's mind leaped just ahead of Francine's words. "I've been worried about what would happen if you came," she said. "Mother said she told the police about you . . ."

The room clamped in suddenly against Cliff, he turned, gasping.

"There's a back way out," Francine said and she darted past him. He followed into the kitchen. "I don't want you hurt," she said wrenching at the bolt on the door. "But I don't know you anymore."

The door was open, he was on a tiny wooden porch, steps, he went down, pumping his legs rapidly, resisting taking the steps two or three at a time. He dared not risk a fall. He hit the bottom step and was into the alley. He heard the rattle of an El train two blocks over, thought he heard voices high above him, he hesitated a moment then turned toward the shorter of the two stretches of alley, north. He ran. Close to the building, keeping in the dimmest shadows. The blue had bled out of the sky. It was going dark—so quickly? Cliff thought—and he ran hard, past a high fence.

Was there a voice above and behind him? He swerved left, out of the shadow, then back in again, expecting the bark of a gun, expecting this all to be wiped suddenly away. Another building abutted on the alley, nowhere to duck in, another fire escape up, but he knew it would trap him. He swerved again, waiting for the moment of transition, the impact of the bullet at the back of his head, that brief moment before it did its work, the moment in which he was first touched. He splashed through a puddle, a radio blared in a window upstairs, he heard the clink of dishes as he ran.

A cross street ahead. He was still alive. There'd been no shot. He sprinted now through the alley, ran hard and straight for the corner and he was aware he was running alone, in an alley, running for his life alone, and he had no rush of feeling at this, none, Lanh was gone, and he was running from her, too. He fixed his eyes on the corner and thought of a jeep full of ARVN soldiers. Would the police— they would be military police, probably—have a car circling the block? He stumbled on a dip near a grating, he staggered, his feet hit flat, hard, on the pavement, he went on, waiting to see a car. He drew near, pulled up, but his momentum pressed him past the edge of the building, onto the sidewalk. The street was empty. He did not look back.

Cliff turned left, began to run. Up the short block was Chicago Avenue and beyond it the sharp slope up to the El tracks. A car, two, passed at the intersection. A taxicab passed. Cliff waved at it but it did not stop. He began to sprint again, he put his head down and pumped hard.

He turned left again at the corner, doubling back south. No cabs before him, no cars. He ran still, ran down the street, past a used car lot, ran and looked over his shoulder. A yellow car, moving, yes. A taxi. Cliff veered into the street, waved at the cab. The taxi pulled over, a car rushed past Cliff, the horn blaring, Cliff dashed toward the cab thinking, Let some little old American lady in her car cut me down, I don't give a shit.

Cliff jerked open the back door of the taxi, closed it behind him quickly and sank into the corner of the seat to keep his head blocked off from view from the rear.

Where to run? To a crowd, the center of the city. "The Loop," Cliff said.

Cliff stepped from the cab into a flow of strangers, a river bed with neon banks, he moved beneath the surface, weightless for a moment. He found his legs still trembling slightly, he found a brassy taste still in his mouth, and he felt a faint exhilaration at the escape, at the pursuit even— he was oddly comforted by the official anger given form by his pursuers. He was a deserter. They know what I've done, he thought. He did not let himself even consider that there may have been no one behind him in the alley, that the door closing in the foyer had been benign.

He looked about him. He would hide now. He would be alone and decide what to do. Up State Street were movie marquees, department stores; at this end were the porn shops, their facades all painted yellow, edged in bulbs that flashed in a running sequence, mimicking in wires and filaments the trills of sex.

Cliff turned the corner, into the splotched lights beneath the El tracks, and found a transient hotel. A few doorways beyond, two women stood—one white one black, their lips dark blooms. Cliff averted his eyes. He stood before a man in a glass cage and asked for a room. The man looked toward the door and waited.

"I'm alone," Cliff said.

The man pulled a key from the wall of pegs behind him and Cliff went up the stairs, avoiding the metal-cage elevator that looked like a small-town lockup. In the third floor corridor he approached a woman plucking at her cleavage, resetting it. He entered her humid atmosphere of perfume and sweat and she smiled at him. Her customer passed a few steps later; his face turned away, his collar open.

Cliff stopped at his room, leaned his head against the door as he fretted at the lock. He had to hide somewhere, be alone, he told himself, but he was regretting this place already. The short-timers moving in the halls. And the room—he knew what it would be. He opened the door, switched on the light. It was tiny, windowless, little more than a bed and a washstand. He switched the light off, closed the door, locked and bolted it in the dark. He lay down on the bed and the dark did not soften, even as his eyes dilated, his mind dilated, he opened up, he felt himself opening wide before the darkness and he could see nothing, think nothing, feel nothing for a time. He could only hear a woman's mocking laugh in a distant room, footsteps pacing somewhere above him, then silence.

He saw Lanh sitting in her bar, sitting with a GI, stroking his head, a Saigon Tea before her, her bare feet curled up under her in the booth. He had never seen her like this. She'd done these things but he'd never actually known her in the bars. And yet he pictured her now in one. He willed this scene. He'd felt empty with Lanh for weeks and he willed this scene. He watched her long fingers curling around a sergeant's neck—a thick neck, rolls of fat—he watched Lanh's fingers tracing the convolutions of the sergeant's ear. Cliff felt a pulse of anger at her and he pressed his fantasy on, preserved that momentary feeling, tried to build on it. He watched Lanh rise with this man, take his hand, lead him to the back of the bar, through a beaded curtain, she turned and hung on his neck, kissed the sergeant—a fat man, wheezing in passion—Cliff saw Lanh's hand fall and squeeze at the man's penis through his trousers.

Cliff sat up with a gasp. Yes Yes. He was feeling

now. His arms rose, his fists clenched, he was angry, jealous, he wanted Lanh, wanted to grab her away, strip her, enter her. He was feeling something again—the emptiness was gone—and he drove himself away from fantasy, pressed toward the Lanh he'd known. She moved silently across the room—afternoon light streaming in the window—the roar of motorcycles from the streets of Saigon—she touched his face and the sound faded away, he could hear her voice. He was sitting in bed that afternoon, just like this, his arms had risen in jealousy—he'd been lost in his own thoughts on an afternoon in Saigon and he'd wanted Lanh so badly that he'd suddenly felt jealous over her past and he'd risen up. She'd had no way of knowing what he was feeling—he'd said nothing—but she came to him anyway—she sensed what was wrong. You are the only man ever to please me, she said. I was frigid before I met you, she said. Sitting in the dark, in this cheap hotel in Chicago, Cliff felt it had been a lie, but she had known to lie in the only way that could have helped him at that moment. She'd known his heart.

He heard voices in the hallway now. Very close. A woman talking in brittle fragments. He heard Lanh stammering in English: want to fuck GI, farmers my country die, talk talk Vietnam. He shut out the words—they were not her—but she had been stripped after all—stripped and marched through the streets and even the gentlest, the kindest, the most intelligent of those who watched could not withhold their ridicule. She had no language now and her mind, her heart, had been sealed shut—she had no country now and everything was alien to her and turned her into a stranger. Cliff shook his head, shook it hard to clear it. He did not understand how this could happen. When he'd gone to Vietnam he'd looked at the sky and wondered at it—it was blue, the clouds were white and they shaped themselves into forms he'd seen before. Somehow he'd expected it all to be different. For this was Vietnam, a profoundly alien land, as incomprehensible as death in a

239

jungle. Then after a time, the familiarity of the sky had come to seem right. There was no difference in countries, in people. That was why he could leave his whole life behind, when the time came—there was continuity after all. But perhaps there wasn't.

He felt the night gape before him. He was lying once more in a bed in a tiny room and he had to decide what to do, where to go. The people of his life pressed into him and he imagined a night like the one he'd spent in Saigon as the communists approached. His parents, Francine, Burr Gillis, and the rest—and Lanh, too—she was part of them all now—but he could not face any of them. And he knew they would only lead him to the same conclusions as before. He tried to go blank, but his feelings whirled on, tossing faces at him until he heard the squeaking of bed springs. Next door. Through the wall he could hear the rhythm beginning, could sense the woman opened wide to the man upon her. Cliff felt Lanh beneath him, folded in his arms, his penis deep inside her, he turned onto his back with her. But she grew insubstantial, she faded into the darkness and Cliff could hear the woman next door—could hear the faint suck of her cunt—even that.

Cliff sat up, put his feet on the floor. His penis was erect. He opened his pants and grasped the shaft of his penis in his hand, moved his hand once, and once again. He felt the room fitting tightly about his body, pressing at him. Beyond, were only sounds, darkness, memories, he was alone, he had run and he was alone and his hand moved along his penis and Cliff thought of closing the loop.

But he pulled his hand away. Lanh was lying in darkness, he knew, nearby. The time had come, he knew, to run again. Lanh existed beyond this room and he would go to her once more.

It was nearly midnight when Cliff climbed the stairs to the apartment. He stood before the door and he raised his hand to knock and found it trembling. The hand surprised him. He could see it only dimly but he turned it, palm toward him, and he waited for it to grow calm. He kept away from the reasons for its quaking. He watched the hand as if it was a stranger grown hysterical in the street. The hand grew steady at last and Cliff decided not to knock. He took out his key, opened the door.

The apartment was faintly lit—a light in the kitchen. He stepped in and he saw Lanh rising up on the bed. She rose to her knees. She was naked. His own body prickled from neck to knees before her. His chest rose and he grew faint. He felt himself shear off; the clutter of rooms, trees, sky, passersby fell away; he was left in a place that was nameless, without language, flagless, mythless. He moved to her and her eyes rose to him. He removed his clothes quickly, trying to hold himself in that void, alone with this naked woman. His penis was still slack but he knew he must touch her. He felt that was the one thing that could remain immutable between them. It was a thing unto itself, he thought, she was a beautiful woman. And his groin began to stir. But only because of a brief smell of earth from outside and a ring of sweat that was spreading at the back of his neck: he had a vision of Vietnam. A flash of sunlight in his first moments of flight, the sun flaring from a pond, a water buffalo beyond, a palm frond, an empty sky, the heat, he felt them all again now, he lay down on the bed, held Lanh; and he swelled with the countryside, with the sprawl of the city, Saigon, their race through the alleyways, he wanted to go back, go back to their alley room, that was their place, Lanh had made him love the very smell of the air, the very heat that beat down the stone walls. This was why his penis rose now, why he pressed against her with a low cry, his breath twisted tight in his chest. In her body he was Vietnamese, he was Vietnamese and all the silences, the empty blacktops, the dying hands across bedspreads, the neat barren script on blue letter paper, all the hulking bodies moving away, the

241

resort hotels, all that dissolved and Cliff beat at Lanh's dry loins, trying to get in, she clutched him and he probed desperately as they waited for her to moisten, for her body to catch up with them as she clutched at his back, her fingers digging deep, she must have known how important this was, the accumulation of countless nights and mornings, the weight of all their years together and apart, of all the accumulated clutter of culture that they tried to sort out and then join by this joining of their bodies.

He was in her now, clutched there softly. She contracted at him, pulsed, and he let himself ease back for a moment, waited for his identity to return—he was part of her, he was Vietnamese now, they were babbling, he realized, they were both babbling in Vietnamese—it's good, yes, my god, my love—and he heard, as if from a great distance, his own voice singing this ancient tongue, singing with the voice of mandarins and monks on hilltops he'd never seen, great forests of mahogany, temple bells, these were all his now—but the bells stopped, the trees remained and the bells ceased and he moved in Lanh and there was only wind and he knew what the monks felt—no, it wasn't the monks' feeling, it was his own—the trees were gone and there was just sky and himself clasping this woman to himself—he was not Vietnamese now, he was simply human—not simply—he was more for a moment—no, he was less—he began to dissolve, there was nowhere to cast his gaze, there were no objects, no senses—he could not exist here, he was floating, his body had dissolved—he fought his way back—he stroked inside Lanh, stroked, he flexed his penis and stroked and she said, Oh god, and he heard her voice, heard its tonal flutter, heard her again at the Forbeses' dinner table. Broken sounds, and she said, Farmers buried in fields. He saw the tiny fortress of stone across the rice paddy. He stood, arms akimbo in the motionless air, and he looked at the gravesite that seemed centuries old and he knew the man had been buried there only last year—the past and the present were the same in this field, time was as still as the air, as still as the heat that pressed at him and he was lost there; and that past for him now—the time when he had stood in that field—was ancient, the world had changed more for him in those five years than it had in twenty centuries for that farmer. And Cliff moved inside Lanh, he laid his face in her hair and he wanted to be Vietnamese again. More than that—he wanted to be human again, connected to a woman only, just a woman. But he heard a car horn bark in the street, and once more, and he heard the refrigerator grinding away— trivial things, they mean nothing, he cried to himself, but they were the things that were imprinted in him—the synapses of culture—the tracks that caught him and pulled him away, back to the dinner table, large there himself, a tall man, taller by a head than the president of Vietnam or Chairman Mao—he tried to wrench himself back, these things had nothing to do with him. But he heard the silence again on the porch just moments before Lanh came down and they were rejoined. He was an American.

"Oh Cliff. Oh god," Lanh said digging at his back, digging at him, throwing her hips up and back, up and back with his own movement. He was numb at the waist, he felt himself moving up and down but there was no sensation now. He cried out at this and Lanh held him tighter, thinking he was coming, Cliff knew. She was wrong about him, at that moment she was totally ignorant of him. He was an American, he thought, and he wondered if that was still true. But he felt weak, he lay against her, his arms would not support him and his hips moved faster and Lanh held tight again. He wanted the orgasm now, though he was afraid because he could feel so little at that moment. He wanted to join her—the moment of release—there was no nationality in an orgasm—he wanted to love her, but he wanted to be something here, something specific, certain—a soldier now and there was a bargirl beneath him. An American soldier and he'd bought Lanh four Saigon Teas and they'd gone to her room and he'd heard the bad drains in the walls, water running all the time, and she looked odd, this tiny little woman and he didn't care—this was what he was paying for—an encounter with the Orient, a scale against his virility—his cock was as thick as her wrist and as long as her foot—a measure for his girl back home—a vision of pink breasts lolling back, the nipples alone as big as this girl's breasts—no winter comforter here, no mulled cider—he'd bribed this woman with an apple—they had no apples here—from the mess hall. Cliff cried out again, raised his head and shook his mind clear. He was not an American. It had all run out—all the power of his past—all the meaning of his own fields, his own rivers, his own buildings and food and dinner conversation and the size of his own hands, his own penis, the size of Quentin's hands, his wife's breasts. Just Lanh, just Lanh, just a woman, just woman, he pulled his head back, searched Lanh's face and she was blank, her eyes were closed, her brow was knit, her face shivered, shivered, shivered as he stroked—how long ago had she come?—she was waiting now, waiting for him—was he still erect? Yes. He could feel himself now, swelling even tighter. It was close. He thrashed about for something to join with in the approaching moment. What was left? This woman? He wanted that, he wanted that. But she looked tired. She had no language to speak. She was faint in the darkness of the room. He came. The release squeezed and squeezed and he found himself attaching only to his own thoughts—and they were full of detritus. Pot shards, bone fragments, a vanished civilization.

Cliff watched the dark ceiling and blinked away tears. He sensed that Lanh, too, was silently weeping and they would not turn their faces, they could not confront each other's regret. But even as he sensed her next to him, even as he wept, he could not hold on to the moment. He was thinking already about highways north, perhaps two days' worth of hitching, a border, then another place to begin.

Her voice sounded distant in the dark room. "Mr. Binh

has asked me to come live with his family for a time," she said.

The voice cut through Cliff's thoughts and he wondered at his growing detachment. Lanh was next to him, her body lay near enough that he could feel its heat without touching her, and yet all they'd been together had already been transformed into night thoughts, into the flow of reverie and regret in a bed in a room in another country.

Cliff rose. He dressed himself and then stood before her. Lanh lay on her back, her face turned to him, her naked body exposed to the knees. He heard a car pass in the street. The window shade flapped at the sill. A dog barked somewhere in the distance. He looked at Lanh and she returned his gaze and they did not move for a long moment.

"I'm going now," he said softly.

Her eyes closed and when they opened, Cliff knew he and Lanh understood each other. He fought back sounds in his throat, wordless sounds, there was no other way for them. Lanh closed her eyes once more and turned her face away. She drew the sheet slowly up her body, covering her thighs, her loins, her breasts, and she clutched it tight in her fist at her throat.

"Where?" she asked, and she looked at him again.

"Canada."

"Will that be a home for you?"

"I don't know."

"You do know." She almost whispered it.

"It won't. No."

She closed her eyes once more, briefly.

"It will be bad for you, as well." Cliff's voice broke, he felt his face growing warm.

"Not as bad as for you," she said.

They were quiet for a moment and their eyes disengaged.

"Go on now," Lanh said. "Get the fuck out of here before we mess this up."

Cliff turned, he moved across the floor, he was down the steps and into the deserted main street of Speedway before he realized that the room had been full of the smell of incense.

The
Best Modern Fiction
from
BALLANTINE